Born and raised in the Detroit area, Steve Hamilton currently works for IBM in upstate New York, where he lives with his wife and two children. An Edgar Award winner, he is the author of several acclaimed Alex McKnight thrillers.

Visit the author's website at:
www.authorstevehamilton.com

A STOLEN SEASON

In Paradise, Michigan, Alex and his occasional partner Leon witness a spectacular boat crash. They drag three men from the wreck and revive them. Later, Alex's friend Vinnie suspects that these strangers are pressurising the local tribes' people into making fraudulent claims for prescription drugs which the men then sell on to addicts. Alex and Vinnie's investigations force the men into desperate action, and one of them winds up dead. Meanwhile, Alex, believing that his cop girlfriend, Natalie, is safe in Toronto working on an undercover operation, doesn't realise the true nature of the op and its link to the drug-traffickers. She is perilously close to having her cover blown. Then she comes face-to-face with three men who could be used to redefine the word vicious . . .

Books by Steve Hamilton
Published by The House of Ulverscroft:

A COLD DAY IN PARADISE
ICE RUN

STEVE HAMILTON

A STOLEN SEASON

Complete and Unabridged

CHARNWOOD
Leicester

First published in Great Britain in 2006 by
Orion, an imprint of
The Orion Publishing Group Limited
London

First Charnwood Edition
published 2007
by arrangement with
The Orion Publishing Group Limited
London

The moral right of the author has been asserted

British Library CIP Data

Hamilton, Steve, *1961 –*
   A stolen season.—Large print ed.—
   Charnwood library series
   1. McKnight, Alex (Fictitious character)—Fiction
   2. Private investigators—Michigan—Fiction
   3. Detective and mystery stories
   4. Large type books
   I. Title
   813.5′4 [F]

   ISBN 978–1–84617–804–7

To Bill and Frank

Acknowledgments

Thanks as always to the 'usual suspects' — Bill Keller and Frank Hayes, Liz and Taylor Brugman, Ruth Cavin and everyone at St. Martin's Press, Jane Wood and everyone at Orion, Jane Chelius, Maggie Griffin, Bob Randisi and the Private Eye Writers of America, all the cool people at IBM, David White, Joel Clark, Cary Gottlieb, Jeff Allen, Rob Brenner, Larry Queipo, former chief of police, Town of Kingston, New York, and Dr. Glenn Hamilton from the Department of Emergency Medicine, Wright State University.

And as always, to Julia, my wife and best friend, to Nicholas, wielder of Soul Edge, and to Antonia, the Princess of Pink.

1

From the beginning, everything about the night was wrong.

Everything.

It was cold. That was the first thing. It was cold and there was a wet fog hanging over the water. The kind of fog that creeps into your bones, no matter how many layers you're wearing. The cold gets into your lungs and chills you from the inside out.

I was in Brimley, too — the last place I'd expect to be. It's normally just a stop on the road, halfway around the bay if you're driving from Paradise to Sault Ste. Marie. There are two restaurants in town, with two different strategies for serving liquor, one of life's essentials on a night like this. Willoughby's has a separate bar in back, and the Cozy switches over at nine o'clock every night, when everyone under twenty-one is kicked out. There's one gas station with a little store on the side, and that's about it, the whole town right there, just down the road from the Bay Mills Indian Community. The rez. On a clear night I could have stood there on the shore and seen the casino lights across the water. But this was anything but a clear night.

I figured Vinnie was probably over there, working at the black-jack tables, keeping order in his own quiet way. He had been a dealer for a few years. Now he was a pit boss. Vinnie's a Bay

Mills Ojibwa, even though he lives off the rez. He's my neighbor, in fact, and one of my three last friends in the world. But I knew I wouldn't be seeing him that night, even if he was just around the bay. I leave the man alone when he's working. Hell, I leave him alone most of the time. That's just the way things are with him.

Normally, I'd be back in Paradise on a night like this, spending my last waking hours at the Glasgow Inn. I'd sit in one of the big overstuffed chairs by the fire. Maybe there'd be a game on the television over the bar. Jackie Connery, the owner of the place and the Supreme Commander, was another friend. Although, unlike Vinnie, I seldom left Jackie alone. He'd never admit it, but Jackie would be lost without me, without my daily commentary on the way he makes breakfast, runs his bar, builds a fire, you name it. He tries to return the favor, but I ignore most of his advice. And his insults. Despite everything, he always has a cold Molson Canadian waiting for me, every single night without fail. He drives across the bridge to Canada once a week to buy a case for me, supposedly on his way to do something else. I think it's just a ritual to him now. An excuse to get out from behind the bar. Either that or he really wants me to have my Molson.

Yeah, a cold beer and my feet up by the fire. That would have been another plan for this night. Instead of standing here on the edge of Waishkey Bay, in a stranger's backyard, looking out at the cold fog. Waishkey Bay opens up into Whitefish Bay, and beyond that lies the vast unbroken surface of the biggest, coldest, deepest lake in the world. Lake Superior. I could hear it out there. I could feel it. I just couldn't see it.

I wrapped my coat tighter around my body and tried to convince myself I didn't need to shiver. I knew once that started, it wouldn't stop until I went inside. I wasn't ready to do that yet. There was too much noise in there. Too much smoke. I wanted to stay out here a little longer, by myself, looking out at the fog and what little I could make out in the night sky. Later, there would be fireworks, maybe invisible but fireworks just the same, right here over Waishkey Bay.

Yes, that was the other strange thing about this night. I was standing here cursing myself for not wearing a warmer coat on the Fourth of July.

It wasn't right. I swear, this was not fair at all. We live for the summers up here. It's the Upper Peninsula of Michigan, for God's sake, as far away from civilization as you can get without leaving the country. The winters last forever up here. Or at least they feel that way. It's brutally, inhumanly cold. The snowstorms gather their strength from the lake and then they unleash themselves on us like they have orders from God to bury us forever. In 1995 we got six feet of snow in one day.

Twenty-four hours.

Six. Feet. Of Snow.

Most years, it doesn't even melt until May. Then we might get a quick flash of spring. The temperature might break forty and we're practically lying on the beach in our bathing suits. That's how desperate we are for a little sunshine. The snow will sneak back a few times and dump a few more inches in the middle of the night. Just teasing us. Then finally the earth will tilt into position and the summer will seem to come all at once. The old joke, how summer was on a Thursday last year. That's how brief it seems. How fleeting.

But God, what a summer it is. For one blink of an eye, this becomes the most beautiful place in the world. There's a light up here. You have to see it to know it. The way it hits the water in the evenings. The way the wind comes off the lake and you can look all the way down a long straight road and see the trees moving one by one.

The sunsets.

The desolate, heartbreaking beauty of this goddamned place. This home of mine.

But not this year. For whatever reason, we're skipping summer altogether. We're rushing right back into those fall months when the lake turns into a monster. Almost overnight, six-foot waves ready to batter the great ships again. To miss out on the promise of summer, it is the cruelest thing imaginable, and everyone, every last person living up here, has been feeling it.

For me, there's even more to regret. But not just now. No use becoming completely suicidal. It'll be there when I finally make it home to my bed. When I close my eyes and remember what her face looks like. When I wonder what she's doing at that very moment, five hundred miles away.

I heard footsteps behind me. I was expecting it to be Leon, my third and last friend in the whole world, and the reason why I was here in Brimley that night. But instead it was the man named Tyler. I had just met him a couple of hours ago, so I didn't know the man. What I did know was that Tyler must have cut quite a figure back in the sixties. He still had long dark hair tied in a braid down his back. Up here in Ojibwa land, that doesn't set you apart too much, but everything else about him did. He was wearing a bright red and green tie-dyed jacket, and it looked like he got his little round eye-glasses from John Lennon's estate sale. From what I gathered, he'd been a musician most of his life, and he'd come up here to be the entertainment director when they opened up the bigger casino in Sault Ste. Marie. He'd bought this old house in Brimley because it had a huge garage, bigger than the house even, with plenty of room for him to work on his old cars. Within a year, he'd quit the job at the casino and had turned half the garage into a state-of-the-art recording studio. He had the whole setup in there, with the sound damping walls and the separate little room for him to sit in with all of his equipment. I couldn't even imagine how much it all cost, or where an old hippie had gotten all that money. But apparently the studio had become a local success story, with musicians from all over the state coming up to record just a few yards away from the lake.

The best part? Aside from this guy building his own recording studio and fixing anything with four wheels, he was also a member of the Coast Guard Auxiliary. Hair and all. Although I guess I shouldn't have been surprised. Any man who can survive up here year-round has to be great at a dozen different things and pretty damned good at a dozen more.

'Can you believe this?' he said. 'It's cold enough to freeze the balls off a monkey. No, wait, that's not right.'

'Brass monkey,' I said. 'My father used to say that.'

'Brass monkey. Whatever that is. I'll try to remember it.'

'Are Leon and the boys ready yet?'

'Almost,' he said, looking back at the garage. He shook his head. 'As ready as they're ever gonna be, I guess. Whaddya think of this, Alex?'

Two hours in his acquaintance, and he was already treating me like a long lost friend. Or a kindred spirit, perhaps. Somebody who seemed to think we had a lot in common, despite our outward appearances. Hell, maybe we did. God knows I could have used another friend. Jackie, Vinnie, and finally Leon. That was the whole deal right there.

Leon — I had met him at the Glasgow one night. Leon with the wild orange hair and the flannel shirt, the big local goofball that nobody had ever taken seriously, not for one second. He had come up to Paradise to fight me in the parking lot, all because he had lost his dream job as a private investigator. The lawyer who was paying him had somehow convinced me to take his place, but the job turned out to be anything but a dream. Not long after that, I found out that Leon actually knew what he was doing. And that

I most definitely did not.

We were partners for a while. I still have some of the business cards he had made up. Prudell-McKnight Investigations, his name first because it sounded better that way. Or so he said. With the two guns on either side of the card, pointing at each other.

Of course, I had no desire to be a PI. With Leon as my partner or not. But that didn't stop the trouble from finding me. I can't even count the number of times Leon helped me. With the computer stuff, or hell, just the fact that he had a gun for me after I threw mine in the lake. I owed him my life.

I started feeling bad about it, the way I'd only go see him if I needed his help with something. I promised myself I'd make a point of taking him out to lunch every so often. Or stopping by his house, even though the sight of me still made his wife nervous.

Or watching him play. That's right. Leon and his band. Just when I thought he was done surprising me, he called me up and told me he was getting his old band together to record a demo.

'What band?' I had said. 'What are you talking about?'

'It's a rock-and-roll band. We used to play together in college.'

'At Lake State? You were in a band?'

'Yeah, we played in all the bars. Didn't I ever tell you about that?'

'What was your band's name, pray tell?'

'We were Leon and the Leopards back then.'

'You're kidding me.'

'But if we really get back together, I'm sure we'll get a new name.'

'Leon,' I had said. 'You are something else.'

'Hey, if I can't do the one thing I love the most . . .'

He didn't have to finish the thought. I knew exactly where he was going. He even tried to do it on his own once. Rented the office, put his name on the door. The whole thing. It didn't work out. He'd been working down at the custom motor shop ever since, selling snow-mobiles.

'Well, music might be a distant second,' he had said. 'Put it that way.'

He was the drummer, which made sense, I guess. If Leon Prudell was going to be in a rock band, it would have to be behind the drums. Just like I had to be a catcher back in my ballplaying days. It just seemed to fit my personality.

'Tell me the truth,' I said to Tyler. 'Are these guys any good?'

'They're a little rough. But they've got . . . something.'

'Uh-huh.'

'They do. It's something.'

'You're a master of diplomacy.'

'You gonna come back inside?'

'I was just getting some air,' I said. Truth was, I had already sat in the studio listening to them for an hour, until my head started to hurt. Between the bright lights, the noise, and for God's sake the cigarette smoke. Either Tyler had people smoking in there in shifts, twenty-four hours a day, or else he was using the place to cure tobacco leaves. I've heard that they've all but banned indoor smoking in some states now, but the idea sure as hell hasn't gotten to Michigan yet.

'It's getting worse,' he said, stepping closer to his dock. 'You can't even see the Point now.'

'The Point? Where's that?'

'It's about a mile out. There was a lumber mill out there, long time ago. You can still see where the bridge was.'

'A bridge?'

'Look down this line. You can see the old pilings.' He gave the air a slow karate chop, and as I followed the line I started to see the dark shapes in the water. There seemed to be two separate lines of them, about five feet apart, running parallel out to where the island must have been.

'What was it, a railroad bridge?'

'Exactly. It was quicker just to go right through the bay, instead of going around. The line ran right through my backyard.'

'When did they close the mill?'

'It burned down one day, around the turn of the century. I've got an old newspaper picture hanging in the house.'

'And they just left those things in the water, all the way out there?'

'They go about halfway. If it wasn't so foggy, you could see where they end. You have to watch out for them when you're out in the boat.'

'I imagine.'

I kept looking at the old wooden pilings in the

water. It looked like the backs of two long sea monsters, swimming side by side into the fog. Then I heard another voice behind me.

'Did the fireworks start yet?' It was Leon. He had a baseball cap on now, with the script *D* of the Detroit Tigers.

'Doesn't matter much,' Tyler said. 'We won't be able to see them. Did you guys decide on a track yet?'

He looked back at the studio. There was a big picture window overlooking the lake, and the light was casting a faint glow on the backyard, all the way down to the water's edge.

'I don't know if we're going to be able to record anything tonight,' he said. 'I'm sorry to waste your time like this.'

'You're not,' Tyler said. 'What else would I be doing on a night like this?'

'It feels like November,' Leon said, rubbing his arms. 'Whatever happened to global warming?'

We heard a faint boom just then, from somewhere around the other side of Waishkey Bay.

'They're trying to do the fireworks,' Tyler said. 'I can't believe it.'

There was another boom. We could see a few red streamers in the air. Just barely. Michigan is already pretty loose with its fireworks laws, and on the reservation it gets even looser. You can fire off just about anything short of an intercontinental missile, but on this night it was a total waste of gunpowder. Whoever it was over there, he fired off five or six more before finally giving up.

'Well, that's it for this year,' Tyler said. 'I think

summer is officially canceled.'

'Wait, what's that sound now?' Leon said.

From inside the studio behind us, somebody ran through a few guitar chords.

'That's your man Eugene,' Tyler said. 'Pretending he's Jimi Hendrix. Does he know how to tune that thing?'

'No, I mean out there,' Leon said.

The guitar stopped. The three of us stood there in the near silence, listening. There was a low droning noise, somewhere out on the bay. It was getting louder.

'It's a boat,' Tyler said.

'Is it safe to be out there?'

'As long as you know where you're going.'

'You can't even *see* where you're going.'

'You have to have the right equipment.'

The noise was getting louder.

'Whoever it is,' Leon said, 'he's going fast.'

'If he's been here before, he can follow one of his old GPS courses . . . But yeah, you're right. Even if you're on a safe line, I don't think you want to be going that fast. You don't know what might get in your way.'

It got louder. It was coming closer to us.

'Wait a minute,' Tyler said. 'It sounds like — '

'He's coming this way,' Leon said.

'He can't. Not this close. He'll run right into the pilings.'

Louder and louder. The unmistakable roar of a powerful boat, and now that it was getting closer, the slapping of the hull against the water.

We saw it. A dark shape, moving fast. Like it was coming right at us. Like it would leap onto

11

the shore and run us over.

'Stop!' Tyler yelled. He ran down onto his dock. 'Cut your motor!'

It was useless. There was no way the driver could hear him. The boat kept coming, and then finally it turned to its port side. It wouldn't hit the dock now. But the pilings.

'Stop! Turn around!'

It didn't. The boat was still just a dark shape in the water, and from where we were standing we could barely tell how big it was. But one thing was certain. The realization probably hit all three of us at exactly the same time. We were about to witness something truly horrible.

I didn't just hear the impact. I felt it in my stomach. It was the long wrenching scrape of the boat's hull against the wooden pilings, far worse than nails on a blackboard. It all happened within two seconds. Before I could even draw another breath the boat had stopped dead. The engine was still churning at the water.

'We need to get out there,' Tyler said. He was already moving.

'Your boat . . .'

'It's on land. I'll get Phil's.' He was heading toward his next-door neighbor's house. 'Call 911! Tell them to send an ambulance and to relay to the Coast Guard.'

Leon pulled a cell phone out of his back pocket and started dialing. As he spoke to the dispatcher, I went down to the dock and looked out at the wreck. It was maybe two hundred yards out. I had no idea how deep the water was. I was wondering if I should dive in, but decided against it. If Tyler could get a boat running, I'd be a lot more helpful riding along with him.

'I'm calling from Brimley,' I heard Leon say into his phone. 'Lakeside Loop, right by where the old bridge went out to the point . . . No, I have no idea . . . No, we can't see anybody. It's too foggy. Yes, we're gonna try that . . . Tyler Barnes is here. He's Coast Guard Auxiliary.'

Tyler came running back down the yard, heading to the dock next to his. Leon was right behind him. By the time I got over there, they already had the boat uncovered and untied.

'Should I go grab the other guys?' Leon said.

'Don't worry about them,' Tyler said. 'We've got to get out there fast.'

'Get in,' I said. It was a runabout, maybe twenty feet long. 'I'll push off.'

Leon jumped into the boat. I gave it a good shove and tried to hop in over the bow. I almost made it, had to hold on tight as one leg went into the water. God, it was cold. I pulled myself up and slid in around the windshield.

'Come on,' Tyler said as he turned the key. The engine clicked but didn't turn over. 'Come on, you son of a bitch.'

'Where's your neighbor?' Leon said. 'Can he start this thing?'

'He's not home,' Tyler said. 'Good thing I know where he hangs his keys.'

He tried to start it again. *Click, click, click.* Then nothing.

'Start, you stupid piece of shit. Turn the hell over.'

'Tyler, those men are probably drowning out

there,' I said. 'We may have to swim for it.'

'Hold on,' he said. 'Just hold on.'

He turned the key again and the engine finally roared to life.

'All right, you pig. Let's move.'

As he pushed the throttle forward, the boat jumped like a startled horse and nearly threw us all overboard.

'Hang on,' he said. 'Let's go see what we can do for these guys. What the hell they were doing out there . . . God, did you see how fast they were going?'

'Be careful,' Leon said. 'Don't run into those things yourself.'

'I know where I'm going. Don't worry.'

It only took us a few seconds to get out to the boat. As we got closer we could hear the whine of their engine. The propeller was still spinning hard.

'We've gotta kill that engine,' Tyler said. 'That's the first thing. Here, Leon. Take this.'

He gave Leon a flashlight. For the first few seconds, the beam did nothing more than reflect in the fog, but as we pulled up to the boat we got our first good look at the damage.

'Holy shit,' Tyler said. 'Look at that thing.'

It was a wooden boat, one of those antique Chris-Crafts. At least twenty-five feet, with that rich polished look you see on the real showpieces. These were the boats they take down to the big Antique Wooden Boat Show in Hessel every summer. Although if this was really one of them, its show days were over. The hull was completely obliterated, with raw wooden planks

14

sticking out in all directions.

The thing was probably worth eighty, maybe a hundred thousand dollars before the wreck. Maybe more. Now it was kindling.

'Do you see anybody yet?' Tyler slowed us down to a crawl.

'Not yet,' Leon said. In the meager light we could make out a canvas top, but it had collapsed. Now it was like a tarp covering the whole cabin.

'This might not be good,' Tyler said. The understatement of the year. I could only imagine what the sudden deceleration had done to whoever was inside this thing. The boat had stopped in an instant, but their bodies would have kept going. And even then, when their bones stopped . . . Their skulls . . . What was inside would still be moving. At that moment, I wouldn't have given fifty cents for their chances of staying alive.

'I'll pull up close,' Tyler said. 'We have to be careful of that engine, though.'

I could see what he meant. The whole boat seemed to be shuddering, as the propeller kept trying in vain to move the whole thing forward.

'Let's get this top off,' Leon said. He was toward the back end of the boat now. I was closer to the front, but the boat was taking on water fast, going down nose first. I had to reach down to grab the canvas. Together we each grabbed on and pulled.

'What the goddamned fuck!' a voice said from inside the boat. 'What happened?'

Leon and I nodded at each other. We pulled

harder on the canvas top. It was heavier than hell, but we were finally able to lift it just enough to see inside.

There were three men in the boat, all of them looking like they'd been thrown forward from where they had been sitting. The one closest to me was lying facedown on the floor, his head in the rising water.

'Grab that guy!' Tyler said. 'Get his head out of the water!'

I jumped into the boat and grabbed him. He was big, and the fact that I was standing in a sinking boat now didn't make things any easier.

'Let go of me!' he said. 'Just leave me alone!'

He knocked my arms away and went back down. With a great heave he threw up everything in his stomach, all over the place. There were beer bottles floating in the water, boat cushions, a fishing pole. And now a few pints of vomit for good measure, spreading all around the boat like an oil spill.

'Cut that engine!' Tyler said.

'I can't get to the controls,' Leon said. 'This guy's out.' He was trying to work his way around the man at the steering wheel. I could see blood on the man's forehead.

'We shouldn't be moving him,' Tyler said. 'But I don't think we have much choice.'

'Let me just get this thing turned off,' Leon said. He tried lifting the man with one arm and reaching for the ignition with the other. He took a small step to shift the man's weight, and that's when everything went crazy. Leon lost his grip and the man fell back onto the throttle, pushing it forward and just about sending us all into outer space. As I fell backward, I saw Tyler jumping into the boat like some sort of long-haired pirate. I heard the wooden hull giving way as the motor drove us against the pilings, felt the cold shock of the water on my back. The only question was how many of us would go down with the boat, or whether the propeller itself would break free and start slicing into human flesh.

I tried to pull myself up, but the big man was trying to do the same and fell right in my lap. Leon was wrestling with his own man, trying to get to the controls. The third man was on his knees now, holding his head like a fighter taking a long eight count.

'Tyler!' I yelled. 'Tyler, cut the engine!'

He climbed over everybody and fell forward, stretching out toward the front of the boat. He reached for the ignition key.

The engine kept churning at the water. The noise was louder than anything else in the world.

Then finally it stopped.

In the sudden silence, I could hear every man breathing. The big man groaned, like he'd be throwing up again any second.

'Is everybody all right?' I said.

'This guy's out,' Leon said, his fingers on the driver's neck. 'But he's alive.'

'These other guys . . . ,' Tyler said. He sat up slowly, holding his shoulder. 'I can't believe they're not out, too. Maybe the boat wasn't going as fast as it looked.'

'Or maybe we're a lot tougher than you think,'

the man on his knees said. He pulled himself up and sat down slowly on the front bench. 'Who are you, anyway? What the hell is going on?'

'Come on,' Tyler said. 'We'll get you to shore.'

'Did you hit us?'

'No, of course not.'

'Did you hit us with your boat? Is that what happened?'

If I could have reached him, I would have smacked him right in the face. 'You hit some old bridge pilings. Now shut up and get in the other boat.'

But when I looked out, I saw Tyler's boat drifting away from us. It had to be fifty feet away by now.

'I got it,' he said. In one smooth motion he was back over the side of the boat, swimming with his head out of the freezing water. Hippie, musician, whatever he was — he was handling everything like a pro. If I had any doubts about him being in the Coast Guard Auxiliary, they were long gone.

'You guys hit us,' the man said again. In the dim light I could see he was in his mid-thirties, maybe. He was wearing a leather bomber jacket. His hair was slicked back on his head, making him look like a drowned rat. The water was up to his waist now, the whole boat going under an inch at a time. 'Goddamn, that's cold.'

'Cap, what are we going to do?' It was the big man. He was apparently done puking.

'They ruined the boat, man. Look at this thing.'

18

'We ruined the boat,' the big man said. 'Didn't you see those things in the water? We ran right into them.'

The man named Cap kept holding onto his head like he had the world's worst hangover. 'I can't even see straight. God, that hurts.'

'What about Harry?'

'What about him?'

'Oh my God, look at him.'

'Holy shit,' Cap said. 'Harry!'

'Is he dead?'

'Harry!'

Both men tried to climb over to the unconscious man. Leon was holding his head up out of the water.

'Be careful!' he said. 'I'm trying to keep him still.'

'Harry! God damn it! Are you alive?'

'He's alive,' Leon said. 'Stop moving the boat until we can get him off.'

'We are so fucked,' the big man said. 'Our lives are over. Do you realize that?'

'Just shut up,' Cap said. 'Okay, Brucie? Will you just shut up?'

'Who are you talking to?'

'Maybe you should both shut up,' I said. 'How about that? Just keep quiet until we can get us all back to shore.'

The big man looked at me. His face was twelve inches from mine. Brucie, the other man called him. What a name for a man the size of a Coke machine. He was about to say something, but the explosion cut him short.

'What the hell is that?'

19

'The fireworks,' Leon said. 'They're starting again.'

There was another explosion, and a faint red glow in the air high above us. Sitting in the ruined wooden boat, it was like we were suddenly transported back to the wrong end of a nineteenth-century sea battle.

'Oh, my head,' Cap said. 'God, that noise is killing me.'

The next few explosions brought a brilliant white light, then another red light, then blue. The fog itself was turning into a very loud ambient light show. It would have been beautiful if we weren't cold and wet, and right below the target zone. One low shot and we'd catch it right in our laps.

'Here's our ride,' Leon said, as Tyler pulled alongside us. We helped the two conscious men into the other boat, and then Leon and I took a few long minutes to carefully lift the third man and pass him over the gunwales. He was deadweight, and we were up to our waists in water now. His head was still bleeding.

'We need to get this man to the hospital,' Tyler said when we were all aboard. 'Did they say they were sending an ambulance, Leon?'

'Yes, they did.'

'Okay, good. I'm sure it'll only take them two or three days to get out here.' He spun the boat around and headed for shore. He was completely soaked from his little late-night swim. He was shivering so hard he could barely grip the steering wheel.

'You guys didn't call the police, did you?' It

was Brucie. In the dim light of the boat, I could see he was about the same age as Cap, with his hair shaved close to his scalp. He had a little gut going, but otherwise he looked as strong as an ape. Aside from the vomit all over his coat, he looked like he could step right out onto a football field.

'The Coast Guard will come around the Point to recover the boat,' Tyler said. 'And the ambulance will take your friend. Hell, they'll want to take all of you, just to be safe. I don't know if the police will come. Does it matter?'

Brucie looked over at Cap. 'No,' he said. 'It doesn't matter.'

Leon's bandmates were waiting for us on the dock. We must have been some sight. We got everybody off the boat and wrapped up in towels. The unconscious man we laid out on the dock. In the dim light from the house, I could see that he was a lot younger than the other two men. He looked like he had just graduated from high school. Tyler covered him with a thick woolen blanket and pressed a clean white cloth against his head. I could see some superficial wounds to his scalp, but God knows what could have happened to him internally. The men all wanted to stay outside with him. So we all stood there on the dock while the fireworks kept exploding in the fog.

'Cap,' Brucie said, 'what if he doesn't make it?'

'He'll make it,' Cap said. 'Just stop talking.'

'What if he's still alive but he's like . . . you

21

know, brain dead. What's going to happen to us then?'

'If you don't shut up,' Cap said, gritting his teeth, 'I'm going to make you brain dead right here on the dock. Okay?'

Brucie kept his mouth shut after that. The time crawled by, until finally the ambulance showed up in Tyler's driveway. I went around and led the men down to the water. A Michigan state trooper showed up a minute later. He wrote a few things down while the EMS guys got the men into the ambulance. Cap and Brucie weren't too sure about going with them. They wanted to drive separately, even though their car must have been a half mile away, at the casino. I was starting to wonder if the trooper would have to break out his nightstick, but the men finally relented and got in the ambulance. My last sight of them was both crammed onto a single bench, squinting in the bright light, while their friend lay on the stretcher in front of them. If there was any gratitude to us for saving their lives . . . well, maybe they'd be sending a nice card the next day.

The trooper stayed a few more minutes. It was the driver himself who had been hurt, so there didn't seem to be a serious crime involved, outside of being criminally stupid enough to drive an expensive wooden boat into an old bridge piling. If they found enough alcohol in the driver's system, they'd have something to ring him up on. But beyond that the whole thing would probably go to the DA and not much else would happen.

'Those pilings,' the trooper said. 'On a night like this? Those guys must not be from around here.'

'I'm surprised it doesn't happen more often,' Tyler said.

'You got that right. Hey, you don't have any coffee, do you? It feels like November out here.'

I never saw the big orange Coast Guard boat show up. I was finally on my way home by then. Around Whitefish Bay, up the lonely dark road to Paradise. The sign in my headlights. WELCOME TO PARADISE, WE'RE GLAD YOU MADE IT! The one blinking light in the center of town.

Then the Glasgow Inn on the right side. It was still open, but I didn't stop. I was still wet enough to be uncomfortable, and besides, I didn't feel like hearing it from Jackie just then. Why I wasn't there all night, what I was doing instead. He'd love the story I'd have to tell him, but it would have to wait until tomorrow.

Come to think of it, some of the evening was almost comical. The way the one guy had asked us if we had hit them. Like we'd actually be out there trying to ram any boats that came by. The big guy throwing up all over the place.

And Leon and the Leopards. That made the whole thing worthwhile, right there. I'd have that over him forever.

I turned onto my access road. There was an almost theatrical mist hanging in the air, like something out of a Frankenstein movie. I passed Vinnie's house. It looked empty. He must have been at the casino still, not yet aware of what had happened out on the bay. I thought he'd probably get a kick out of the whole story, too.

That's what I thought. And would go on thinking until the next morning.

Then after that . . . Hell, if I had known . . .

It seems like an impossible question now, but what were we supposed to do that night, let all three men drown?

I came to my cabin. It was the first of six, all built by my father back in the sixties and seventies. This first one was the one I helped him build myself, back when I was eighteen years old and thought I knew everything, which explains the imperfect fitting of the logs and the cold drafts that come whistling through the walls on a windy night.

When I was out of my truck, I had to wait a few moments while my eyes adjusted to the total darkness. Pine trees, birch trees, an old logging road. A small shed out back and my snowplow sitting up on cinderblocks. And my cabin. That's all there was.

Nobody there waiting up for me.

I checked the answering machine as soon as I got inside. A green glowing zero on the display. She still hadn't called.

I didn't want to think about, didn't want to wonder where she was at that moment, or what she was doing. It was becoming a routine for me, all the things I tried to keep out of my mind. I was getting pretty good at it.

Until I finally lay down in my bed, and turned out the lights. Then they were all there, the doubts and the worries and the mortal fear, having their way with me until I finally fell asleep.

And then on this night, the dream. Me back on the shore, standing in the fog. Thicker in the dream, so thick I can't even see my feet. The sound of something on the water, something I can't see. Just like when the boat was coming, although somehow I know this thing is bigger and moving twice as fast. I can't move. I don't know which way to run, even if I could. I'm just waiting for it, as it gets closer and closer. The thing, whatever it is. Coming right at me, out of the fog.

2

Two months earlier, a fine day in May, the snow finally gone and spring officially in the air. You could feel it. That was her last day in Blind River, as we packed up the old house forever.

There weren't a lot of happy memories there, but it was the only home she ever knew. It was the very same house I had found my way to on a cold and snowless New Year's Eve, five months before, driving up across the International Bridge and following the shore of the North Channel until I finally arrived in this little town. An old logging town with a statue of two men hooking logs in the water. I came that night with a lump in my throat and no clear idea of what I was doing, or if this woman would have any interest in seeing me on her doorstep.

Natalie was her name. Natalie Reynaud.

She was a police officer, a member of the Ontario Provincial Police Force. I had met her when I had come up to northern Ontario with Vinnie, to look for his brother. The results of that search were tragic for everyone involved, Natalie included. She did the one thing that no cop is ever supposed to do. She walked away from a case while they buried her partner.

It doesn't matter what the circumstances might be. Who's at fault. What you could or couldn't have done. Your partner's life is your greatest responsibility as a cop. If he ends up dead, you failed. Simple as that.

I knew this myself. I knew it all too well. On a different police force in a different country, in a different time. Back in 1984, in Detroit, just before crack cocaine made its big debut, when the auto industry was still in a severe slump, the local economy in ruins, when the summer days were too hot and the nights gave no relief. My partner Franklin and I, responding to a simple nuisance call, an emotionally disturbed man who was bothering everyone at the hospital, hiding behind the plants in the emergency room. We found his apartment on Woodward Avenue, sat down with him at his kitchen table, tried to talk to him man to man. The aluminum foil all over the walls, that was our first clue he had precious little connection to the planet Earth.

He had the gun taped to the underside of the table. An Uzi automatic with a .22-caliber conversion kit, retrieved from the Dumpster in his alley. A minute, maybe two, an eternity as we tried to talk some sense into him. Rehearsing my draw in my head, over and over, waiting for the right moment to shoot him in the chest.

He shot Franklin first. Then me. The purr of the automatic weapon, no louder than a sewing machine. Both of us on the floor, looking up at the ceiling. No aluminum foil on the ceiling. I remember that.

Franklin dying next to me, the light going out in his eyes. The hospital, the recovery. Three bullets in my body, the shoulder, the top of the lung, the cavity behind the heart.

The bullet behind my heart still there. It was

too dangerous to try to take it out. Whenever I think about it now, it's a constant reminder of my failure that night. Franklin is in the ground, a wife and a daughter left behind. I walked away from the force and right into a liquor bottle. It's not a terribly original story, and certainly not something I'm proud of. On top of that, I developed a preoccupation with painkillers. To this day I'll still get little cravings for that codeine buzz. The warm embrace that makes you feel like nothing can ever hurt you.

It took a long time for me to be myself again. Or at least something resembling a real human being. I came up here to Paradise to sell off my father's cabins, this lonely place at the mercy of a cold inland sea. The desolation, it somehow felt like home to me. I've been here ever since.

The years passed, each one much like the last. I rented out the cabins to people from downstate. Tourists in the summer, hunters in the fall, snowmobilers in the winter. I chopped wood and kept the cabins clean. That plus the disability checks from the Detroit Police Force, it was enough to live on. I spent my evenings at the Glasgow Inn.

That all changed when I got talked into being a private investigator. Trying it on for size, anyway. As an ex-cop, I was qualified in the state of Michigan. I tried it, it blew up in my face, and it's been one trouble after the next ever since.

Until Natalie.

The first time I saw her, she was jumping out of a moving float-plane as it came in to dock. One simple movement and I could see that this woman was an athlete. It turned out she was a hockey player back in college. A hockey player who led her team in penalty minutes — that summed her up pretty well right there.

She has green eyes. She has a little scar on her chin. What hockey player doesn't have scars? She has brown hair, and she usually has it tied up. When she reaches up to unpin it and it falls down to her shoulders . . . Well, let's just say the image stays with me for a while.

She was a good cop until her partner was killed. Then she took a leave of absence. At the time, I felt like maybe I was the only person in the world who could understand exactly what she was going through. Which is why I showed up at her house on New Year's Eve with a bottle of champagne in my hand.

It was cold outside. Neither of us wanted to be alone. We ended up on the floor of her guest bedroom. That was the beginning.

Things happened after that. Her own past caught up to her, much as mine had. When we finally got through it, it was like we had more in common than ever. I was starting to imagine what it would be like to spend the rest of my life with her. A miracle in itself, that I'd even think that. But then it came time for her to make a choice.

It was time for her to decide if she was ever going to go back to being a cop.

Her commanding officer was a man named Henry Moreland. He was a staff sergeant in the Ontario Provincial Police, stationed up in Hearst. He was the one who sent her out on leave, and now he was the one who was asking her to come back. He believed very strongly that if she didn't do it soon, it would never happen. That if she waited too long, she'd never again be the kind of person who could wear that badge.

Staff Sergeant Moreland and I had had our differences: he seemed to think I was at least partly responsible for all the trouble Natalie had been through. But this was one thing we could agree on. I knew he was right in this case. Even more, I knew the cost of *not* going back. I didn't want it to happen to Natalie. I didn't want her to lose that part of her life forever, and to always wonder if she should have tried to be a cop again.

I wanted her to go back. I hated the thought of her going away, of not knowing how long I'd have to wait to see her again. I hated it, but God help me, I told her to go. I told her to go.

So one more trip out to Blind River, to help her finally close up the house for good. The place was sold. A few last boxes to load up, then she'd say goodbye to it forever.

We went back upstairs one more time, to the room where we first spent the night together. The room was empty now, a sad, late afternoon light streaming through the window. We lay on the floor, just like the first time. But the air wasn't cold now. We weren't feeling desperate and lost, and unsure of what we were doing.

It was slow this time. A couple of hours later, we went outside and looked around the place one more time. We didn't go into the barn. There weren't any good memories there for either of us. No need to relive them.

When it was finally time to go, neither of us knew what to say. Toronto was a long haul. That's where Moreland was assigning her — about as far away as she could go and still be in Ontario. I couldn't help wondering if it was intentional. Hell, if she were a Mountie, he'd probably be sending her to British Columbia, or the Yukon Territory.

I didn't know if this would work. I didn't know if I could still be a part of her life if she was five hundred miles away. All I did know was that, while being alone was something I had grown accustomed to, now it would feel different. Every day, I'd wonder how she was doing. How the job was going. How she was dealing with the city.

We'd talk on the phone every night. That was the promise. I said goodbye to her and told her to take care of herself. I told her not to drive like an off-duty cop all the way to Toronto. 'You always drive too fast,' I told her.

'Yeah,' she said, 'look who's talking.'

I kissed her and told her to get on the road.

I watched her get in her Jeep and start it. She looked at me for a long time. I thought she was going to roll down her window, but then she seemed to change her mind. She pulled down the driveway and turned onto the main road.

I got in my truck and followed her. I never caught up to her. She was driving too fast.

It was a beautiful day in May. It was beautiful enough to make you believe that summer was right around the corner. That was the promise.

That was the hope.

★ ★ ★

She called me that night, as soon as she hit Toronto. She was lonely already, she said. She had no idea what she was doing there. She called me again the next night, after reporting in to the station. Things were a lot different. Toronto's a real city, after all. There's traffic, and noise, and tall buildings. Like any other city, there are good parts and bad, the streets with good food and music and everything you could want, and the streets you don't walk down alone after dark. Coming from Blind River, it must have felt like a different world.

She wanted me to come out to see her. I said I would. Eventually. My gut told me I should wait a little while, let her get settled, let her find her own place before I came and made things more complicated.

But God I wanted to see her.

I talked to her every single night for a month straight. She was working the day shift in the center of the city, right next to Chinatown. The precinct was right on Queen Street. She was doing foot patrol, getting to know the place.

Then June 21, the first official night of summer. The sun hadn't shone in Paradise yet. The temperature hadn't even cracked sixty yet. But it was early still. There was plenty of time for summer to arrive. At least that's how it felt then.

No, it wasn't the weather that got to me that night. It was the fact that she didn't call, for the first time since moving to Toronto.

I called her number. The phone rang a few

32

times. I hung up and went to bed.

The next day, I was surprised by how bad I felt. I didn't want to admit that the phone calls were so important to me. I didn't want to feel like I was depending on them. That they were the only part of the day that really mattered to me. I was starting to think, maybe it's time to go pay her a visit.

She called that night.

'Alex.'

'Natalie, what happened? Are you okay?' The words coming out too strong, before I could stop them.

'I'm fine, I'm fine. I'm sorry about last night. A bunch of us, we went out for drinks, and it got kinda late.'

'I understand,' I said. 'It's no big deal.' I was starting to feel a little off balance. I held on to the phone tight, listening to her quiet voice from five hundred miles away.

'We got talking about what kind of work we'd all done before. I had a couple of beers in me, you've got to understand.'

'Yeah?'

'Normally I don't make a big deal about it, but I started telling everyone about the undercover work I did up in Hearst.'

'You never told me you did undercover work.'

'It was just the one time. This was years ago, when I could still pass for young.'

'Oh, come on, Natalie.'

'I'm serious. On this assignment, I had to be a biker chick.'

'You're kidding me.'

33

'No, I'm not. There was a gang I tried to get close to.'

'A Canadian biker gang?'

'Yeah, why not?'

'I'm picturing a really polite version of the Hell's Angels.'

'Alex — '

'With mufflers on their bikes so they don't make too much noise.'

'How about making crystal meth in a bathtub and selling it to teenagers? Is that polite enough for you? How about beating the hell out of people with metal pipes?'

'I'm sorry.'

'You guys in the States,' she said. At least she was starting to sound a little more like herself again.

'Go on with your story.'

'There was this woman, she was riding with the leader of the gang. They called him rabbit or weasel or something. Some kind of rodent. Anyway, the idea was that if I could get close to her . . . I mean, it was so hard to keep track of these guys. They were always on the move. But if I could help pin them all down on a buy, you know, a definite place and time. We'd nail them.'

'So what happened?'

'Nothing. The guy died on his motorcycle, just about tore his head right off his body. The woman lived for a few days before she finally died, too.'

'So no bust. They never suspected you were a cop?'

'I don't think they ever did, no. I guess I was pretty good at it.'

That was the night, the first night I heard about Natalie's talent for undercover work. I had no idea, although it shouldn't have surprised me. If there's anybody I've ever known who could pass as a biker chick . . .

Yeah, I would have paid to see that one.

I could tell she was tired, so I let her go. She told me she missed me. I said the same. She told me she was going to work crowd control at some big summer festival the next day. The most boring assignment you can draw, moving crowds of people around like cattle, except cattle have better manners. It's even worse than writing parking tickets.

Little did she know, the next day she'd hit the cop jackpot.

★ ★ ★

In Paradise, it was the second day of a summer that hadn't arrived yet. In Toronto, it was the biggest day of Natalie's professional life. I thought about her all day, as I finished the roof on the cabin. I sat in the Glasgow and watched the clock, and I said to myself, this is not a good thing. You sitting here and waiting for it to get dark so you can go home and wait by the phone. This is not the right state of mind.

I couldn't help it.

She called at ten o'clock that night. I could tell something was up. There was a certain energy in her voice. Something I hadn't heard

35

since she moved out there.

'I told you, I was just going to do crowd control today,' she said. 'I was ready for the longest day of my life.'

'I remember.'

'I get to work, and my CO says I need you to go up to the Mounties' office on Yonge Street. I'm thinking, what the hell is this? What did I do wrong now?'

'The Mounties . . . I thought they only worked in provinces without their own police.'

'No, they have a regional office here. For anything national. Or international.'

'What did they want with you?'

'That's what I'm getting to. I go up there, and they take me to the operations room. There's about thirty people in the room, all sitting in chairs. There's a podium up front, a big projector screen. The whole works. They're obviously right in the middle of something. They're showing pictures of people on the screen. But as soon as I go in, everything stops and they're all looking at me.'

She paused for a moment. I didn't say anything. I listened to the faint hum on the line, the sound of the distance between us, until she spoke again.

'The man up front, his name was Keller. He's some kind of special operations commander for the Royal Mounted. He introduced himself, and then he says to everybody in the room, he says, this is Natalie Reynaud of the OPP. She has a certain talent I think you'll all be interested to hear about. I'm thinking, what the hell is going on here? I felt like I'd been called down to the principal's office.'

'I imagine.'

'He says to me, tell us about your previous undercover experience.'

'The stuff you were talking about last night.'

'Yes. He says tell us all about it, so I gave him the whole story. How I had hooked up with these bikers in Hearst. First through the woman and then the leader and everyone else . . . How it never amounted to anything.'

'Because they ended up dead.'

'Exactly. But somebody I was drinking with last night, they must have tipped off Keller, because he got on the phone to the Mountie who had run that operation up in Hearst, way back when. That guy must have given me quite a recommendation, because all of a sudden I'm a natural-born undercover agent.'

'I'm not surprised, Natalie. I'm sure you were great at it.'

'I don't know about that. But next thing I know, they turn on the projector and there's this woman's face on the screen. She's really attractive. Just killer. They say her name is Rhapsody. Which is such a perfect name, isn't it? Doesn't that make her sound like somebody who should be answering the phone at a beauty salon?'

'Sounds more like a stripper to me.'

'Yeah, maybe you're right. Appearing in the lounge tonight, 'Rhapsody in Blue.' '

'I take it that's not what she did for a living?'

'Apparently not. According to Keller, she's

hooked up with a man named Antoine Laraque. And Laraque is the reason why everybody's in that room.'

'Drugs again? Like the biker guy?'

'No, not drugs. Guns.'

'In Canada?'

'I'm telling you, Alex. You wouldn't believe it here. This whole city is going crazy with guns right now. All these gang members, especially in Rexdale, Scarborough . . . It's like they're catching up with the American cities all of a sudden. It's like they picked up Detroit and dropped it in Ontario.'

'Hey, that's my old hometown you're talking about.'

'I'm sorry, but you know what I mean.'

'Sad to say . . . But yes, I do.'

'In fact, as it turned out, half the people in that room were from the States. There's this big joint operation between the ATF and Royal Mounted. Because, of course, you know where all the guns are coming from.'

'Of course,' I said. 'But this sounds like big-league stuff. What exactly do they want you to do? You're not telling me this whole group got together just because you — '

'No, no. The operation's been active for a good two months now. They've got this one Mountie, a guy named Don Resnik. He's a real undercover pro. They were thinking they'd try to use him to make some kind of contact.'

'But then what? You came along? All of a sudden they're changing the plan?'

'They think I'll have a better shot at it. I'm a

new face in town. Nobody will recognize me, and they said if I have this ability to make a connection with another woman . . . Maybe if I have the right kind of backstory to work with . . . Like maybe I'm here in town trying to set up some kind of deal.'

'Natalie, doesn't this sound kind of far-fetched to you? Do you think these people are going to fall for this?'

'We haven't gotten that far yet. Right now, it's just a little test, to see if I can make the contact. But if you think about it . . . I'm the perfect cover, aren't I?'

'How's that?'

'A woman gun dealer . . . Who's going to suspect she's really a cop? It's the ultimate double fake-out.'

'Women cops work undercover all the time. Everybody knows that.'

'Yeah, and it's usually what? A hooker working the corner, right?'

I thought it over for about two seconds. I hadn't seen many solicitation stings back in my own day, but hell, prostitution was usually the least of our problems in Detroit. In any case, I knew she was right. I couldn't think of one single time a female officer had posed as anything else.

'So when does this happen?' I said. 'When do you try to connect with Rhapsody?'

'Tomorrow.' I could hear the excitement in her voice. And the nerves.

'Just like that? What are you going to do, start talking to her at the supermarket?'

'Actually, it's a coffee shop. She stops in there

every morning. I've got this whole script made up. I better go over it again before I go to bed.'

I had a mixture of feelings that night. I was proud of her. I knew how important the operation must have been to everyone involved. If so many guns were really flooding the city, I knew what the effects would be. I knew that all too well. Beyond that, I was envious. She was getting into the kind of police work I would have killed to do myself, back in the day.

But more than anything else, I was scared to death.

★ ★ ★

Another cold day in Paradise. Jackie was starting to get a little cranky about it. I got my first cancellation. I was almost done with the roof. I wasn't much use to anyone, though, because all I could think about was Natalie going undercover in Toronto, trying to connect with this woman named Rhapsody, and then, beyond her, with a network of international gun smugglers. I had to try pretty hard to imagine a worse group of human beings to fool around with.

I think I hit my fingers with my hammer about four times before Vinnie finally stopped by and asked me what the hell was wrong with me. I gave him the quick version. I was up on the ladder, finishing up a row of wooden shingles. The sun was trying to fight its way through the gray clouds, finally giving up for the day. Summer was still on back order.

'She'll be fine,' Vinnie told me. 'You know

they'll be right behind her.'

'Yeah, I know,' I said. 'I know that.' Like I really believed it. Right behind her. Tell that to my old partner.

When we were done, we had dinner at the Glasgow. We sat by the fire. My hands were sore from the cold and the hard work and from hitting them with the goddamned hammer. When it was late enough, I wished everyone a good night and went back home. The phone was ringing when I opened the door, so at least I didn't have to sit there again like a high school kid.

'Alex,' she said, 'tell me what you did today.'

'Never mind me. What happened with the undercover thing?'

'Please. You first. I want to hear about you so I can clear my head a little.'

'What's there to say? I worked on the cabin with Vinnie.'

'Tell me everything. What did you do?'

She wasn't going to let me go, so I told her the spellbinding tale of how we nailed on some more wooden shingles.

'Is it still cold there?'

'It's unbelievable,' I said. 'I've never seen it like this before. It's almost July.'

'It was actually kinda nice here. It was a great day for making new friends.'

'How did it go down?'

'Good, good. I think. I don't know.'

'Tell me what happened.'

'I was in the coffee shop. I was sitting at a corner table, with a laptop. We had one car

41

parked on the street outside, couple of guys in plain clothes. One with a newspaper, the other with a cell phone. She usually stops in around nine or nine thirty, so I was there at eight thirty, just to be sure.'

'Were you nervous?'

'No, not at all. Terrified, maybe. But not nervous.'

'I got it. So go on.'

'I was sitting there for an hour. By nine thirty, there was no sign of her. I kept sitting there, waiting. I was thinking maybe she wasn't going to stop in today. Or maybe, hell, it's crazy but I was wondering if she made us before she even opened the door. Just smelled something funny and kept walking.'

'There's no way.'

'I know. I'm just saying, it's the kind of thing that goes through your head. Anyway, it was almost ten, so I figured we'd have to shut it down. Then she came in. You should have seen her, Alex. She had this white jacket on, black skirt, this blouse that was sort of like a Dalmatian print. Like that woman in the movie. What was her name?'

'What movie?'

'With the Dalmatians. Cruella De Vill. Like her. Except younger. And better looking.'

'Whatever you say.'

'Black-and-white shoes. She even had a white streak in her hair. She was just so . . . put together. Like it was almost too much but not quite. Somehow it looked good on her.'

'What were you wearing?'

'Oh, I was all in black. They bought me this nice black suit, with a short skirt. Black stockings, shoes, the works.'

'I'm trying to picture that,' I said. I had a strong suspicion she looked pretty great dressed like that. It gave me a hollow feeling in my gut.

'They got me a real Coach bag, too. Black, of course. The idea was to show a little flash, but I don't know. Seeing her walk in, I felt totally outclassed.'

'There's no woman on this earth who could outclass you, Natalie.'

She didn't say anything for a moment. 'Yeah,' she finally said. 'Well . . . '

'Keep going.'

'She generally doesn't spend much time there. She gets her coffee and leaves. So I made like I was coming back to get a refill. I was standing right behind her. You should have smelled this perfume, Alex. It smelled almost like Opium, but the top note was different.'

'You're losing me now.'

'Sorry, it's just that . . . I mean, it's funny how much you notice when all your senses are on red alert, you know?'

'Uh-huh.'

'I waited a few seconds, and then I said, 'You're Rhapsody.' She turned around, and she said, 'Do I know you?' She was pretty cold about it, too. Like she wasn't sure if I was wasting her time. I said, 'I hit Kingston right around the time you left. I saw you around for a few days.' '

'Kingston?'

'The women's penitentiary. In Kingston,

43

Ontario. It's closed down now. But the backstory was that I was going in the same week she was going out. Like five years ago.'

'What were you in for?'

'Jailhouse etiquette is not to ask that question, even when you get out. But if it came up, I was in for grand theft and assault.'

'I can see that.'

'Yeah, thanks. Anyway, the whole point of today was for me to just say hello, let her know I recognized her. So maybe the next day, if I was there again — '

'You could strike up another conversation.'

'That was the idea. But she came right out and asked me what I was doing in town, if I lived there now. I told her no, I was just in town for a few days, working on putting a deal together.'

'A deal?'

'Yeah. She asked what business I was in. I said, 'Personal protection.' '

'Very nice.'

'Then I said, 'How about you?' She said, 'Oh, I'm into all sorts of things these days. It's good to be diverse, don't you think?' '

'She said that?'

'She was so smooth, Alex. And here I am with my knees knocking together.'

'Natalie — '

'I had a good exit line, though. As she was leaving, I said to her, 'Nice shoes.' You think Resnik would have thought of that?'

'Natalie, are you sure about all of this? I mean, what's supposed to happen next?'

'Eventually, if we get to it, I'm going to be

there in Toronto, trying to move some guns across the border. I'll have a supplier in Michigan, and I'll be trying to connect with the right person so I can put a deal together. I'll be staying at the downtown Hilton with my muscle.'

'Your muscle?'

'Yeah, Resnik gets to play that part. He's about six foot five, and he looks like he could wrestle a grizzly bear. He's a real good guy, though. Ordinarily, you'd expect him to resent me for coming in and taking over the lead role. But he's been fine with it.'

'Natalie, I'm sorry, but this all sounds crazy to me.'

'You sound like my CO now.'

'Your CO thinks it's crazy, too? Oh, that's a good sign.'

'He's just looking out for me, Alex. A few days ago, I was the new kid on the block. Now I'm going undercover.'

'You're undercover, all right. If this goes any further, you're gonna be about as deep undercover as you can get.'

'They'll take over a whole floor of the hotel, Alex. There'll be men in the rooms on both sides, and across the hall. Cameras, microphones, the whole deal. I'll be the safest woman in Toronto.'

'Yeah, until the bad guys show up.'

'They had another homicide today,' she said. 'Out in Regent Park, with a gun from the States. That's twelve already this year. Twelve people shot dead and it's not even July yet.'

'I hear what you're saying, but — '

'They told me I could keep the clothes when we're done. Not bad, eh? What do you think?'

What I thought was that she was making jokes about it because she had no idea what she was getting into. That she was even more scared than I was, if that were even possible.

'Natalie, for God's sake. Are you gonna be careful?'

'Of course I am. When we're all done here, you're going to come out and visit me, right?'

'Sure. Of course I will.'

'I've got to go to bed now, Alex. I need to meet with everybody again first, then get ready for another meet at the coffee shop.'

'You're gonna call me tomorrow night?'

'I honestly don't know. I'll try to call if I get a chance. But things might happen fast here. Once I get in the hotel, we'll be pretty much working this thing around the clock. It's like my whole life will be on hold for a while.'

'I understand. Call me when you can.'

'I will. Just don't wait up for me, okay? It's going to be hard enough.'

'Hard enough? What do you mean?'

'I'm sorry. That sounds bad.'

'Just tell me.'

'I've got to do this, Alex. Okay? I've got to do this the only way I can. I can't be thinking about anything else tomorrow.'

'All right,' I said. 'I got it.'

'I wish you were here right now. I really do.'

'Me, too.'

'I'll talk to you later.'

I didn't want to end the call like that. But I

didn't know what else to say. I didn't want to put any more pressure on her, didn't want to add any more weight to her burden. I said good night and that was it.

A week later, and I still hadn't spoken to her. She'd leave a message every couple of days. Always during the day, never at night. I'm okay, she'd say, things are moving fast, talk to you soon. I couldn't call her back, of course. At any moment she might have been in character, with Rhapsody or God knows who else right there in the room with her.

Seven days, and the only time I wasn't thinking about her were those few minutes on the night of July 4, when I was pulling those guys off the sinking boat. Otherwise, no matter what I was doing, working on the cabin with Vinnie, sitting at the Glasgow, lying in my bed and staring at the ceiling, she'd be right there in my head and I'd be wondering if she was safe.

Seven days with me going quietly insane while Natalie put her head in the lion's mouth.

3

The morning after the boat wreck, I woke up so goddamned sore, it was like I had been in the wreck myself. My arms hurt, my back hurt, and it felt like I had somehow pulled both hamstrings. Getting out of bed was comical. I got in a hot shower and let the water pound on me until I loosened up a little bit. When I was dressing I looked outside and saw the trees bending. That plus a light rain I knew would feel like cold buckshot in the wind. It's July 5, I told myself. This is not a hallucination. It's really the middle of the damned summer.

A cup of coffee and I was out the door. I could have gone down to the Glasgow for breakfast, but I wanted to get two hours of work done before I did that. I got in the truck and headed down the access road, past the second cabin my father had built, then the third, the fourth, and the fifth. They were all empty now. The people who had booked them had looked in the newspaper, had seen a high of maybe fifty-two degrees, a low of thirty-nine. They had decided they could just stay home and be miserable instead of coming all the way up here. I couldn't blame them.

I came to the last cabin, a half mile down the road. I had been rebuilding it for the past few months. Vinnie had been helping me when he could. Things had once gotten a little sideways between the two of us, and this is how we made up. He showed up to help one morning, and without saying a word we were good again.

When I got out of the truck, I spent a few minutes looking around the outside. The little grooves I had cut on the bottom logs were doing their job, collecting the rain and letting it drip off away from the foundation. Thank God the roof was on now, was all I could say this morning. There's no way we could get up there today and work on it without killing ourselves.

I went inside the place. It was still just a rough shell at this point. I had been trying to restore it to its full glory, to make it the best cabin in the Upper Peninsula again. This was my father's masterpiece, after all. When it was burned down . . . Well, it had become an obsession with me to rebuild it.

I went inside and took my coat off. About five minutes later, I knew I either had to put the coat back on or build a fire. I wasn't sure which was more ridiculous, but I figured the fire would make things a little cozier at least. I put some paper and wood in the new stove and lit it. That's when Vinnie showed up. Vinnie LeBlanc, in his old denim coat with the strip of fur around the collar. His hair was tied in a ponytail today.

'Why aren't you using the fireplace?' he said. He was the kind of guy who never said good morning. Or goodbye.

'I wasn't sure how long I'd be here.'

'Is that draft still coming down? You've got to fix the flue on this thing.' He bent down and looked up the airway. This fireplace had always been his favorite part of the cabin. The way my old man had saved up all the rocks he had dug up over the years, until he had finally taken on this monumental task of building a two-story fire-place by hand. I couldn't even imagine how he had done it alone. Hell, for that matter, how he had done *any* of this alone. Clearing the property, building these cabins, each one better than the last. It must have been therapy for him, after my mother had died. Something to do instead of sitting at the window, staring out at the street.

'What are you going to start on today?' Vinnie said. 'The stairs?'

'I thought we should get the flooring in first. Then we can do the stairs.'

He looked up at the beams crossing the room above our heads. 'You want to put the second floor in before you even build the stairs to get to them?'

'That's what ladders are for. It'll be easier to do the stairs after we have something to build up to.'

'You just want to get the floor in so it'll look almost done. I'm telling you, it's a bad decision.'

'What are you talking about?'

'You're too impulsive. You know that. You don't do things in the right order.'

I stood there looking at him. 'You're being a little abrupt this morning,' I said. 'Even for you.'

'Abrupt? Who says 'abrupt'?'

'What's the matter, Vinnie?'

'Nothing,' he said. He didn't look me in the

eye. 'Let's get some work done. We can do it your way if you really want to.'

As he bent down to pick up his tool belt, I heard the little grunt he let out. I saw him stand back up a little stiffly.

'Vinnie, what happened to you?'

'Nothing. Come on, let's do it.'

'Stop,' I said. I went over to him and grabbed him by the shoulders. Up close I could see the bruise on his face, just outside his left eye.

'Who did this?'

He looked away. 'It's nothing.'

'You got clocked pretty good here. Who was it?'

'Some guys at the casino. We had a little altercation last night.'

'Some guys? How many?'

'There were three of them. They were all at one table, getting totally lit up, making a racket. I asked them to turn it down a notch, but they didn't seem very cooperative.'

'Three men, you say?'

'Yeah. One of them looked underage. The other two were real hard cases. I eventually had to ask them to leave, and I tried to escort them outside personally. That's when things got a little out of hand.'

'Just out of curiosity, was one of them rather large?'

He started rubbing the side of his face, where the bruise was. 'Yeah, one of them.'

'Did they happen to leave on a boat?'

He stopped dead. 'Yes, they did. How did you know that?'

'You're gonna hate me for this,' I said. 'But I think I helped save their lives.'

★　★　★

We started on the stairs. I told Vinnie I was just humoring him, but deep down I knew he was right. He usually is. We got in a couple of hours, but I was working on an empty stomach. So we left everything where it was for a while. I asked him if he wanted to join me at the Glasgow. He probably spent more time there than anybody, not counting Jackie and myself, but today he begged off. He wanted to go down to the rez and check up on his mother. Ever since his brother died, it was something he made a point of doing at least once every day or two. I couldn't even imagine how many times he got asked why he wasn't living on the rez himself now. Sometimes I wondered what his answer was, when it was just Vinnie and his family and they really wanted to know why he was living up here in Paradise.

He told me he'd be back after lunch, that he'd meet me there. So I went down to the Glasgow on my own. Past my empty cabins, with the wood split and stacked next to each front door, waiting for somebody to decide it was worth making the trip again. There's a spot right where you turn onto the main road — you can see the lake through a break in the trees. The wind was kicking up three-foot breakers now. The sky was such a dark shade of gray, it was like you couldn't even imagine the sun ever coming out again.

I pulled into the lot and went inside. The place was empty. I stood there in the doorway wondering where Jackie was, until finally he came out of the kitchen, carrying a case of beer.

'It's you,' he said. A typical greeting. Born in Scotland, he had come to Michigan as a teenager. Fifty-odd years later, you could still hear a slight burr in his voice.

'Where is everybody?'

'Who the hell knows? If they live here, they're probably at home in a deep depression. And if they don't live here, they'd be crazy to come.'

That pretty much summed up Jackie's attitude these days. He was taking it hard. Not just because there weren't any tourists around. Hell, he probably didn't mind that part at all. But Jackie loved the summers up here, maybe more than anybody I could think of. He's the guy who would pull his car over to watch a sunset.

Maybe it was in his blood, some Scottish thing. A better appreciation for the kind of day they didn't often see back in Glasgow. Or maybe he was just a tough old bird who had made it through another winter and expected a little sunshine.

'And where were you last night, anyway?' he said. He set down the beer and started putting the bottles in the refrigerator below the bar.

'Any chance of me getting an omelet?'

'Go right ahead. You know where the kitchen is.'

'Come on, Jackie.'

'The one night I actually could have used some company,' he said. He banged another bottle in the refrigerator. 'There wasn't a single soul in this place. Can you believe that? First night I've ever seen that happen.'

'Cheese and ham. Green peppers if you have them.'

He stopped what he was doing, just long enough to glare at me.

'Come on,' I said. 'It'll take your mind off your troubles.'

'Use the small pan,' he said. 'And don't burn anything. It only takes a couple of minutes.'

'Jackie . . . '

'Why are you limping, anyway? Did you go find some trouble somewhere?'

'You can ask Vinnie about it later. He's the one with the bruises.'

'I'm asking you.'

'Jackie, are you seriously not going to make me an omelet?'

'Two eggs, Alex. It's so easy even you can do it.'

'Fine. You're obviously too busy out here with all your customers.'

He slammed the case down, a little clue that maybe I was pushing my luck. I went back into the kitchen and started rummaging around. I found the right pan, then I took out two eggs and broke them.

Not a minute had gone by, and Jackie was right there next to me. 'What are you doing? Didn't you ever learn how to break an egg?'

'It's not that hard.'

'Get out of the way.' He pushed me aside and started taking the little bits of eggshell out of the pan. 'You don't have the heat high enough, either. I swear, you're the most useless human being I've ever seen.'

'Oh, I forgot to say . . . Good morning.'

He threw in the green peppers. 'You need to wait with the cheese, too. Until the very end. You getting all this?'

'If I start doing all this for myself, you won't even have a reason to get out of bed in the morning.'

He took his spatula and worked it around the edges. This was the part that always threw me. This was when I'd usually give up and just scramble them.

'Have you talked to her?' he said.

I didn't answer. I was surprised he had even asked. Jackie was the veteran of a bad marriage and an even worse divorce, and at this point in his life I didn't figure he'd be changing his opinion on relationships with the opposite sex.

'Not in a while.'

He nodded. 'It's hard. Toronto's a long way.'

'There's more to it. She's working.'

'It's a long way, Alex. There doesn't have to be any other reason.'

I wasn't sure what to say to that. Or if I could even argue his point.

He put the cheese in and folded the omelet perfectly. 'Get out of my kitchen.'

'You're a prince.'

'Yeah, yeah. Go sit down.'

'I think Vinnie might need one, too. He'll probably be here later.'

'Is that right?'

'Yeah. Your customer service needs a little work.'

I left the kitchen before he could hit me with the pan. I sat down in one of the overstuffed chairs, put my feet up by the fire.

Jackie came back out with the omelet. He set the plate down on the little table. He stood there looking a little lost for a moment, like he didn't know what to do next.

'You should be enjoying this,' I said. 'Nobody else to worry about for a while. Hell, you could even close the place and go somewhere.'

He sat down in the other chair, made a sound like my suggestion was the most ridiculous thing he'd ever heard.

'It just feels strange,' he said.

'By strange you mean . . . cold.'

'No. It's more than that. Did you see that sky out there? It looks like the world's gonna end soon.'

'For God's sake, you should go to Florida. Or where's your son these days? Boston? You should go visit him.'

'It's just . . . wrong, Alex.' He sat back in his chair. 'Something in the air is just plain broken.'

That was the cheerful thought that hung in the air for the next hour or so. Jackie stayed by the fire. I kept my feet up. I could have gone back up and worked on my own, but I was in no hurry. Wait until Vinnie shows up, I told myself. And I hope he takes his time.

The wind picked up outside. It would be raining soon. It would be the rain that blows sideways and makes you colder than any winter

56

snowstorm ever could.

Something in the air, Jackie had said. Just plain broken.

The door opened. Two men came in. I didn't recognize them at first. I thought it was just two strangers stopping by for lunch, or for a drink. Then I saw the damage. The first man through the door had a bandage on the left side of his face, right along the jawline. The big one had his right wrist wrapped up with an Ace bandage.

The third one . . . He wasn't here, but then he was the one who was unconscious when we found them.

The first guy was wearing the same leather bomber jacket. He was a little shorter than I remembered. He looked around the place, then came right over to me. 'You're McKnight,' he said. 'I remember you.'

'How did you know my name?' I didn't get up from the chair.

'I was over by your friend Tyler's place today. I wanted to find out who you are. And Mr. Prudell, too.'

'Yeah?'

'My name's Caplan, by the way. You can call me Cap. This is Bruce,' he said, indicating the big guy. Bruce nodded to me. With his wrist all wrapped up, he didn't look inclined to shake my hand.

'Reason we're here,' Cap said, 'is we just want to thank you. You know, for helping us out.'

'It's all right,' I said. 'You didn't have to come all the way up here.'

'Seriously, man. Least we can do is buy you a drink.'

'That's not necessary.'

'I insist. Please.' He stood there, his arm straight out as an invitation to the bar.

'No, really.'

'Where's the bartender, anyway?'

'I'm right here,' Jackie said. He got up from the chair. 'Come on, Alex. Show the men some consideration. If they want to buy you a drink, let them.'

'That's right,' Cap said. 'You should listen to this man.'

'That'll be the day,' Jackie said. He went back behind the bar.

I got up slowly, wishing hard that I had told Jackie a little more about what had happened the night before. Maybe then he wouldn't have been so fast with the hospitality.

'What are you having, Mr. McKnight? May I call you Alex?'

'Jackie knows what I drink.'

Cap took one stool at the bar. The big man, Bruce, took another, leaving one open for me, right between them.

'Here you go,' Jackie said, setting me up with a cold Canadian. 'Are you gonna share some of your private stash with your friends here?'

I gave him a look that should have taken ten years off his life. But before another word could be said he was taking out two more Canadian beers and putting them on the bar.

'What do we have here?' Cap said.

'Alex only drinks beer that's been bottled in

58

Canada,' Jackie said. 'See if you guys can tell the difference.'

I kept staring at Jackie. I couldn't imagine why he was acting like a good host all of a sudden. He certainly didn't use it on most people. Hell, if it was wintertime and you stopped in for one, he'd probably be yelling at you about the snow on your boots before you closed the door behind you.

It was the day, I thought. The strange, strange day, and the fact that he hadn't seen a real paying customer all week. It was going to his head.

'This is outstanding,' Bruce said. He was holding the bottle in his huge hand, looking down at it with admiration. 'Absolutely outstanding.'

'I agree,' Cap said. There was something about the way he talked. He was too self-aware, too smooth for his own good. I thought I had him figured pretty well, the type of guy I'd run into my whole life, in high school, in baseball, then later on both sides of the badge. Three inches too short, always trying too hard to make up for it. All car and haircut, and not much else.

Yeah, I thought I had him pegged.

'Did Alex tell you how we met last night?' Cap said to Jackie.

'No, he didn't.'

'Well . . . we were out in a boat. It was pretty dark. And foggy.'

'Last night?' Jackie said. 'You were out in a boat? You're kidding me.'

'Pretty dumb, I know. We paid for it, believe

59

me. Yes, sir. We were at the casino down in Bay Mills, and we ended up going out across the bay.'

'Don't tell me,' Jackie said. 'Those old bridge pilings . . . '

'Is that what those things are? We never even saw them. Next thing I know, we were stopped dead and the goddamned boat was sinking.'

'What kind of boat was it?'

'Ah, some old thing,' Cap said. 'A wooden boat.'

'A Chris-Craft,' I said. 'It looked like somebody had put a lot of work into it.'

'Wait a minute,' Jackie said. 'You guys drove an antique Chris-Craft into those pilings?'

'Whose boat is it, anyway?' I said.

Cap looked at me. 'It's Harry's boat.'

'It's his dad's boat,' Bruce said.

'It *was* his boat,' Cap said.

'Harry was the driver.'

'Yes.'

'How many drinks did he have before you guys went out?'

Cap hesitated again. 'Two drinks. Maybe three. Harry can hold his liquor. Believe me, he wasn't drunk.'

'How old is he?'

'He's legal, don't worry. He looks younger than he is.'

'And where is he now? Is he still in the hospital?'

'Yes. In Sault Ste. Marie. I'm sure he'll be fine.'

'Do you know that for a fact?'

'I don't know what you mean, Alex.'

'Did you talk to the doctor?'

'I talked to Harry. He'll be fine.'

'He looked pretty banged up last night. I'm surprised he's even awake today.'

'Alex, as I told you, we just came out here to show our appreciation.'

'That didn't seem to be your attitude last night,' I said. 'As I recall, you accused us of hitting you. Like we'd actually be out there on the bay, waiting for someone to come by so we could ram them.'

Cap didn't say anything. He kept looking at me, straight in the eye. Jackie stood on the other end of the bar, watching us. He must have been wondering what the hell was going on.

'I think we're getting off on the wrong foot here,' Cap finally said. 'Everything happened so fast last night. I think we were all a little in shock or something.'

'Yeah. Or something.'

He started tapping his fingertips on the beer bottle. 'Okay,' he said, drawing out the word. There was a little smile on his face.

'Before you guys got in the boat,' I said, 'did you happen to run into a little trouble at the casino?'

'What do you mean?'

'At the Bay Mills Casino. Did you happen to have a little altercation with someone who works there?'

'There may have been a little misunderstanding. Some Indian trying to act like a tough guy.'

'The pit boss, you mean.'

'Yeah, whatever. Without the casino he'd

probably be selling little totem poles to tourists.'

'I kinda doubt that. Anyway, he's a friend of mine. You guys gave him some nice bruises.'

'This *is* a small town,' Cap said. 'Didn't I tell you, Brucie?'

I didn't see the big man's reaction. I was still looking at Cap.

'Why are you really here?' I said.

'I told you.'

'Okay, then. You bought me a drink.'

'Maybe there is one more thing.'

'Surprise.'

I saw it in his eyes just then. The little flash of anger. It came quick, like it wasn't that far away to begin with. Not far away at all.

'There was a box in the boat,' he said. 'About this big.' He held up his hands about four feet apart.

'What about it?'

'It was yellow and black. Airtight. You know, designed to float.'

'What was in it?'

'Some valuables. Wallets, cash, that kind of thing. It's just a box to keep things safe. Like a lockbox.'

'I never heard of a lockbox that floats.'

'It was in a boat,' he said. He seemed to be measuring his voice carefully now. 'Everything in a boat should float, don't you think?'

'You may have a point. But why are you telling me all this?'

'I was just wondering if you happened to see it.'

'No, I didn't.'

'It was in the front of the boat,' he said. 'At one point, I remember seeing it. I was going to grab it, but that was when the other guy jumped in to turn off the motor. And then after that I think we were all pretty occupied with Harry. You know, making sure he was still alive and everything. I never saw the box after that.'

'I never saw it at all. It probably just floated away.'

'I'm not sure about that.'

'Or else it sank. It might have gotten damaged and filled up with water.'

'You're answering pretty quick. Are you sure you don't want to think about it?'

I counted to three in my head. 'I didn't see it. I didn't touch it. I don't know anything about it. I can't help you.'

He finally blinked. He looked down at his bottle. I could see the veins in his forearms standing out as he worked his hands. If something was going to happen here, it was me and Jackie against the two of them. And the biggest man in the room was right behind me.

'Do you . . . ,' he started to say, slowly, 'have any idea . . . '

'Cap,' Bruce said.

'Shut up, Brucie. I'm talking to the man. I think he needs to understand some things.'

'Or not,' I said. 'I think I'll just stay in the dark, if you don't mind. I'd like you both to leave now.'

'He needs to understand, Brucie. The man needs some enlightenment.'

There was an old baseball bat under the

63

counter. Jackie had had it there for years, and never had to use it. Not once. At that moment, I couldn't help wondering if it was still there.

'He really, really needs to understand.' He was working his hands harder and harder. Opening them and closing them. The only question now was how fast I could hit him with my bottle, and then what the big guy would do to the back of my head.

That's when the door opened and Vinnie walked in.

4

Five hundred miles. Paradise, Michigan, to Toronto, Ontario. Across the International Bridge, then up around the North Channel, right through Blind River in fact, past the house where Natalie grew up. Turning south finally around Sudbury, down the eastern edge of Lake Huron, through Big Chute, through Barrie. Finally coming to the city itself, on the northern shore of Lake Ontario.

Or if you're a bird, you fly right over all that water. Like many other things in this life, how much quicker it is if you don't have to go around something so unimaginably big.

Or in my case . . . It's almost immediate. I'm already there, in my mind, a thousand times every day. When I open my eyes in the morning, cold sunlight in my cabin window, I'm thinking about her doing the same in her own bed. Somehow I can feel that she is awake at the same moment I am. I can hear the shower as she steps into it. I know how long it takes her to be ready to face the day. Her hair dried, a few brush strokes across her cheeks. That's all she needs. How much she hates to waste time.

I know when she's driving her Jeep. The music she is listening to. The sounds of a city all around her. It's a miracle that I know this, moment to moment. A miracle both wonderful and terrible at the same time. After so many years, to feel this way.

I don't know how long it can last. Even now, I can feel it start to fade sometimes. A faraway station on the radio, lost in the air. In the mornings especially, when she goes to the operations room instead of to the precinct. Her whole routine different now. I have to ask her about it after the fact to fill in the blanks. That she has to take more time in the morning to put herself together. That she's already wearing her undercover clothes when she drives into the city. That she's still meeting with the task force before she heads out to the coffee shop.

It's become a regular thing now. Seeing Rhapsody there, spending a few minutes at one of the tables. It's hard for me to imagine how that would feel, to be on stage every day. To be somebody completely different from yourself. I don't know how long it will take for Natalie to win Rhapsody's trust, assuming she ever does. How long it will take, with just a few words every morning, to steer things around to a certain type of merchandise that might find its way from the States to Toronto for the right price.

Five hundred miles away from me, it's all coming together, day by day. Natalie is inching her way closer to the man they call Antoine Laraque.

★ ★ ★

It took about five seconds for the men to remember where they'd seen Vinnie before. That

66

was just enough time for Jackie to grab his bat from under the bar, and for me to slide out from between Cap and his pal Brucie. Now it was two against three plus a baseball bat, on our home field.

Cap played it cool. He took another long pull off his beer, like he had never had any other intentions. Vinnie kept standing in the doorway, looking like something out of an old western. Brucie just looked at Jackie and his bat, like the sight was vaguely amusing.

'I get the impression,' Cap said finally, 'that we're not welcome here anymore.'

'Leave this bar,' Jackie said. 'Leave it now.'

'How much for the beers?'

'Just. Leave.'

Cap put the bottle down. He gave his friend a little tilt of his head and then aimed for the door. When he got to Vinnie, he looked him up and down for a moment. 'We have to stop meeting like this,' Cap said.

Vinnie didn't say anything. He stepped aside slowly and let them pass. They opened the door and left the place. Through the window I could see them getting into one of those big Cadillac Escalades. It was black with silver trim.

'What did they want?' Vinnie said.

'They wanted to buy me a drink,' I said. 'So Jackie gave them some of my beer.'

'How the hell was I supposed to know better?' Jackie said, putting the bat away. 'You could have said something.'

'Is that all they wanted?' Vinnie said. 'It looked

67

like they were getting ready to tear this place apart.'

'After they expressed their gratitude, they sort of moved on to another topic. Apparently, there was some kind of floating box in the boat last night. They seemed to think I might know something about it.'

'Did you?'

'I honestly never saw it.'

'A floating box. What the hell could have been in there?'

'They said it was just their wallets and cash.'

'Who gets in a boat, takes out their wallet, and puts it in a box?'

'Yeah, it sounded a little fishy to me, too.'

Vinnie thought about it for a while. 'I'm gonna head out,' he said. 'We can get back to work tomorrow, eh?'

'What are you going to do?'

'I just want to check on something.'

'On what? Vinnie, for God's sake, you're not gonna do something stupid, are you?'

'No, I just want to go see somebody, make sure she's all right. A woman who was working at the casino last night.'

'You want me to come with you?'

'No, she might not talk to me if you're there.'

'Vinnie, you're not going after them now, are you? Am I gonna have to bail you out of jail again?'

'One time, Alex. One time in my whole life. You make it sound like I get put in jail every week.'

'I'm just saying. If you're gonna go do

something stupid, let me know first. So we can do it together.'

'Okay, I promise. I'll see you later.'

And then he was gone, too. I finished my beer and watched Jackie trying to calm himself down.

'I would have hit the big guy,' he said. 'I swear to God. If he had laid a hand on you, I would have broken that bat right over his head.'

'Nothing like a wood bat,' I said. 'Don't you hate the sound those aluminum bats make?'

'What?'

'When you hit him, it would have been 'clang!' I hate that sound.'

'You're worse than Vinnie.'

'No, I think it's a tie.' I got up, went back to the chair by the fire, and grabbed my coat.

'Where are you going?'

'Same deal,' I said. 'I've gotta go check on somebody, too.'

★   ★   ★

I thought about what the man had said as I drove. He needs to understand, Brucie. The man needs some enlightenment. Unless it was the most useless bluff in the history of bluffing, this man named Cap knew something important. Maybe he was important himself. Although, hell, I didn't even know his last name. I had no idea who the hell this man was.

The rain started. I took Lakeshore Drive, my favorite lonely road in the world, but today the view was nothing but a study in gray. Water. Sky. The whole mood of the day.

I took the road all the way down to Brimley. I could have stopped at the reservation, tried to find Vinnie, but I let him be. Instead I went to Tyler's house. I parked in front, happy not to see the black Escalade there. Although from what they had said, it sounded like they had already paid a visit here. I knocked on the front door.

A woman answered. She was about five foot nothing, and she looked like she came from the same hippie culture as Tyler. She had a wonderful smile, though. The kind of smile that makes you feel welcome. On a day like this, it was exactly what I needed.

'Is Tyler here?' I said.

'He's in the studio. Come on around.'

She opened the door farther, and together we walked around the house to the back, where the big garage was. 'How do you like this weather?'

'I think we should all get our money back.'

'It'll warm up soon. It always does.'

'I hope you're right,' I said. I was thinking maybe I should hang around this woman for the rest of the day. Maybe some of her optimism would rub off.

Tyler was in the studio, earphones on his head and a cigarette in his mouth. In the daylight I could see out the big picture window. There in the cold water were the two rows of dark wooden pilings leading out toward the point. I couldn't see the boat, at least not in the water. But there was something on the shore, covered by a large blue tarpaulin.

'Alex!' he said when he saw me. He took the

70

earphones off. 'Did those jackasses pay you a visit, too?'

'I'm afraid so. It sounds like they were here earlier.'

'I'm sorry about that, man. I would have called you if I had your number. I don't think I ever got your last name.'

'It's McKnight.'

'This is Liz,' he said. 'The old lady.'

'The next time he calls me 'the old lady',' she said as she shook my hand, 'I'm going to throw him in the lake.'

'Come on outside,' Tyler said. 'You gotta see this.'

We went out to the backyard, to the same spot we had been standing when it all happened the night before.

'The Coast Guard finally came around midnight,' he said. He started moving the rocks that were holding the tarpaulin in place. 'After everyone else had already left. They were gonna put out lighted warning buoys.'

'Not that anyone else would be stupid enough to go out there,' Liz said.

'So I told them, just see if you can pull the wreck loose. I'll tow it closer and then pull it onto the shore with my winch. It was so low in the water, I wasn't sure they'd get it free. But eventually they did. And here it is.'

He pulled the tarpaulin off with a flourish, like he was unveiling a great piece of art. Actually, that's exactly what this thing was — but it was a piece of art that had been rammed full speed into a wooden post. In the light of day, the damage was spectacular. The hull was opened up halfway down the centerline, the planks either broken clean through or splintered in every direction. In some places, you could see the unfinished wood, the way it must have looked decades ago, before it was varnished.

'Can you believe this?' He ran his hand across the topside, where the wood was still smooth and perfect. 'All the work somebody must have put into this thing.'

'And the money,' Liz said.

'I had to cover it up last night,' he said. 'It's just obscene. It hurts me to look at it.'

'Can you imagine how hard they must have hit that thing? I can't believe those guys lived through it.'

'I wonder how the driver is. They said he was in the hospital, but they didn't even know how he was doing today.'

'Yeah, I wouldn't be real happy with those guys,' I said, 'if they were my friends.'

'I'm not too happy with them myself. They showed up here this morning and wanted to see the boat. I was thinking they might want to salvage the motor or something, but no, they just started looking inside the thing. Then they started looking on the shoreline. Eventually, God, they must have gone down a half mile in each direction, looking in the water. Going through everybody's backyards and out on the docks. They even wanted me to get Phil's boat and take them out to where the wreck happened. I told them there was nothing to see out there. That's when they started to get weird on us. You

72

know, like when they first got here, they were telling us how grateful they were for the help last night. But then they started talking about some box they were looking for.'

'A floating lockbox,' Liz said.

'Whatever the hell that is. They didn't seem to believe we didn't know anything about it.'

'That sounds familiar,' I said.

'We told them there was nothing else we could do. But they didn't seem to like that. Eventually, we had to persuade them to leave the property.'

'Okay, and how did you do that?' I was having a hard time picturing how these two could be so persuasive. Unless . . .

'I brought out one of our shotguns,' Liz said. 'I believe it was the Remington.'

'Yeah, the over-and-under,' Tyler said. 'You should have seen the look on their faces when she racked that thing. They changed their tune pretty fast.'

They were both smiling at the memory now. God love them, I thought. Only in Michigan.

'Well, I hope you guys are going to be careful,' I said. 'They could come back.'

'Let them come,' Liz said. 'I'm a good shot.'

I took out one of the cards Leon had made for us and gave it to them. I told them to call me if they ever saw the men again.

'What's this?' Tyler said. 'You and Leon are private investigators?'

'We were,' I said. 'For about five minutes. Which reminds me . . . Oh no . . . '

'What is it?'

'If they came to see you, and they came to see me . . .'

'You're right, they probably stopped by Leon's place,' Tyler said. 'Is that a problem?'

'That all depends,' I said, 'on who was home.'

★ ★ ★

From Brimley I kept heading east on Six Mile Road, past the old abandoned railroad car, through the last of the Hiawatha National Forest, and then out into the open hay fields. I didn't know how this weather would affect the crop this year, but I didn't imagine it would help any.

I crossed the highway and drove through Sault Ste. Marie — 'the Soo,' as the locals call it. Up to Three Mile Road, and into the parking lot for the Custom Motor Shop. That's where Leon worked these days. It was a far cry from his dream job, but the man had a family to feed. The place looked pretty quiet today. No surprise given the miserable weather. When I went in, they told me that Leon had left early. In fact, he had received a phone call, and had left in a hurry without saying a word.

Exactly what I was afraid of. I got back in the truck and headed south. The first small town down the road was Rosedale. That's where Leon lived, in a little house on a dead-end road, with a tire swing hanging from the big oak tree in the front yard.

I parked the car in the driveway, right behind Leon's little crappy red Chevy Nova. I rang the

74

front bell. Leon's wife Eleanor opened the door, and her face told me everything I needed to know.

'Before you say a word — ,' I said.

'Hello, Alex.' Eleanor Prudell was a large woman, to put it mildly. She was also probably the strongest woman I had ever met. I had seen her lift Leon right off the bed once, back when he had two broken ankles. And Leon had to go at least 240.

Eleanor loved me. I knew that. She would have done anything in the world for me. But at the same time, she couldn't help associating me with some very bad moments in her life. She knew all about Leon's desire to be a private investigator. She tried to understand when he opened up that office in the Soo, even though she knew the business would almost certainly fail. She could have lived with all of that, but the real problems began whenever I was involved. Even though it was Leon's idea that we be partners, even though I never bought into the private investigator thing to begin with, it was always me who somehow managed to find trouble. It was always me who came asking Leon for help. Which usually meant something dangerous. The time we got shot at out on the lake, that was probably the worst of it. Of course, Leon didn't absolutely *have* to tell her everything. But he did.

'I take it you got a visit today,' I said.

'There were two of them,' she said. 'I was here alone.'

'What did they say?'

'Our kids could have been here. Thank God

they're at camp today.'

'Ellie, what did they say?'

'They wanted to know where Leon was. They said they had to ask him some questions.'

'Well, on the plus side, you probably could have taken both of them at once.'

'That's not funny.'

'I know. Look . . . '

That's when Leon appeared behind her. 'Alex,' he said. 'What's going on? Is everything okay?'

'I was checking to see if you're all right,' I said. 'Did you tell Ellie what happened last night?'

'Yes.'

'Especially the part about you inviting me out to Tyler's studio, and then how the boat crashed and we saved those guys?'

'Right, and how none of this was your fault, for once.'

'Yeah, that's great. Thank you.'

Eleanor came out the door and hugged me. The trick is to inhale quickly so you don't end up with any broken ribs.

'Damn you, Alex. I just . . . '

She looked away from me. She was genuinely scared to death by all this, and I guess I couldn't blame her.

'It's okay,' I said. 'We'll make sure they don't come back here. I promise you.'

She nodded her head. She put her hand on my arm, then she turned and went back inside the house. That left me and Leon standing there on the porch.

'I'm sorry,' I said. 'I don't know what else to say.'

'Don't worry about it. Really. She'll be fine.'

'Leon, what did we get ourselves into here, anyway? I thought we were just helping those guys out. It's not like we could have left them out there.'

'I guess we should have, eh? We should have let them drown.'

'As it turns out, Vinnie already has a little history with these guys.' I gave him the rundown, with Vinnie throwing them out of the casino last night. And then walking in on them today, at the Glasgow.

'Do you think he'll go after them now?'

'I'd put money on it.'

'You need to borrow a gun again?'

'No, Leon. Come on.'

'I'm serious. You might need it. You have no idea who these guys really are, or what they're capable of doing.'

'Hold on to it. If I need it, I'll call you.'

'If you need it, you won't have time to call me.' A classic Leon line if there ever was one.

'Thank you. But no, I don't need a gun. I'll talk to you later.'

'Suit yourself,' he said. 'But don't blame me if you end up dead.'

⋆ ⋆ ⋆

As I started to drive home, I couldn't help wondering if Leon was right. Like he said, we had no idea who these guys really were. Or what they would do.

I moved from that to wondering how Natalie was doing. What she was doing at that very moment. And if she was safe.

Natalie.

Then, for the hundredth time, wondering if this thing was going to work out, or if I was just fooling myself. Leon and Eleanor — now that was a real relationship. It takes about two seconds to see how much they mean to each other.

Tyler and Liz. That was real, too. They spend every single day together. They go to sleep together. They wake up together. They scare away bad guys with shotguns together. God damn.

What am I even thinking here? That me and Natalie will be like that someday? It's almost impossible to imagine.

That's what was going through my head as I drove back to Paradise. I'd stop in at the Glasgow, where I belonged. Me and Jackie, the two lonely bachelors.

That's when my cell phone rang.

I fumbled around for it, tried to answer it, dropped it, picked it up again, finally got the damned thing on and next to my ear. I didn't even check the caller ID.

'Hello?'

'Alex? It's Vinnie.'

'What happened?' I said. In one instant I had visions of him in jail, of me trying to find a bail bondsman again. The last time around, it had been Leon, but he didn't do that anymore.

'Where are you?' he said. 'Can you come to the Soo?'

'I'm just leaving. I was going back to Paradise.'

'Well, turn around. I've got somebody here I want you to meet.'

'Who is it? What are you talking about?'

'Just meet us at the Kewadin. I think you should hear what this woman has to say.'

5

When the Bay Mills Indian Community opened up the King's Club in 1984, the first Indian-owned casino in all of North America, it was a complete bust. The casino closed within two months. They regrouped and tried again, and now there are twenty Indian-owned casinos in Michigan alone, and for that matter hundreds more around the country.

The Bay Mills tribe parlayed the success of the King's Club into the Bay Mills Casino and Resort, complete with a hotel, theater, spa, golf course, the works. Not long after that, the Sault tribe, a newly formed Ojibwa community down the road, announced plans to build their own casino. That's how the Kewadin came to be. It's a lot bigger than the Bay Mills casino. It has a lot more lights out front, and it's as close to a real Vegas-style facility as you're ever going to see around here. It's also the source of an unofficial rivalry between the two tribes.

Even the name is a problem. 'Kewadin' is the Ojibwa word for 'north' — although in their language, it's more than just a point on the compass. It's everything you associate with the north. The winter, the cold, the very spirit of northerliness. I heard Vinnie's cousin Buck complaining about this once. When you give something a real Ojibwa name, it's like you're calling forth the power behind that name. To him, and to a lot of other Bay Mills members, giving a casino a real Ojibwa name was almost unthinkable.

I had no idea why Vinnie would even be there, let alone why he'd want me to meet him there. But that's where I was headed.

The rain had stopped. I could see the glow of the place a long time before I finally got there. It was down on the southern end of the Soo, with a lot of trees and a few smaller buildings surrounding it. The casino itself had a tall roofline shaped into several triangles that looked like tepees. The design always struck me as a little self-mocking, but what the hell. If it didn't bother them, who was I to complain?

Normally, the place would be packed on a summer night, but the parking lot wasn't even half full. I'd seen more cars here at midnight, in the middle of February. I pulled in not far from the front door, killed the engine, and got out. I had no idea where I was supposed to meet Vinnie and the mystery woman, so I just walked in.

There were two separate gaming rooms on either side of the center hallway. The slot machines were ringing with those hollow notes that don't sound like anything else in the world, followed by the occasional crashing of coins against a metal tray. I poked my head into the original room, didn't see Vinnie anywhere. I crossed the hall and went into the newer Paradise Room. More of the same, and no Vinnie.

I was tempted to go sit at the bar and wait for

him, but the bar there in the Paradise Room is as long as a runway, with birds and palm trees and whatever the hell else all lit up in neon, and of course it's surrounded by slot machines. Everything Jackie's bar isn't. So instead I walked back out into the hallway and through to the hotel. It's a long walk, but when I finally got there, I saw Vinnie sitting in the lobby. A woman was sitting across from him, with her hands folded in her lap. She was in her thirties maybe, with dark hair, dark eyes, the cheekbones . . . It was obvious she was a tribal member.

'Alex,' he said. 'How far out of town were you?'

'Sorry, I was looking for you. It's a big building.'

'This is Theresa LaFleur.'

She was slow getting up, and even as she shook my hand I got the feeling she was less than thrilled to meet me. Or maybe I was just imagining it.

'Why did you want me to come, Vinnie? What's going on?'

'We need to talk somewhere,' he said. 'But not here. Terry, how about the restaurant? Would that work?'

'Yes, fine,' she said. 'Let's go.'

Vinnie led us to the hotel restaurant. The walls were all covered in logs and there was a huge bear head over the fireplace. The hostess tried to seat us up front, but Vinnie asked for a booth as far away from the door as possible. I was starting to wonder just what the hell was going on, and why he was making us all act like spies.

Vinnie sat next to Theresa. I sat across from them. We waited until the drinks were ordered. Then I finally got the story.

'Terry has something to tell you,' Vinnie said. 'So that you'll understand what's going on.'

'Okay.'

'Mr. McKnight,' she said, 'before I start, I want you to understand something. We are not specifically talking about anybody. This is all hypothetical.'

'I don't follow you.'

'Terry works at the clinic across the street,' Vinnie said. 'It doesn't matter what she does there. She just has something to say to us about something that might theoretically be happening there. But the medical information laws are very strict on this sort of thing.'

'Okay,' I said. 'I get it. We're not talking about anybody in particular. Go ahead.'

'All right, let's just use you as an example, if you don't mind. Let's say that you're a member of the Sault tribe. You live here in town, and you come to the clinic for your medical care. One day, you come in and you say, 'Doctor, I really messed up my back. I was lifting something and I felt the muscles tighten up. I'm in total agony now.' The doctor might take an X-ray, but maybe he doesn't see any problem there. No slipped disk or anything. But still, you can pull those muscles pretty easily, and if you do it bad enough, it can really be painful. Have you ever done that?'

'Not that bad,' I said. 'But enough I can imagine if I did.'

'Did you take painkillers for it?'

'Just aspirin.'

'Okay, well let's say you *really* hurt those muscles. You can't even move. So the doctor gives you something stronger. Tylenol 3 . . . maybe even Vicodin . . . Are you with me so far?'

'I think so.' I looked at Vinnie. He said nothing.

'Are you aware that tribal members get their prescriptions for free, Mr. McKnight?'

'I didn't know that, no.'

'Well, they do. So even though your back is messed up and you can't even stand up straight, at least you're getting some pretty strong drugs without having to pay for them. If the drugs help you get better, then great. But if you develop a problem with them . . . '

'Yeah?'

'Then getting a lot of them for free is not necessarily going to be a good thing.'

'No, I imagine not.' I looked at Vinnie. I couldn't believe he'd tell her about my own history, my own little issue with the 'Vike' when I was recovering from the shooting. But at this point I couldn't rule it out.

'So imagine you keep coming back,' she said. 'You keep telling the doctor that your back isn't better yet. The doctor has no way of knowing how bad your back really feels . . . '

'So he keeps giving me the drugs,' I said. 'But eventually he'll start to suspect something.'

'Eventually, yes. Of course. So maybe he finds some reason to give you a blood test. If you've got an abnormally high level of the drug in your system, he'll know that you're abusing them.'

'I understand what you're saying. Believe me. I don't know who we're talking about, and I guess I'm not supposed to even ask. But what does this have to do with me? Or Vinnie?'

She looked around the room. Then she lowered her voice a little bit and delivered the punch line. 'What if the drug test was perfectly clean?'

'I don't follow you.'

'Clean test. No drugs at all. Not a trace.'

I thought about it for a moment. 'So I'm not taking the drugs at all . . . Even though I keep asking for them . . . I'm either giving them to someone else or — '

'Stop right there,' she said. 'You don't even have to say it.'

'Okay. So, look . . . If this is happening, you need to tell somebody about it. Not me. Not Vinnie. You tell whoever's in charge of the clinic, and you tell the police.'

'I can't do that.'

'Why not?'

She shot Vinnie a quick glance. 'I told this to Vinnie because I thought he could help. It was his choice to involve you. If he wants to tell you anything else, that's up to him. But I'm done here.'

She started to get up from the booth, stopped herself, and sat down again.

'One thing you have to understand,' she said. 'These are serious drugs, and if you become dependent on them, you'll do anything to keep getting them. Do you understand what I'm saying? You'll do *anything*.'

'Terry, I understand. I'm just trying to — '

'If it was the patient who had the problem, then we'd be able to do something directly. The pressure would be on us to fix it, because we're the ones supplying the drugs. You follow me? But if it's somebody else out there, somebody we don't even know . . . Then it's out of our control. And the pressure gets put on the person who's passing along the pills. They're stuck right in the middle.'

This time she got up for good.

'Right in the middle,' she said. 'And God help them.'

Then she was out the door.

* * *

A few minutes later, we were out the door, too. Vinnie's truck is a lot newer and a lot cleaner than mine, but the real reason he was driving was because he was the only one who knew where we were going next. Once again, I was just along for the ride.

It was late in the day now. Dark gray instead of light gray, and a few degrees colder. It looked like it was going to start raining again any second.

'At some point,' I said, 'you're going to tell me where we're going next, right?'

'You can probably figure it out.' He was taking us due north, to the heart of the Soo.

'We're gonna meet the middleman. Or is it the

middlewoman? Will you tell me that much, at least?'

'Her name is Caroline.'

'Okay. How do you know her?'

'She works at Bay Mills. She wants to deal blackjack someday.'

'Why does she live here in town?'

'She's not a Bay Mills member. She's Sault.'

'Wait, if she's a Sault member — '

'She was working at the Kewadin,' he said, 'but she ran into some trouble there. So she came over to Bay Mills.'

'Ran into some trouble?'

'She had a drinking problem. Now she's clean. But she sort of wore out her welcome there, so we took her on at our place. It actually happens quite a bit. Both ways. I know a few Bay Mills people who work at the Kewadin now.'

'Despite the rivalry?'

'We're all part of the same family. We take care of each other, no matter what.'

That much I didn't doubt. I'd seen it in action enough times to know. Apparently I was about to see it yet again.

'So we're going to go see this Caroline,' I said. 'So tell me, why exactly am I part of this? Aside from being an all-around good guy to ride along with you . . . '

'Because I promised you,' he said. He kept his eyes straight ahead as we drove down the quiet, dark streets.

'Promised me what?'

'That I wouldn't do anything stupid without you.'

'This is good. I'm glad you take everything I say so literally.'

'There's another reason.'

'What's that?'

'You know about this stuff.'

'What stuff?'

'Painkillers. Vicodin.'

I looked over at him. 'Are you serious?'

'Let me ask you this . . . Would you recognize if somebody was high on Vicodin?'

This is great, I thought. All of a sudden I'm the consultant from the Betty Ford Clinic.

'First of all,' I said, 'you don't really get high on it. It's more like you get . . . I don't know . . . you get 'warm' on it.'

'Warm?'

'That's the best word I can think of. It just makes everything feel . . . good. Like you're wrapped up in a security blanket.'

'What happens if it wears off? And you don't have any more pills?'

'Well, you understand, I never got to the point where it was a huge issue. I had a little thing with it, way back when. After I got shot and it felt like my whole life was falling apart.'

'Okay, but you can imagine — '

'I can imagine that it would be hell. If you were really hooked on it, it would be like somebody taking away your oxygen.'

'The guys from the boat,' he said. 'Do you think there's a chance at least one of them is taking this stuff?'

'I was wondering when we'd get around to them.'

'They were with Caroline last night. Right before I threw them out.'

'You didn't tell me that.'

'I'm telling you now. That's what I was checking out today. I knew Terry's been working at the clinic, so she was the first person I went to see. I think she was waiting to tell somebody.'

I shook my head at that one. I didn't say what I was thinking. I didn't have to.

'You heard her,' Vinnie said. 'Caroline could be caught right in the middle here. Those guys could really hurt her. I know it. Did you look in their eyes today?'

'All the more reason — '

'To send her to prison for selling drugs?'

'If what you're saying is true, then these guys are using her. She'll get off easy.'

'If they don't kill her, and if the judge doesn't look at her prior record.'

'You said she had a drinking problem.'

'That was one of her problems,' he said. 'She's had others.'

'It sounds like she's making her own bed, Vinnie. She sees an opportunity and she's taking it.'

He took his foot off the gas. He pulled over to the side of the road, stopping slowly. A big difference between him and me right there: if it was me driving, I would have slammed on the brakes and bounced his head off the dashboard.

'I can turn around and take you back to your truck,' he said, 'and I can go talk to her alone. Or you can come with me. Your call.'

'Does this woman know what you're trying to do for her?'

'I guess she'll find out.'

'She's lucky,' I said. 'I'll tell her that myself.'

★ ★ ★

The house was on Seymour Street. From the dull streaks on the aluminum siding to the peeling paint on the wood trim, it was a testament to what Northern Michigan weather will do to your house if you don't take care of it. Vinnie knocked on the front door. Nobody answered.

'Eddie's truck's here,' he said. It was there in the driveway, and it made mine look like it just came off the showroom floor.

Vinnie knocked again. From deep inside the house we heard somebody yelling.

'Sounds like he said, 'Come in,' doesn't it?'

'Sure, why not?'

He opened the door and stepped in. As I followed him, I picked up the smell of cigarettes and beer, as well as something that had burned in the oven. There wasn't much to the living room. An old couch, a coffee table that should have been taken apart and put in the wood stove, two folding chairs. The television was on, but nobody was there to watch it.

'Hello?' Vinnie said.

'Who's there?' It was a man's voice, from the kitchen.

Vinnie went around the corner without answering. The man was sitting at the kitchen table, an open beer in one hand, a cigarette in the other. A cloud of smoke hung just below the ceiling.

'What are you doing here?' he said. He was wearing an old blue bathrobe, his bare legs just visible below the table. I didn't know if he was white, or Indian, or some of both. He looked thirty years old going on fifty.

'I'm looking for Caroline,' Vinnie said. It was obvious he knew this man, but I didn't get the feeling he was going to introduce me to him.

'She's at work.'

'No, she's not. This is her night off, remember?'

'I guess you'd know better than I would.' The man stubbed his cigarette in the ashtray.

'You don't know where she is?'

'If she ain't at work, and she's not with you . . . '

'Why would she be with me, Eddie?'

He didn't answer. Instead he took a long pull off the beer. 'You want one?'

'You know I don't drink.'

'Pardon me. It slipped my mind.'

Vinnie stood there. He didn't say anything. He didn't move a muscle. The man sat at the table and wouldn't look him in the eye.

'Eddie,' Vinnie finally said, 'are you working?'

'In this weather?'

'There are other jobs.'

'Get out.'

'Are you even looking for something else?'

'I said get out.'

Vinnie kept looking at him. I knew all about

Vinnie's long fuse. I figured it was already lit, since maybe late last night when he threw those guys out of the casino. I was wondering how much longer it would burn. Finally, he turned away and went to the door. I followed him outside.

When we were back in his truck, he started it and put it in gear.

'I take it you and Eddie have a history,' I said.

'Not really.'

'What about you and Caroline? This whole thing is starting to make a little more sense now.'

'It was a long time ago.'

'You got her the job at Bay Mills, didn't you?'

'She's a good friend of mine, Alex. She always will be. I was just trying to help her out.'

'So what now?'

'I want to check one place.' He was heading to the water, to the locks and the heart of town.

'You think you know where she is?'

'Yeah, I'm pretty sure. There was a time you could always find her at the Palace.'

There are at least a dozen bars in Sault Ste. Marie. There are eight of them on Portage Avenue alone. The Palace is just a couple of doors down from the Ojibway Hotel. Vinnie parked the car on the street.

Right behind a black Cadillac Escalade.

It wasn't a surprise. Not at all. I already had a gut feeling we'd be running into these guys again. If we had jumped in an airplane and flown to Anchorage, they would have been parked outside the first bar we walked into.

'Before we go in,' I said, 'just tell me one thing.'

'What is it?'

'Who are these guys? I've never seen them before. Have you?'

'No.'

'So what are they doing here? You don't have to come all the way up to the U.P. just to buy some pills.'

'I don't know why they're here, Alex. I don't care.'

We got out of the truck. Behind the bar, a great freighter was moving slowly through the locks. I didn't have time to look twice at it, because Vinnie was already opening the door. When we were inside the place, it didn't take long to find them. There was a table for six in the back corner, between the jukebox and the pool table. There were three men at the table — the two we already knew so well, and now a third, his head wrapped up in so many bandages it looked like he was wearing a white turban. It had to be the driver of the boat. Alive and well, or alive at least. And out of the hospital.

There were three women at the table. They all looked enough alike they could have been sisters. But only one of them even noticed us as we stood there. She started to smile, probably reflex. Then all the color drained out of her face.

'Vinnie,' she said. 'What are you doing here?'

Vinnie said two words to her. Slowly.

'Leave. Now.'

She took the two other women with her. Most of the other drinkers left as well. That was a very good idea, it turned out. Because Vinnie's long fuse had just burned to its end.

6

I can make a long list of all the bad things that have happened in my life. My mother dying when I was a kid, a partner dead, a bullet next to my heart, a failed marriage. Those would be the items on the top of the list. Somewhere below those would be never getting an at bat in the major leagues, never telling my father I loved him, and, oh yeah, getting talked into becoming a private investigator. I'm not sure exactly where spending a night in jail would rank, but it would probably make the top twenty.

There are three holding cells in the basement of the City-County Building. When Vinnie and I were brought down here, there was already one man in the cell. He was sleeping on one of the three beds, and the loud clang of the metal door didn't wake him. The poisonous smell of alcohol hung all around him, so it wasn't much of a mystery.

My hands hurt like hell, but Vinnie's hands looked even worse. He sat on one of the beds with his back against the concrete wall, his hands tucked under his armpits. He didn't say much all night. I knew better than to try to talk to him, so all I could do was count the hours until sunrise. Eventually, I lay down and tried to sleep. When I closed my eyes I saw Vinnie going at it with the man named Cap. He was going at it like I'd never seen him before, like he seriously didn't want his man to walk away alive.

I was having my own problems with the big man named Bruce. If he had had two good hands, he probably would have taken me apart. But his taped-up strained right wrist didn't help him much, especially after I grabbed onto his thumb and twisted it backward. Funny how a large dose of pain will take the fight right out of some guys.

The drunk slept. Vinnie stared straight ahead at nothing, lost inside his own head. I just sat there and wondered how this would get written up in the paper. They have this senior reporter at the *Soo Evening News* who likes to get creative with the police blotter. For this particular item, he'd probably describe a 'violent altercation' at a 'local watering hole.' Or perhaps even a 'spectacular melee' at an 'after-hours drinking establishment.' Whatever words he used, it would go on to say that Vincent LeBlanc and Alex McKnight, both of Paradise, were taken into custody and spent the night at the Chippewa County Jail. And that the other participants were all released.

The time passed. There was no way to see if the sun was up yet. But somehow I knew it was morning. The guard was nowhere in sight, so I had no choice but to use the toilet in the middle of the cell. A new low in my life, to be exceeded one minute later when the drunk finally woke up and threw up on my shoes. Then it got even worse.

Chief Maven showed up.

The chief and I already had a colorful history,

of course. For some reason we had taken an almost instantaneous chemical dislike to each other. The only thing going for me was the fact that everyone else seemed to hate him, too.

He stood at the bars and looked through at both of us.

'Good morning, Chief,' I said.

'What happened to your shoes?'

'Are you going to let us out of here now?'

'I got to see you in this very cell once before, remember?'

'Chief — '

'I never thought I'd get to see it again.'

'If you're not going to let us out, then — '

'I will,' he said. 'Eventually. Just give me a chance to burn this image into my mind. It'll keep me warm all winter.'

Some days I could almost understand why he had such a big chip on his shoulder. He was the chief of police for the second-biggest town in the Upper Peninsula, but he had to share a building with the county guys. He didn't even have his own jail. The state police down the street got most of the serious cases, not to mention the U.S. Customs office at the bridge and the Coast Guard on the locks. He was low man on the totem pole and it had to eat at him every time he went into his little cement box of an office.

Yeah, some days I could actually feel for the man. But today was not one of those days.

He slid the key into the lock and opened the door. Vinnie and I both stepped out. I was surprised at how good it felt to be out of the cell, even if Maven was responsible for it. As he led us down the hall, I looked back at the drunk. He was back on the bed, fast asleep.

'This way,' Maven said. He led us up the stairs and right to his office. I knew it all too well, especially the crappy little waiting area just outside it, with the hard plastic chair and the magazines a decade out of date.

He opened his office door and waved us inside. There were two more hard plastic chairs waiting for us, facing his desk. 'You gentlemen have a seat. I'll be right back.'

'Come on, Chief,' I said. 'You don't have to play the waiting game today, all right?'

'I can take you back downstairs to the cell if you'd rather wait there.'

We sat down. He closed the door and left us there.

Chief Maven had never wasted much effort decorating his office. It had four gray cement walls. There were no pictures. There wasn't even a window. How the man could ever spend time in this room, I didn't know.

'I got you into this,' Vinnie said.

'He speaks.'

'I'm just saying I'm sorry.'

'Don't worry about it. Seriously. I think I owed you a few.'

'I'm in no position to ask,' he said. 'But I'll ask anyway.'

'Shoot.'

'If we tell him everything, it'll put Caroline in a tight spot.'

'Potentially.'

'You know it will.'

'So what do you want me to say?'

'Just put it on me. It was my fault.'

'Vinnie, does this woman mean that much to you?'

'I told you before. She's a good friend.'

'Let me guess. There was a time she was something more.'

'You could say that.'

'When was this?'

'A long time ago. Before you came up here.'

'You were kids, then.'

'Pretty much, yes. It didn't feel like it at the time. We were pretty heavy there for a while. I guess you could say we were engaged.'

'What happened?'

'We were both drinking back then. All the time. I decided to get straight, but she didn't. I mean, maybe she tried, but . . . '

'You had to end things.'

'I tried to help her,' he said.

'I'm sure you did. But if she was still drinking . . . '

'I feel like I failed her, Alex. It's like I could only save myself. I had to leave her behind.'

'So even now, when she makes this problem for herself . . . '

'I think you'd do the same. I know you would.'

I didn't try to argue. He had me dead on that one.

We didn't say anything else until Chief Maven came back a few minutes later. He sat down behind his desk like it was a hugely painful inconvenience for him to be there.

'Why were we held overnight?' I said.

'Because you trashed a bar. I'd call that a no-brainer.'

'Neither of us was drunk.'

Maven looked back and forth between us. 'So I understand. Mr. LeBlanc, you were quite sober as well, right?'

'Yes,' Vinnie said. It occurred to me that Vinnie had probably never had this pleasure before, a personal visit to the legendary Chief Roy Maven's office. From the sound of his voice, it sounded like Vinnie was taking to it about as well as I had my first time.

'We spent the night in jail,' I said. 'The other guys were released at the scene.'

'The bartender said you guys came in and attacked them. What were they supposed to do?'

'There's more to it than that.'

'Yeah, I kinda figured there might be, McKnight. That's why you're sitting here.'

I hesitated.

'I'm all ears,' he said.

'They were harassing people at the casino,' Vinnie said. I was surprised when he jumped in, but now there was no stopping him. 'A couple of nights ago. I had to throw them out. Yesterday, they came up to Paradise and tried to pick a fight with Alex. Even though he helped save their lives the night before, when they wrecked their boat.'

'Those were the guys on Waishkey Bay?' Maven said. 'Where that old bridge runs through the water?'

'The old pilings, yes.'

'So why did they try to pick a fight?'

'Who knows? They thought Alex took something valuable from the wreck. Some kind of box that was in the boat. Which he didn't, of course. But instead of being thankful, here they were threatening him. I showed up at the Glasgow Inn just in time.'

'Is that right, McKnight? This man saved your ass? Probably not the first time, eh?'

I wasn't sure what to say.

Maven didn't wait for me. 'So how did this whole thing end up here in my town?'

'Like I said, I threw them out of Bay Mills. I figured they'd end up at the Kewadin. I recognized their vehicle outside the Palace.'

'So you went in and attacked them.'

'I confronted them, yes. They were going to come back, Chief. It was only a matter of time. You should have seen these guys. You should have heard what they were saying to Alex. I was just trying to look out for my friend. I take full responsibility for what happened.'

'Now wait a minute — ,' I said.

'You should be ashamed of yourself,' Maven said to me. 'You don't deserve to have a friend like this.'

'Just hold on.' Count to three, I told myself. Don't leap over the desk and strangle him.

'I will grant you one thing,' Maven said. 'There is something not quite kosher about these boys. Besides being stupid enough to run a boat into an old bridge.'

'Who are they, anyway?' Vinnie said. 'Where are they from?'

'All three are from downstate, from around

101

Detroit. I'd say they're just up here for vacation, but hell, with the weather we've been having?'

'They're from Detroit? Where are they staying up here?'

Maven looked at him. 'Just hold on right there, Mr. LeBlanc. That's the kind of trick McKnight would pull. You've got to understand, this whole thing has to stop right here. Somebody's going to get seriously hurt, or even killed.'

'All they have to do is leave,' Vinnie said. 'Just go on back home.'

'They may do just that. I hope they do. But at the same time, I have to warn you. If you go after them again, I'll throw away the key. Do I make myself clear?'

'You're not charging us?'

'I could. Your friends had no interest in filing assault charges, but I could still ring you up for disturbing the peace, destruction of property . . . Which reminds me, the Palace has a list of damages here. I trust you guys will take care of that?'

'Yes,' I said. 'Of course.'

'Good. Do we have an understanding on what you're *not* going to do next?'

'Yes,' I said.

'Mr. LeBlanc?'

Vinnie thought about it. 'Yes, Chief.'

'I keep telling myself,' Maven said. 'The next time I have McKnight in my office, that's the day I retire.'

'Maybe you should,' I said. 'Go someplace where they actually have summers.'

'That would make you happy, wouldn't it. Seeing me leave.'

'I think you'd miss me.'

'It's always a pleasure, McKnight.' He stood up and opened the door for us. 'Now get the hell out of here.'

We did. We went outside, each of us taking a deep breath of fresh air. It wasn't raining, but there was a cold wind coming off the lake. The Palace was close enough to walk to. We got in Vinnie's truck, still parked on the street from the night before, and then he took me over to the Kewadin.

'You need to get some ice on your hands,' I said. As he drove I could see how cut up and swollen they were. Both of them.

'I will.'

'You surprised me in there. You played Maven like a drum.'

'It wasn't hard. He obviously dislikes you so much. Anything that makes you look bad he's gonna fall for.'

'Yeah, good thinking.' I shook my head and looked out my window at the miserable day.

When we got to the Kewadin, he pulled up next to my truck. The parking lot was still half empty.

'What are you going to do now?' I said.

'I'm not sure. Maybe go see if Caroline's okay.'

'You're not going after them, are you?'

'How could I? I don't know where they are.'

'Vinnie . . . '

'I'll see you later. If you're around, maybe we

103

can get some work done.'

'I'll be there,' I said. I started to get out.

'Please don't do anything.'

'I'll see you at the Glasgow.'

I closed the door and watched him drive off. I could only wonder when I'd see him again, and if he'd be in one piece.

★ ★ ★

When I got back to Paradise, I thought about stopping in at the Glasgow. I would have killed for one of Jackie's omelets just then. But I went up to my cabin first and I was glad that I did. There was a message on my machine. It was from Natalie.

'Alex . . . You're not there . . . I just wanted to see how you're doing. You asked me to call you tonight. I guess you're out. Anyway, things are getting hot here. We might be making a move soon. Finally. I'll try to call you tomorrow. Have a good night. Bye.'

She sounded a little lost. Maybe a little pissed-off that I wasn't there, after I bugged her to call me so much the last time I talked to her. I couldn't blame her. She probably thought I was down at the Glasgow, drinking beer while my phone rang off the hook. Little did she know.

I got some ice out, wrapped it up in a towel, and put the whole thing over the knuckles on my right hand. I lay down on the bed. I could hear the wind blowing. I thought I heard it start to rain again, but couldn't be sure. I was content to stay inside for now and wonder.

You don't sleep well in jail. That's one thing I had learned. I felt like I could stay right here on the bed for a week.

But no . . .

I should do something . . .

What? What should I do? What . . .

When I woke up, the ice had melted. I was holding a wet towel. My hand was still sore, and now I was hungry as all hell. I looked at the clock. I had slept for more than three hours.

I took a shower, put clean clothes on, and looked for anything edible I might have in my refrigerator.

You're stalling, I thought. You're looking for an excuse to stay here in case Natalie calls.

My choices were a can of baked beans or spaghetti with no sauce. I'll go to the Glasgow, I thought. Check on Vinnie on my way down there, see if he's home yet. Eat something, then come back. She probably won't call until tonight, anyway.

As I was on my way out the door, the phone rang.

It was her.

'Alex,' she said, 'you're there.'

'Yes. Sorry I missed you last night. Things got a little crazy . . . '

'I wish you had a better cell phone. It would make things a lot easier.'

'I told you, cell phones work like crap around here.'

'Bad cell phones do. I'm telling you, next time I see you, we're getting you a new one.'

'Next time you see me? I like the sound of that . . . '

'I don't have much time to talk today,' she said. 'I was thinking I'd just leave a message again, tell you that we're finally moving. We're pretty close to taking them down, and I'm not sure when you'll hear from me again.'

'How long have you guys been setting this up? I never worked any undercover, but from what I remember hearing, the longer the setup, the more chance of getting compromised.'

'You're sounding like my CO again.'

'Natalie . . . '

'I know, I know. It wasn't the plan. But we've gotten this close. We can't back out now after all this work.'

'Is something going to happen today?'

'Maybe. I don't know. I have to hook up with Rhapsody. She'll know what the next move is.'

I closed my eyes. I didn't want to tell her I thought the whole thing was crazy. I didn't want to plant any doubts in her mind when she was this close to the payoff.

'Just be careful,' I said. 'If anything looks off . . . '

'I know, Alex. I'll pull the plug.'

'But nothing will go wrong. Don't worry. You'll be fine.'

There was a long silence. I couldn't imagine what she was thinking. I waited for her to say something else.

'So what did you do last night?' she finally asked. 'Were you hanging out with Vinnie and Jackie?'

'Well . . . Vinnie.'

'I bet you guys were working on the cabin.'

'No, actually, we were in jail.'

'Excuse me?'

'Listen, it's a long story. I'll tell you all about it when I see you, okay?'

'You're telling me to be careful here and you're the one getting thrown in jail?'

'Okay, I know it looks bad on paper.'

'What, you got drunk, you got in a fight . . . My God, Alex.'

'I wasn't drunk. Come on.'

'This is almost kinda funny. I should be laughing.'

'Yeah, it's hilarious.'

'Are you going to be charged with anything?'

'No,' I said. 'Chief Maven let us go this morning.'

'Chief Maven . . . That's beautiful. Did you say 'hi' for me?'

'Your name didn't come up, no.'

'Okay, I've got to go now.'

'Natalie. Please. Do you want the whole story now?'

'I really have to go. Don is here. We're getting ready to roll.'

'Okay,' I said. 'Okay. Give me a call later, please? Let me know how you're doing?'

'I'll try. Unless things get crazy. Just do me a favor, eh?'

'What's that?'

'Try to stay out of jail tonight.'

★　★　★

107

When I finally headed down to the Glasgow, I looked for Vinnie's truck as I passed his house. It wasn't there. The sun was going down now. It was officially time to start getting worried.

I was hoping maybe he'd be down at the Glasgow. No such luck. Jackie said he hadn't seen him all day.

'You weren't here again last night,' he added. 'That's two nights in a row. A new record.'

'It might be a hat trick,' I said. 'I've gotta go find Vinnie before he does something *really* stupid.'

It was almost dark by the time I got to the rez. I cruised down the main street, past Vinnie's mother's place. No sign of his truck. I checked both casinos. Nothing.

'God damn you, Vinnie. Please tell me you're not tracking those guys down.'

There was only one place left to go. I headed east to the Soo. I had nothing to think about all the way there except the way Natalie sounded on the phone, and what she'd be getting herself into next. Maybe even right now, as I was driving down this lonely road. Maybe right this very moment, she's five hundred miles away, in the dark corners of a big city, putting it all on the line.

Thinking so much about Natalie and Toronto . . . It was a jarring segue when I hit Sault Ste. Marie. I think of the place as a city, but it's not. Not by a long shot. It's a small village on the edge of the water, the last stop before you leave the country. A true border town, dwarfed by its sister with the same name on the other side of

108

the river. Sault Ste. Marie, Ontario, is a good four times bigger. All the clubs are over there. The music and the dancing girls. You know you're in the minor leagues when you have to go over to Canada to find the real nightlife.

The only bright lights in town were at the Kewadin, as usual. I didn't see Vinnie's truck there. I drove up Seymour Street, past Caroline's house. The place looked completely dark, like nobody had lived there in years. If I hadn't been there myself the night before, if I hadn't stood in the kitchen and seen Caroline's husband smoking his cigarette and drinking his beer, I would have sworn that this was an abandoned house.

I parked the truck on the street, got out, and knocked on the door, just in case. There was no answer.

'Come on, Vinnie. Where the hell are you?'

I got back in the truck, drove down Portage Avenue. I slowed down in front of all eight bars. Then I cut back and drove by the Antlers. I was running out of options.

'All right, I'm done, Vinnie. If you want to do this that badly, I can't help you.'

I drove back to Paradise. I was getting tired again. I went through Brimley, through the rez. Up around the edge of the bay, with the water looking dark and cold in my headlights. If I was hoping he'd be there at the Glasgow, I was disappointed. If I was hoping his truck would be parked in front of his cabin . . . No dice. The man was still out there somewhere, doing God knows what.

And Natalie . . . I can't call you. I can't even call your station to ask if you're safe. I have no idea what the hell is happening to you.

Yeah, this is wonderful, I thought. I'll be bouncing back and forth between both of these little worries all night long.

No rest. No sleep.

Just me alone in a cold cabin with a silent phone, going quietly insane.

7

I didn't know all of the details, but this was the night when Natalie Reynaud first met the man named Antoine Laraque. It's an almost lyrical name, something that would fit a writer, or a dancer. I can picture the car moving down a dark street in Toronto. The car has to be black. The driver has to be a man paid well to be doing it. The lights ahead, Chinatown, then the harbor. Most of the big hotels there, near the convention center. The Hilton is three blocks from the water. The elevators are glass, running up the outside of the building. You can see the whole city as you go up higher and higher. The stadium. The CN Tower. Beyond the city the vast expanse of the lake.

Two people going up the elevator, while the driver waits below. Antoine Laraque and Rhapsody Rowan. I don't know if either of them enjoy the view on the way up, or if either of them even notice it. Somehow I picture dark sunglasses on both of them, even though it is night.

I don't know what it took to bring the two of them up to the fifteenth floor of the Hilton that night. If you think about it, it's an inherently risky move. You're way off your home turf, in a confined space, cut off from your vehicle fifteen floors below you. It takes a certain level of trust to make such a move, especially when the person waiting for you is someone you didn't even know a month ago. It takes trust, or if that's running thin, then it takes the promise of great riches or great power or preferably both.

Or hell, just cold blood. Maybe that's all it takes.

I can't imagine what Natalie was feeling. An actor goes on stage, plays a part. If it's not convincing, the audience starts to slip away. If it's really bad, they might stand up and boo. They generally don't take out guns and start firing. Or they don't wrap their arms around the actors' necks, point the guns at their temples, and use them as human shields. The Actors Guild would definitely not go for that.

It's Natalie Reynaud and her partner, Don Resnik, in a room on the fifteenth floor. The room is wired for both sound and video. The backups are stationed in the adjoining rooms. The rest of the floor is empty, except for one man in a bathrobe, posing as a guest going down to the end of the hall for ice. He's there to make sure the hallway doesn't seem *too* empty. The man's service revolver is hidden underneath his robe.

The whole point of the operation, of course, is to catch Antoine Laraque offering some amount of Canadian dollars, some specific number of 'loonies' to use the local slang, in exchange for a large number of automatic handguns, to be delivered sometime thereafter. The double fake-out, as Natalie herself called it, setting up a woman to be the contact. It's so unusual it has to be convincing.

The other important part of the operation — the size of the net, as they call it. A big net instead of a small net. When the police move in, the idea is to bust all four of them, Natalie included. You do this just in case there's a chance to keep the identity intact, to have the fictional character get out on bail, or on a technicality, or whatever else, to go back on the street and set another trap. That's when the real acting begins, when Natalie plays the part of a career criminal getting taken down. If she can sell that one, then she's really earning her Oscar.

If it goes well, then nobody gets hurt. They get a clear and unimpeachable offer on tape. Maybe with Rhapsody on the hook, she flips and helps put Laraque away for the rest of his life. Rhapsody, the woman with more lives than a dozen alley cats put together.

That's the plan. Set the trap, catch the big mouse. Take a few hundred guns off the streets of Toronto. Save lives. Maybe even build some careers for the officers involved.

Of course I didn't know anything about it at the time. I'd hear all about it much later, in vivid detail.

How the mouse walked right into the trap, and then how he walked away.

Vinnie's night, on the other hand . . . He was a lot closer to home, and I'd get the whole story as soon as I opened my eyes.

★　★　★

I fell off the chair. It took me a moment to realize what had happened, where I was. I had finally dozed off, or at least I had slipped into that half sleep with the half dreams about the real events in your life. Me in jail, but instead of Maven standing there, it was Natalie. For some reason she was smiling at me. Vinnie was in the cell next to me, a row of bars between us. He was calling my name. Then I was falling.

I looked around me. Why was I lying on the floor?

God, Vinnie . . .

I was still in my clothes, so I was out the door in ten seconds. The sun was just coming up, to start another losing battle against the cold morning mist. It was too early to be out there. Too early to be doing anything at all, but I had to see if he was home.

His house was only about a quarter mile down the road, but the days I could have run that distance in less than a minute were a distant memory, so I got in the truck, fired it up, and drove around the bend to his house.

Vinnie's truck was in the driveway. That was the good news.

The driver's-side door was open, but I didn't see Vinnie anywhere. That was the bad news. Probably very bad news.

I pulled up behind his truck, slammed mine into park and got out. I went to his door, opened it without knocking.

'Vinnie.'

There was no answer. I didn't see him anywhere.

'Where are you?'

A muffled sound, from somewhere. I looked around the place, couldn't find him. Until I got to the bathroom. He was there, on the floor, his head over the toilet.

'Vinnie,' I said. 'What's the matter?'

I bent down next to him. As I put my hand on his back, the unmistakable smell of alcohol hit me. Which would have made sense for just about anybody else. But before I could figure that one out, he looked up at me.

'Oh my God,' I said when I saw his face. 'What the hell happened?'

His left eye was completely swollen shut, his right eye almost as bad. I couldn't tell how bad his bottom lip was with all the blood on it. Instead of answering me, he went back to spitting the blood into the toilet. The water was pink.

'Talk to me. What did they do to you?'

'Whazzit look like, Alex?' It was hard for him to talk.

'I mean, how bad? Did they break anything? Did you lose any teeth?'

'Whed I can feel anyfing, I tell you.'

'I'll get some ice.'

I went to his freezer and got both ice trays. When I came back, he was sitting on the floor, his back against the tub.

'We'll get the swelling down,' I said. 'That's the first thing.'

I was about to start wrapping the ice in a towel, but when I looked at him again I figured, hell, I wouldn't even know where to begin.

Instead, I dumped the ice in the sink and filled it with cold water.

'Can you stand up?' I said.

He shrugged one shoulder.

'Come on. I'll help you.'

I pulled him up to his feet. He swayed back and forth a few times like he'd pass out, until he finally found his legs and we got him over to the sink.

'You ready for this?'

He went down facefirst into the ice water. He stayed down a lot longer than I would have. I was about to yank his head out when he finally came up for air. There was blood in the water, blood dripping on the edge of the sink, blood on the floor. He took a few uneven breaths and then put his face in the sink again.

I left him for a moment, went back to the kitchen and grabbed the roll of paper towels. He was coming up for air again when I got back. I stopped him for a moment so I could get a better look at his face. It was hard to tell exactly where he was bleeding.

'Open your mouth.'

He did.

'I don't see any teeth gone,' I said. 'I think your gums are cut up, though. Here . . . ' I ran some fresh water on a big wad of paper towels and handed it to him. He worked it carefully into his mouth and held it there. When he took it back out it was red.

'Keep doing that.' I gave him some more paper towels. 'When we get that stopped, we'll start icing your eyes.'

He spit more blood in the toilet and then put the paper towel in his mouth again.

'Vinnie, you don't have to answer this right now if you don't want to, but how come you smell like a gin mill?'

He looked at me out of the one eye he could still see through. 'Vey pord idod me.'

'What?'

He shook his head and waved me away. I'll get the story later, I thought. Right now, it's time to do something else. I went out to the kitchen and picked up his cordless phone.

'Whaf that for?' he said as he came out of the bathroom.

'I'm calling the police.'

'No. No poleef.'

'I'm calling.'

I started to dial. Instead of fighting me for the receiver he went over to the base unit and unplugged it.

'Vinnie, don't be an idiot.'

'What are the poleef gonna do?' He took the towels out of his mouth.

'Arrest them? Charge them with assault?'

'I went after them. They defended themselves. They just did a lot better job of it this time.'

'Why did you do this alone? What's the matter with you?'

'I wasn't planning on it, Alex. But even if I was . . . Hell, I got you in enough trouble already.'

'Oh, cut that shit out. You should know better. If you were gonna go after them, you should have brought me with you. Period.'

'I told you, I didn't go after them. They

117

showed up at Caroline's house.'

'When?'

'I don't know. Late.'

I thought back to the night before, how deserted the house looked when I stopped to knock on the door. 'It must have been after midnight,' I said. 'I drove by looking for you.'

'Why did you do that?'

'Why do you think? What were you doing there, anyway?'

'I was trying to get her to stop what she's doing.'

'You know what she needs to do now.'

'No.'

'I don't understand. How much further are you going to go to protect her?'

He wiped more blood off his mouth. 'They poured it on me.'

'Excuse me?'

'You asked about the liquor smell before. I was trying to tell you they poured it on me. I smell like I took a fucking bath in it.'

I didn't have to ask for details. I could picture it all, the whole ugly thing. Or at least the general idea. Beating the hell out of him and then pouring the firewater on the Indian.

I put the receiver back in its charger. I didn't bother trying to plug the thing back in. Instead I pulled what was left of the ice out of the sink and wrapped it in a kitchen towel.

'Did you take anything yet?'

'No.'

I went and got him four ibuprofen out of the bathroom. 'Here,' I said. 'Take these and

118

keep icing your eyes.'

'Where are you going?'

'I'll be right back.'

'Alex, do not call the police.'

'I won't.'

'I'm serious.'

'I'm not calling the police. I promise.'

'And don't go after them. We don't even know where they are, anyway.'

'Vinnie, sit down and put the ice on your face, okay? When I get back, we'll talk about where they are, and who's going after who.'

'After whom.'

I stopped at the door. 'It's a good thing you're already beat up.'

'Yeah, good thing.'

'Ice,' I said. When I was outside, I went over to his truck and closed the driver's-side door. The thud was as solid as the decision I had just made.

Once again, for the thousandth time in my miserable life, it was time to do something stupid.

8

This is what I was thinking ... After all the sitting around I had been doing, waiting for Natalie to call, waiting for Vinnie to get home ... All the danger that both of these two people were in — the woman that I loved and the man who was as close to me as a brother ...

Here, finally, was one thing I could do. For one of them, at least.

I went back to my cabin, took a shower, put some clean clothes on. I knew there was no rush. No reason to hurry. Stay cool, slow yourself down a little bit. Eat something so you have your strength. Put yourself together so you can do this right.

I went back to Vinnie's cabin. He was sitting right where I had left him, holding the towel full of ice against his face.

'You're gonna be a real sight for a few days,' I told him.

'We'll see what we can make our friend Cap look like.'

'That's not going to happen.'

He didn't say anything to that. He moved the ice from one eye to the other.

'Do you have any idea where I can find those guys?'

'No,' he said. 'I don't.'

'Vinnie ... '

'I don't, Alex. If you wait until tonight, they'll

120

probably show up somewhere in town. One of the casinos, or at Caroline's house again.'

'Why did they go there? Did she invite them?'

'I don't know,' he said. 'As soon as I saw them pull up . . . Well, as you can imagine, things went downhill pretty fast.'

'Her husband, what's his name again? Eddie? Was he there?'

'Yeah, he was there.'

'I don't suppose he tried to help you fight them off.'

'I don't actually recall him doing that, no.'

I thought about it for a minute. I could have done what he said, just wait until that night, hope to find them somewhere in town. Or else . . .

'Wait a minute,' I said. 'Wouldn't Caroline know where they are?'

He looked at me as well as he could with one good eye. 'You're not going after them alone.'

'Look who's talking.'

'I'm serious.'

'I'm not going after them,' I said. 'Not really.' Not in the way you're thinking of, anyway . . . It was close enough to the truth, I could say it with a straight face.

'What are you going to do?'

'I'll tell you after I do it. I promise.'

'I'm coming with you,' he said. He took the ice away from his face. His beaten-up wreck of a face.

'You stupid idiot . . . What the hell were you thinking?'

'I've never wanted to kill a man before,' he

said. 'I think I could do it now, Alex. I honestly think I could do it.'

'I believe you. That's why you're staying here.'

A few minutes later, I was out the door. He had fresh ice. He had water. He had soup. He had the bottle of ibuprofen.

I had the keys to his truck.

Before I left, I stole them. I didn't want him to follow me down there. Then it occurred to me that he might have a spare key, so I opened the hood on his truck and disconnected the battery terminals.

Then I figured, yeah, that'll slow him down for two minutes. I went back to my truck, got the big wire cutters and snipped off both connectors.

Now you're grounded, I thought.

I headed out to the main road as the sun cleared the trees. Hell, maybe the temperature would break sixty today. There was always hope. I headed east yet again, tearing up the same old road to the Soo. An empty road, as straight as if drawn with a ruler. I drove even faster than usual, which is saying something. I'm not just an ex-cop, but an ex-cop who took three bullets on the job, so there isn't a state trooper, county deputy, or local police officer in the state of Michigan who would give me a speeding ticket.

Okay, maybe there was one particular chief of police who would gladly ring me up, but as far I knew he never sat out here with a radar gun.

It was just after ten when I hit Sault Ste. Marie. I drove to Caroline's house on Seymour Street. This time I saw Eddie's beat-up old truck in the driveway. I pulled in behind it.

Nobody answered when I knocked on the door. I knocked again, louder. Finally, I heard movement somewhere inside. When the interior door opened, there was Eddie, looking like he'd just spent the last few hours laid out on a morgue table.

'The hell you want, man.' He had sweat pants on and no shirt. Which was the last thing I needed to see at this hour. Or any hour.

'Remember me?'

'You're Vinnie's friend.' His voice was slightly muffled through the glass storm door.

'Very good. Where's Caroline?'

'She's sleeping.'

'Wake her up.'

'No way.'

I grabbed the storm door handle a split second before Eddie. We had a brief tug-of-war until I got it open and stepped inside the place. I was ready to nail him if I had to, but he was already moving backward.

'The fuck you doing,' he said. 'What's the matter with you?'

'What happened here last night?'

'It was Vinnie's fault, man. He shouldn't have been here.'

'He was trying to look out for your wife. Because obviously you're not going to.'

'You can't come in here and talk to me like that.'

'And yet somehow I'm doing just that. Go wake up your wife.'

'I'm gonna call the police.'

'You go ahead. We'll all have a lot to talk about.'

'What's going on out here?' Caroline said. She came into the room wearing an old blue bathrobe. Her eyes were still swollen with sleep, her dark hair all over the place.

'It's what's-his-face,' Eddie said. 'Vinnie's buddy. I told him you were asleep.'

'My name is Alex,' I said. 'I think we met briefly at the bar.'

'Yeah,' she said, 'right before you guys took the place apart.'

'That wasn't exactly my idea. But speaking of Vinnie — '

'I'm putting some clothes on,' Eddie said. 'If you don't mind.'

'Go right ahead,' I said. 'There's a couple of things I need to ask your wife about.'

When Eddie left the room, Caroline kept standing there. She didn't invite me into the kitchen for coffee. She didn't ask me to sit down. She looked down at the carpet and rubbed the back of her neck.

'Where are they?' I said.

'Who?'

'You know who I'm talking about.'

'I don't know.'

'I think you do.'

'Please go,' she said.

From another room I could hear Eddie banging drawers. It sounded like he was getting dressed in a hurry.

'I'll go when you tell me where to find them.'

'Why do you want to know that?'

124

'You know why. They beat the hell out of Vinnie.'

'You want them to do the same to you?'

'That's not my plan.'

I heard a door slam. Then footsteps outside.

'You should stay away from those guys,' she said.

'So should you.'

She shook her head. She still hadn't looked me in the eye.

'I know what you're doing,' I said. 'With the prescription medicine.' I didn't want to rat out Theresa, the woman from the clinic, but I would if I had to.

'You don't know anything.'

'How much money are you making?'

'It's none of your business.'

'I can't imagine it's worth it.'

'Like I have a choice.'

I thought about that one for a minute. Then I heard Eddie starting his truck. What the hell, I thought. I'm parked right behind him.

I went to the front window and looked out, just in time to see him backing up a few inches, clipping my bumper, and then gunning the truck forward in a sharp turn across his own front yard. When he hit the street he was gone in two seconds.

'Where's he going?' I said.

'I think you make him nervous.'

I turned and looked at her. This time, I really saw her for the first time. It wasn't the sleep that had made her eyes so swollen. As I moved closer to her, I could see the purple bruises. I had officially never seen so many bruises on so many people in one week before.

'Did Eddie do that to you?'

'Please go now.'

'He's making you do this,' I said. If he were still here, I'd very much want to bounce him off every wall in the room. 'He's making you get the pills and sell them. Am I right?'

'I'm not talking about it. I don't even know you.'

'You don't have to do this. Any of it. You can leave here right now.'

'Get out.'

'I'm serious. Vinnie will help you. I'll help you.'

'I said get out.'

'Okay,' I said. 'If you don't want us to help you . . . Fine. Just tell me where they are and I'll go.'

'I'm not telling you anything.'

'I know Vinnie won't talk to the police about what you're doing, Caroline, but I will. Do you understand me? I'll call Chief Maven right now.'

'Why are you doing this to me?'

'I have no choice. The next time Vinnie runs into those guys, either they'll kill him or he'll kill one of them. Either way, his life is over. Don't you care about that?'

She didn't answer. She was starting to rock back and forth now.

'So tell me where they are,' I said, 'and I'll leave you alone.'

'You're an asshole.'

'Yeah, sometimes. When I have to be. Tell me where they are.'

'They're in Hessel.'

'Hessel? Are you serious?'

'The kid, Harry, his father's got a summer-house down there.'

'Where is it?'

'It's a maze down there. All those little islands.'

'I know that. Is the house on one of the islands?'

'No, there's a road that goes down from the center of town. It branches a couple of times.'

'Draw me a map.'

She gave out a long sigh like she was the most tired and beaten-down person who ever lived. 'You want a map,' she said. 'Why don't I just chauffeur you down there myself?'

'No, thanks. The map will do.'

She went into the kitchen and drew it on the back of a pizza menu. She handed it to me without looking at me, then sat down at the kitchen table.

'Thank you,' I said. 'I'll come back sometime, if you want me to.'

'Why would I want that?'

'I told you. I can help you.'

'You can't help me.' Her voice was flat, like she was reciting a simple fact that anyone with any sense could see.

'I can try. I'll start by smacking your husband a few times.'

That almost got her to smile.

'Just say the word,' I said. 'Just let me go do this other thing first.'

She nodded her head. That was all I was going

to get from her. I left her sitting there at the table, went out the front door to my truck. Eddie had left a set of tire tracks across the thin grass, and as I stood in front of the truck I could see where he had dented my bumper.

'Oh yeah,' I said out loud. 'I'll definitely be watching out for you, Eddie.'

★   ★   ★

Before heading down to Hessel, I had one more stop to make. I drove over to the Custom Motor Shop, but Leon wasn't there. His boss Harlow told me that business was so slow, they had to cut him loose for a while. With the lousy weather, who was going to buy a boat? I almost told him I knew a few guys who were looking for a new boat, but I didn't feel like explaining the joke. So I just thanked him and left.

Exactly what I was afraid of, I thought. I have to go to the house again.

Eleanor answered the door. That same cloud came over her face as soon as she saw me. I wondered how many perfectly innocent visits I'd have to make for that cloud to go away. Whatever the number, today wouldn't be the start of them. I was there to borrow a gun.

I asked Leon to be discreet about it, not to parade through the house with the gun in his hand. He brought it out to me in a shoe box, but I don't think Ellie was fooled. It's not like I make a habit of borrowing shoes from the man.

I hate guns, that's the thing. I hate everything

about them, even though I carried one every day for eight years. When I threw my last gun into the lake, I was in no rush to replace it. So now here I was, using a loaner from my ex-partner. I had my driver's-side window open, hoping he'd just give me the box so I could be on my way. Instead, he opened up the passenger door and got in the truck with me.

'What are you doing?' I said.

'I'm not giving you this until we talk.'

'Leon, come on.'

'Tell me the situation.'

'Leon . . . '

'It's the men from the boat,' he said. 'That much I can guess. Last I saw of them, they were going around looking for that stupid lockbox. What's happened since then to make you need a gun?'

I gave him the short version. How the men were getting the pills from Caroline. How close to her Vinnie had been, way back when. Then how he'd gotten himself beat up the night before.

'How bad is it?'

'They got him pretty bad. But he'll live.'

Leon shook his head. 'So you're going to go make the same mistake.'

'I was hoping a gun in my hand would make a slight difference.'

'Think it all the way through, Alex. You're upping the ante here.'

'Yeah?'

'You stick a gun in their faces, tell them to stay away from Vinnie, to stay away from this woman on the reservation . . . What do you think happens?'

'Well . . . '

'I've seen those guys. Lord knows you have. You don't think it'll be like poking a stick in a bee's nest?'

'Okay, Leon. So what do you suggest?'

He thought about it for a minute. 'First way I can think of . . . '

'What is it?'

'If you hurt them, Alex. I mean if you hurt them so bad you get right into their souls . . . '

'That does have its appeal right now. If you could have seen Vinnie . . . '

'No, I mean you'd really have to beat them within an inch of their lives,' he said. 'To these guys, you'd have become the devil himself. So bad they'd shiver every time they thought of you.'

'I don't know about that.'

'You can't do it, Alex. You can't go that far. I know I couldn't.'

'So what does that leave me?'

'Well, there's one other way I can think of. You remember my little principle for maximizing a perceived threat?'

'Oh no,' I said. 'Please don't tell me. Not that thing . . . What was it?'

'The illusion of overwhelming force.'

'Every time we try that one, it blows up in our faces. Remember?'

'We've had bad luck with it, I admit. Something always breaks the spell. But the idea itself is solid.'

'I can't believe I'm even going to ask,' I said, 'but how would it work this time?'

'It's simple. You have to make these guys believe that it would be in their best interest to stay as far away as possible. That messing with you, or Vinnie, or anybody else you care to name would be the biggest mistake of their lives.'

'I thought that's what I was gonna do.'

'As what? A guy who rents out cabins?'

'More than that. An ex-cop, for one thing.'

'That won't do it, Alex. These are bad guys. You gotta go in a lot harder than that, know what I mean? You gotta go in like this is something you do every day and twice on Sundays.'

A classic Leonism, I thought. Somebody should write this stuff down.

'It would help if I went with you,' he said. 'We could double the effect.'

'You're not coming with me.'

'I really think I should.'

'Leon, I appreciate it. Really, I do. You've saved my ass more times than I can count. But I can't keep dragging you into things, okay? I can't keep putting your wife through this.'

'I'll tell her we're going fishing.'

'She can see right through you, Leon. Through me, too. I'm doing this alone.'

He looked out the window at his house. He was about to say something, but he stopped himself before he made a sound.

'Thank you for the gun,' I said. 'I'll bring it back when I'm done.'

'Okay,' he said. He put the shoe box down on the seat. 'Be careful, all right?'

131

'You know I will.'

He opened the door. As he was about to step out, he turned back to me.

'You know what was in that lockbox, right?'

'If I had to guess . . . Money.'

'To buy what?'

'More drugs. Big-time drugs.'

'From where?'

'Not the reservation? . . .'

'Of course not. This thing with the woman . . . It can't be more than a bottle or two at a time, right? I bet they're just taking those pills themselves.'

'You're probably right,' I said. 'Anything more than that, it would never get past the doctors on the reservation. So hell, how much money could even be involved here?'

'Small time stuff,' Leon said. 'But if you had some real money and you were in the market for a big score, where would you go?'

I shook my head.

'Assuming it was that same kind of stuff . . . prescription painkillers . . . Vicodin . . . Hell, just about anything these days.'

'Canada,' I said.

'Exactly. They've got a ton of it over there. And American dollars will buy a lot more of it.'

It was starting to make more sense to me. It was an open border, with a thousand different places to slip through unnoticed. Natalie was dealing with her own version of the story, but in a completely different way. Different merchandise, going in the opposite direction, but the same basic idea. Hell, even her own grandfather had been part of it, back when the liquor was coming across from Ontario during Prohibition.

'That's why they were in the boat,' I said. The irony of it, that those old wooden Chris-Crafts were once the rumrunner's choice, all those years ago when they were the fastest thing on the water.

'On a foggy night. Maybe they couldn't get across the water yet, so they were waiting . . . Killing time at the casino, rounding up a few pills, just for themselves.'

'But now if their box of money is at the bottom of the lake . . . '

'They're in a tough spot. They probably don't know *what* to do. They might be afraid to go back empty-handed.'

'So maybe I can give them a little nudge.'

'Exactly,' Leon said. He got out of the truck. 'Make them feel a little homesick.'

'Thank you again.'

'One more thing . . . I probably shouldn't even have to say this, but make sure you load the gun.'

'They won't know if it's not loaded.'

'Yeah, but *you'll* know. It'll make a big difference, believe me.'

He was right again. He almost always was. I took the gun and I left him standing there in his driveway. As I looked back in the rearview mirror, I could see him watching me until I was out of sight.

9

I left the gun in the box all the way down there. Hessel is about fifty miles due south, so it didn't take long. Once I got there, though, I had to pull out Caroline's map to find the house. The Les Cheneaux Islands are scattered all along the Lake Huron shoreline — I'd once heard somebody say there are thirty-six main islands, with almost as many little peninsulas jutting out from the mainland. Overall, there were hundreds of channels running through the whole area, some of them wide and inviting, some rocky and shallow. It was a beautiful part of the state, but easy to get hopelessly lost in.

I left the main road in Hessel, past the big marina where they had the Antique Wooden Boat Show every August. We were still a month away, but I had to wonder what they'd do this year if the weather didn't improve. If summer never really came.

It was past noon now. I knew I was close to the house. The secondary road ran down one of the thin peninsulas, with lots of trees on both sides of the road, driveways, signs with cute names on them. Gaston's Getaway. Ratlinburg's Retreat. These were all summer places, and from the looks of them they were summer places for people who had a lot of money. I knew this place was booming, but I had never been down all the way to water, had never seen the money firsthand.

I watched the numbers on the mailboxes until I figured I was about a quarter mile away from the house I was looking for. I didn't want to risk driving by it, so I pulled down a driveway and left my truck in the high weeds so the owner of the place could get by me if he had to. If it came to that I'd give him some story about breaking down on the road and pulling off.

Of course, if this was really a summerhouse, the owner probably wasn't here anyway. It's one thing to escape the heat of the Detroit suburbs. It's another to exchange it for what feels like a chilly day in March.

I took the gun out of the shoebox. Leon's Ruger P95 semiautomatic. I picked up a cartridge, felt its weight in my hand. I heard Leon's words in my head. There was no point in carrying it if I couldn't depend on it when I needed it.

That's when it all caught up to me. I am sitting here in my truck with a gun in my hand.

'You're actually going to do this,' I said to myself. I pictured Vinnie's bloody face.

'Damned right I am.' I slid the cartridge into the gun and got out of the truck.

I had a light jacket on, partly so I could hide the gun when I tucked it into my waistband. I walked back to the main road, hung a right, and kept walking down toward the house. I listened carefully for the sound of a vehicle. If I had to, I could make it into the brush before anybody on the road saw me. But there was no traffic that morning. The whole place seemed to be deserted. Again, not a huge surprise, given the way the day felt.

The house was a little farther down than I thought it would be. I had to be even more careful now as I made my way along the driveway. I was about halfway to the end when I saw the house. It was a big post-and-beam-style cabin, maybe a little over the top with all the windows and the complicated roof. But it had definitely set someone back a few bucks.

When I got a little closer, I could see three vehicles — a red Viper, a silver Mercedes, and the black Escalade I already knew so well. I stopped and waited to see any signs of life in the house. There were a few lights on inside, but what the hell. Wasting electricity was probably pretty low on their list of sins. I made myself wait a few more minutes, then I approached the house. Peeking in the first window I came to, I saw a big open living room, lots of empty bottles on the table, plenty of trash all over the place. I kept working my way around the perimeter, looking in each window. More lights on, more mess. No people.

In back of the place, there was a deck and a scruffy yard with a horseshoe pit, a few dozen empty beer bottles scattered at both ends. Then, beyond that, a dock on the channel. I was sure the wooden boat had been kept there. The dock was empty now. I could see the tops of two more houses on the other side of the channel, but I was pretty sure nobody could see me standing here, or anything that I was about to do.

So far so good.

I went onto the back deck, past the gas grill that was in serious need of cleaning, and tried the back door. It was unlocked.

I opened it slowly. I took the gun out of my waistband. This was definitely feeling like something serious now. I made my way through the living room to the big spiral staircase by the fireplace. Whoever built this place had spared no expense, but somehow it all didn't seem to work together. The staircase was too big, too overdone, and not in the right place. It was too far from the natural flow of traffic. And the bricks they chose for the fireplace . . .

Enough, I thought. This is not why you're here.

I went up the stairs, poked my head in each of the three bedrooms. Three empty beds, all in total disarray. There were lots more bottles, some questionable reading material, and in one room the distinct lingering odor of marijuana. The good news, I said to myself, was that these guys had never tried to rent a cabin from me.

Once I knew that the place was empty, I went back downstairs and looked everything over more carefully. On the kitchen counter I found a boat key attached to a bobber. Must be a duplicate, I thought, for that boat that looks like a piece of modern art now. I found more cigarettes, an overflowing ashtray. I found more empty beer bottles. Lousy American beer, of course.

Then I found three pill bottles. All labeled Vicodin, with all the usual warnings about mixing with alcohol or operating a vehicle or heavy machinery. Sure enough, two of the bottles had been prescribed to Caroline. They were empty. The third had been prescribed to someone named Roseanne Felise. It was still half full. Or half empty, depending on how badly you needed those pills.

I slipped the bottle into my pocket, figuring I could give it to Vinnie later. It would be a good conversation starter if he decided to pay a visit to Ms. Felise.

I found something even more interesting on the kitchen table. Someone had spread out a large map showing all the waterways between Michigan and Ontario. The Les Cheneaux Islands, the top of Lake Huron, from Mackinac Island all the way over to St. Joseph Island in Canada. The St. Marys River, up through the locks, into Whitefish Bay. It was all there, with detailed information on water depths and areas of danger.

I looked closely and saw the old bridge pilings clearly marked in Waishkey Bay. It's a good map, guys, but it can't help you if you don't read it.

'Where are you right now, anyway?' I said out loud. My voice sounded strange to me in the empty house.

'And more important, how long am I gonna have to sit here until you get back?'

If they were gone for the day, I realized, I was going to be stuck here for hours. I took out my cell phone, looked at the display. It was going back and forth between a faint digital signal and a faint analog roam. I didn't even know if Natalie would be able to reach me. If she called.

Damn, I wanted to do something, anything, so bad. But now I'd have to wait. This would drive me right over the edge.

Unless I left and came back later. Sneak back out now, come back in the evening. Damn.

Fortunately, I didn't have to wrestle with my options for long. I heard footsteps on the front porch.

'You're here,' I said. 'For once, you're gonna do me a favor.'

I checked the gun. I got myself ready. It was showtime.

I was thinking I should let all three of them come in first. Get them all together in one confined space. I needed to hide out for a minute here . . . But where?

The spiral staircase, I thought. Right behind here. It's big enough to hide me, and it's out of the way. Perfect.

I stepped behind it and waited. My heart was a jackhammer.

Breathe, man. Just breathe. Nice and easy. You're cold. You're a freakin' ice cube.

I heard them arguing outside. 'How much longer we gotta stay here, huh? I'm going crazy here.' A deep voice. I was guessing it was the big guy, Brucie. 'I can't stand this fucking place.'

'I don't even want to hear it, all right? Just shut the fuck up.'

I peeked around the edge, didn't see any of them coming in yet. Where the hell were they?

One man came through the door. It was Cap. He opened up the refrigerator for a second, then closed it. Then he came into the main room. He was heading right for me. Still no sign of anybody else behind him.

This wasn't the way I wanted it to work, but what the hell. It was time to improvise, and just seeing this guy's face again . . . Hitting him right in the mouth would feel like Christmas.

I waited until he was about to take the first step on the stairs. There was still nobody else in the house. I switched the gun to my left hand, stepped out from behind the staircase and saw the surprise on his face for about half of one second. I was already stepping into the punch, a right hook that caught him square on the chin. It was solid enough to rattle my teeth — I couldn't imagine what it felt like to him.

Anybody else in the world, anybody, it would have been a cheap sucker punch. But for this guy I was willing to forgive myself. He went down hard and stayed on his back, his eyes wide open. I left him there and went into the kitchen to wait for his friends.

I grabbed one of the beer bottles and waited next to the door. I heard them both coming in together. The kid was first. He still had the bandages on his head, like a turban. He was carrying a white Styrofoam cooler. The big guy Brucie came in right behind him. 'Next time he tells me to shut up — ,' I heard him say. He didn't get the chance to finish it, because I shattered the beer bottle across the back of his head. A move right out of an old western, but it seemed to work. He went down about halfway, suspended there for a moment with his head between his knees. I gave him one good push

140

with my foot, right in the backside, and sent him down on the kitchen floor. The kid stood there the whole time, still holding the cooler.

'I assume you won't be giving me a problem here,' I said.

He nodded. That was it.

'Good. Go sit down on the couch.'

He did as he was told. Brucie started to get up on his hands and knees, so I put the gun to the back of his head. Everything Leon had said, it all came to me at once. Classic Leon stuff, but right now it was something to hold on to. Do this like it's something I do every day, he had said, and twice on Sundays.

'You're going to crawl over to the couch,' I said. 'Nice and slow.'

'What the fuck!'

'Get going. Or would you like me to shoot you?'

He started to get up, so I gave him a boot again. He started crawling.

'That's better. On the couch with Harry.' I looked over at the kid. He was sitting on the couch with the cooler in his lap. 'That's your name, right?'

He nodded. He was looking straight ahead. He still hadn't said a word.

'You can put the cooler down.'

He put it down at his feet and sat back up straight. His body was so stiff he looked like a statue of a young man wearing a turban.

Bruce finally made his way to the couch and sat down next to him. Cap was starting to get up now. He was rubbing his jaw.

'You, too,' I said to him. 'On the couch.'

'You're dead. You are an absolute dead man.'

'Whatever you say. Just get on the couch.'

He pulled himself up and crossed the room.

'It's a little cozy,' I said when they were all squeezed onto the couch. 'But this won't take long.'

I've seen enough men with guns in my life — the man who really gets your attention isn't the one who holds on tight with both hands, waving it around like he's more scared of the thing than you are. No, the man who makes your heart stop is the man who holds a gun like it's a part of him, like it's no more unusual to be pointing a deadly weapon at your chest than it would be to hold a cigar or a pen. That's the effect I was going for. I was about to see if it worked.

'What the fuck do you want?' Cap said. He was still rubbing his jaw.

I pulled up one of the club chairs and sat on the edge. I rubbed a piece of lint from the barrel of the gun. 'Harry, this is your father's house, right?'

The kid flinched when I said his name.

'His summerhouse?'

He nodded.

'You're not taking very good care of it.'

He swallowed hard. If it was possible for him to look any more miserable than he already was, he was giving it a good try.

'Is that why you came here?' Cap said, giving off so much heat he was practically glowing. 'To give us housekeeping tips?'

'That's a good line,' I said to him. 'You have a natural talent.'

He didn't answer. He didn't even blink.

'Anybody ever shoot you before?'

Silence.

'I had it happen to me once. You want to find out how it feels?'

He nodded his head up and down, very slowly.

'Okay, you'll be first,' I said. 'Anybody does something stupid, you get the first one.'

He smiled at me. I did my best to smile right back.

'What are you guys doing up here? Besides buying pills and beating people up?'

'Your buddy jumped us,' Brucie said. 'What are we supposed to do?'

'Shut up, Brucie,' Cap said.

'I'm just saying.'

'Don't even try. I'll do the talking here.'

'All right,' I said, 'let's try to focus, guys. We need to come to an understanding here. The next time you're thinking about coming up to one of the reservations, or to Sault Ste. Marie, or hell, let's just say anywhere in Chippewa County . . . '

'You got us all wrong,' Cap said. 'We're just some guys on vacation.'

I pointed the gun at him. 'How about this, Cap? The next time you say that, I'm going to shoot you in the face. Do you really want to give me an excuse? Because I'll do it with great pleasure, believe me.'

He looked at me for a long, long moment. Brucie was staring at the gun in my hand. Harry looked like he was about to be sick.

'Okay, here's your problem,' Cap said. He sat back in his seat and ran his hands together. 'You're not convincing at all. I mean, just listen to you . . . ' He slid into an exaggerated Yooper accent. ''One false move, I shoot you, eh?' It doesn't work.'

I was about to tell him that I didn't talk like that, that I was from Detroit just like him. But then I realized that the last thing I should do was start arguing with him. This whole thing was not going the way I wanted.

'You can't say 'shoot,' anyway,' he went on. 'It's an extremely lame word. It just sounds like you're avoiding what a gun really does, which is kill somebody. You see what I'm getting at? It's Alex, right? Isn't that your name? If you're the real thing, Alex, you'd be pointing that gun at me and saying, 'I'm going to *kill* you.' Doesn't that sound a lot more believable?'

I smiled at him. I could feel the sweat on my hands now. It was already getting to the point where I might have to do something drastic, like fire a round and take a little chunk out of somebody. But then all hell might have broken loose and I'd really have a serious situation on my hands.

Before I could decide, I saw something change in Brucie's eyes. He was looking over my shoulder.

I was about to turn when I felt the cold steel pressed against my temple.

'Drop it now,' a voice said from behind me, 'or I'll blow your brains out.'

I dropped the gun. There was a bearskin rug on the floor. The gun hit the rug with a soft thud.

'Pick it up, Cap.'

Cap pulled himself off the sofa. 'Hello, Mr. Gray,' he said. He moved slowly, looking me in the eye as he bent down to pick up the gun. When I was safely disarmed, the man took the gun from my head and stepped around me.

He was tall. He was heavy. He was wearing a gray suit. His hair was gray. His eyes were gray. The fact that his name was apparently Mr. Gray was a bit more than my mind could handle at that moment. I had no idea what kind of trouble I had gotten myself into this time.

Mr. Gray looked down at me like I was something on the bottom of his shoe. 'Where do I begin?' he said.

I was expecting a few questions from him, but he walked away from me and stood over the three men on the couch. He had put his gun away, somewhere deep in the recesses of his jacket.

'Number one, what the hell happened to your head?'

'A little accident, Dad.'

'A little accident.' He turned back at me, like suddenly I was his sympathetic audience.

'In the boat.'

'You had an accident in the boat.'

'Yes.'

'Which boat would you be referring to?'

Harry didn't answer.

Mr. Gray looked at me again. 'Something tells

me I'm not going to like this.'

'It was the wooden boat.'

He nodded his head. 'My antique Chris-Craft. The one I refinished by hand myself.'

'I'm sorry. There were these pilings in the water.'

'I called your roommates last night,' Mr. Gray said. 'When I finally got a straight answer, imagine my surprise when I found out you were up here.'

'I couldn't do it anymore. I'm sorry.'

'You left school?'

'Yes.'

'What's your name?' he said to me.

'My name is Alex.'

'You have kids?'

'No, I don't.'

He nodded his head. 'Good thinking.'

'I was going to tell you,' Harry said.

'Oh, I'm sure you were intending to,' Mr. Gray said. 'I have no doubt about that. I'm just wondering if that would have actually happened before you came up here and got yourself killed.'

Harry didn't answer.

'Let me guess,' his father said. 'You wanted to see the real world. Hang out with two tough guys. Drink some beer. Play some black-jack at the Indian casinos.'

Harry stayed silent. He looked down at the floor.

'How about hookers? You get any hookers up here yet?'

'Mr. Gray,' Cap said.

'I'm not talking to you yet,' he said. There

wasn't a hint of anger in his voice. He sounded almost amused. Cap shut his mouth and kept it shut.

Yeah, this was the effect I was going for myself, I thought. Now here was the real thing, in person.

And I am totally fucked right now.

'Harold,' Mr. Gray said, 'I would like you to go out and wait in the car for me.'

'I can't stand up,' he said.

'Why would that be?'

'I sort of wet my pants.'

'You wanted some real life, Harold. Here it is. Now go get in the car.'

'But I have my car here.'

'You can leave it for now.'

'I need my car.'

'I said you can leave it here.'

'Can I go upstairs and change, at least?'

'No, I think a ride back to Detroit in wet pants will be a good object lesson for you.' He looked at me again. 'Don't you agree?'

I didn't say anything.

Harry stood up. The dark stain down his pants was unmistakable. He gave Cap and Brucie a small nod and then left the room. I heard the front door open and shut. Now it was just the four of us and somehow the room felt ten degrees colder.

'Caplan,' Mr. Gray said. 'Bruce.'

Cap looked up at him. Bruce didn't dare. Mr. Gray went over to Bruce in two quick steps and grabbed him by the neck. With his back to me now, I couldn't see what took place between

147

them. A few seconds later, he moved over to Cap. He stood over him for a while, but didn't touch him.

'Before we discuss what you guys have done to my house,' he finally said, 'and to my boat, and why in the world you would let my son come up here without calling me immediately . . . '

He turned to me once more, and now it was like he was really seeing me for the first time.

'Please tell me who this gentleman is, and why he had a gun pointed at my son's head.'

'Actually, I have no quarrel with your son,' I said, finally speaking up. 'If you'll let me explain.'

'That won't be necessary. Alex, was it? What's your last name?'

'McKnight.'

He thought about it for a second. 'No, I've never heard that name before. What do you do for a living?'

'I was a cop once. Then a private investigator.'

'Is that right?'

'My partner knows I'm here right now,' I said. It was time to find some way to climb out of this. 'He's expecting me to call him about now.'

'I'm sure he is.'

'I'm serious, Mr. Gray.'

He put his hand up to shush me, a simple gesture like a man waving away the man trying to top off his water glass.

'I think it would be a good idea,' he said to Cap and Brucie, 'if I removed myself from this situation as quickly as possible. If I don't, I'm honestly afraid that I'll end up killing both of you. You take care of our guest, you come back

148

here and you clean this place up, and you give me a call when you're done. At that point, I'll tell you what we'll be doing next. Do you think you guys could do that much without totally fucking it up?'

Take care of our guest, he says. This was not sounding good at all. It was time to start looking a little harder for a quick exit, no matter what I had to do.

Mr. Gray left the place without giving me another glance. As soon as the door closed behind him, Brucie started breathing again.

'We're dead,' he said.

'Relax,' Cap said.

'We are totally, completely dead.'

Cap looked at Leon's gun. 'Is this piece of shit loaded?' The way he took out the cartridge, it was obvious this was not the first time he had handled a gun.

'What are we going to do with him?' Brucie said, nodding in my direction.

'You heard the man,' Cap said, slamming the cartridge back in Leon's gun. 'Let's go take care of him.'

10

Brucie drove the car. The black Escalade. I didn't have much chance to enjoy the luxury. Cap was next to me in the backseat, holding Leon's gun. I had no idea where we were going.

Neither did Brucie, even though he was at the wheel. 'Where are we going?' he said. He spoke quietly, with a perfect calm that sounded almost resigned.

'I know the place,' Cap said. With his free hand he rubbed his jaw.

'You gonna tell me where?'

'Just drive. I'll tell you.'

'We need a place by the water,' Brucie said. 'With nobody around for miles.'

'I think that's the whole goddamned Upper Peninsula.'

Brucie didn't react to that one. He kept driving.

I tried to study Cap without making it obvious. Gun in right hand. Maybe thirty inches away from me, a lot of room back here in this big vehicle. If he was distracted for a second, could I get the gun away from him?

Hell, what other shot did I have? I needed to wait for the right moment, maybe when he was talking to Brucie, maybe looking out at where we were going. Anything.

But no, he kept watching me closely. No expression on his face at all. Brucie kept driving.

The speed limit on this road was fifty-five. He was going fifty-four.

It was so obvious to me now. I was a cop once. I saw plenty of criminals. I saw enough regular-issue bad guys to last a lifetime. But only once in a great while did I see men like this.

They were professionals. If either one of them had ever had a moral compass, it had been carefully dismantled until nothing was left. Now they were driving me to a safe place, far away from anyone else so they could kill me with my own borrowed gun and leave my body to rot in the water. They were driving like it was a trip to the hardware store. How did I not see this in them from the very beginning?

We were going east now on M-134. It was a lonely highway, just trees and occasional views of Lake Huron. The sky was getting cloudier, like it would rain again soon. We came to Port Dolomite, passing the big limestone quarry, the high walls of white stone. This will be the place, I thought. It makes perfect sense, find some abandoned corner of the quarry, shoot your man, and leave his body there.

Leave his body there.

I started to feel dizzy. I couldn't breathe.

Think, Alex. Think. There has to be a way out of this.

We passed one entrance to the quarry, then another. There were security gates everywhere. Brucie kept driving until it was just the trees and the water and the sound of the car again.

'That one stretch of road,' Brucie said. 'The other day, when we were out driving around.'

'What I'm thinking,' Cap said.

I kept waiting for him to take his eyes off of me. Just for one moment. I could go for the gun, try to twist that bad hand, take the gun, and shoot him quickly. Then either make Brucie stop or shoot him in the head and take my chances.

At the same time, while I watched and waited, the seconds ticking by, there was another part of my mind thinking about Natalie, playing back everything we had ever done together. From the moment I had first laid eyes on her. On that lake in northern Ontario, seeing her jump off that plane onto the dock. The way she moved. The way she looked in that old farmhouse, when I drove all the way up there to find her and to share a bottle of champagne on a lonely New Year's Eve.

She wasn't here with me now. From the sadness of it, the loneliness, to a strange calm I felt when I realized what a good thing that was. She wasn't here to take this last ride with me, wouldn't be standing next to me when the bullets started to fly. She was five hundred miles away, and now for the first time that distance was a comfort to me.

She'll be okay, I thought. She'll feel bad when she hears what happened to me. Then she'll get over it and she'll go on with her life. This thing we were trying to hold on to, this impossible, unworkable thing — it will be nothing but a memory.

We were heading into the heart of the DeTour State Forest Campground, the darkness under the trees making everything look colder. What little sun there was, all but gone.

'Hey, Cap,' Brucie said.

'What is it?' He didn't take his eyes off of me. The barrel of the gun still thirty inches away, his hand rock solid. If I went for it, I'd have no chance. My options were running out.

'I want him.'

'What do you mean?'

'I'm saying, I want to do him.'

'What are you talking about?'

'It's always you doing this part,' Brucie said. 'Me waiting with the car. I want to switch it around this time.'

'This is my gig. You've never done it. Not one goddamned time.'

'That's what I'm saying. It's about time. You remember in the bar?'

'What about it?'

'When they came after us. You got the Indian, remember?'

'Yeah, so?'

'So this guy took my bad arm and tried to twist it right off. I can still feel it. Not to mention a fucking beer bottle on the back of my head. You know what I'm saying? I've got some personal motivation here.'

'Number one, I seem to recall getting sucker punched today,' Cap said. 'You don't think I have some personal motivation, too? And number two . . . '

'What?'

'As soon as you start talking about personal motivation, I know you're not ready. This isn't junior high school, Brucie.'

Brucie thought about it for a few seconds. He started to slow the car down. There was a turnoff ahead.

'I want him,' he finally said. 'It's your turn to wait in the car for once. That's the way it's gonna be. You got a problem?'

'There's no reason to talk like that. If you want him so bad, go ahead. Knock yourself out, man.'

Brucie made a right turn. It was a narrow road, leading down toward the water.

'Leave the gun with him after you're done,' Cap said. 'It's his, so it can't come back to us.'

'Yeah, no kidding.'

'Wipe off your prints, though.'

'Gee, I never would have thought of that.'

Cap shook his head and smiled at me. 'The man's always been too sensitive,' he said. Like I should be in on the joke.

'I'll go down here as far as I can,' Brucie said. The road was overgrown. I could hear the branches scratching at the sides of the vehicle.

'This is far enough,' Cap said. He glanced behind us, then forward, checking out the empty access road. I had a fraction of a second, but it was gone before I could move.

Cap tightened his grip on the gun, as if reading my mind. 'You should feel honored,' he said to me. 'Brucie's gonna break his cherry on you.'

Natalie and me in the guest bedroom. The first time.

Natalie and me having dinner at the Ojibway Hotel.

Natalie and me on the island. When I almost lost her.

The road got even tighter. A large branch slapped at the windshield.

'You can stop now,' Cap said, 'before you destroy the car.'

'I'm getting off the road, genius.'

'Nobody can see you now.'

'Like hell.'

'The car's black. Nobody can see you.'

Brucie jammed on the brakes. If he had been going any faster, Cap would have been thrown into the front seat and things would have gotten interesting.

'The fuck's the matter with you?' Cap said.

'Time to swap,' Brucie said. 'You can be the chauffeur now.'

'Yeah, time to swap, so I can back this thing all the way out of here.'

Brucie opened his door and came around to our side.

'Come on,' Cap said to me. 'Slide out my way. Nice and easy.'

He opened up his door and got out. He kept it open and waited for me, passing the gun to Brucie.

When I was standing level with him, Cap looked me in the eye. 'Sweet dreams,' he said. I wanted to hit him again. Or better yet, I wanted to grab my keys and rake them right across his neck.

'Hurry it up,' Brucie said. He backed away into the brush so I wouldn't be too close to him as we all maneuvered ourselves around. Cap

155

went to the driver's side. Brucie waved me away from the vehicle and closed the door.

'Walk,' he said. 'That way.' He pointed down toward the water.

I walked. He stayed behind me. The way I was figuring it now, I had one last chance to improvise something. Create some sort of distraction, turn around and go for the gun. Either take it from him or knock it away long enough to make a break for it.

At least there was only one man to worry about now. My odds were that much better.

Yeah, right. I was fooling myself. I knew that. These were the last steps of my life. This air the last I would breathe.

I tripped and almost went down. With the sudden movement, I was sure I'd get it right then, square in the back. But it didn't happen. I regained my footing and kept walking. I could see the edge of the water now. Lake Huron, sister to Lake Superior. I never would have dreamed this would be the last lake I'd ever see.

Natalie on the phone with me. The sound of her voice, so far away. To hear it one more time . . .

No, Alex. Don't give in to this. This is not the way to go out.

'Aren't you going to say anything?' Brucie said.

'If you're expecting me to beg,' I said, 'it's not going to happen.' I didn't turn to face him. I kept walking.

'You're taking it like a man. I'll give you that much.'

I wondered how this was going to happen. How many seconds I had left. It was dark here in the trees.

'You shouldn't have come to the house,' he said.

'No kidding.'

'You did this for your Indian friend?'

'Yes.'

A few seconds passed.

'I had a friend like that once,' he said.

'If that's true, you probably didn't deserve him.'

A short laugh from behind me. 'Tough to the end, eh?'

'I'd like to see how tough you'd be without the gun,' I said. It was a reach at this point, but what the hell. It was worth a shot.

He laughed again. 'Yeah, I bet you would.'

Pine needles under my feet. The smell of fresh water. The cold air in my lungs. I was starting to feel dizzy.

'Stop here,' Brucie said.

I stopped. We were overlooking the water now, on a little bluff about twenty feet above the shoreline. The waves were two feet high, maybe three. It was a tame lake compared to Superior. Smaller waves, warmer water. I could see a sailboat in the distance. The sail bright yellow against a gray sky.

Clouds. No sun.

I would never see the sun again.

'It's not much of a cliff,' Brucie said, 'but it's as good as we're gonna find up here, eh?'

'If you're gonna do it, do it,' I said. I turned to face him.

'Don't you want to know why I told Cap I was gonna do this?'

'You gave him your reason.'

'There's more to it.'

'Like what?'

'I knew what he would have done to you if it was him. The thing you gotta remember about Cap . . . Fuck, man . . . '

He shook his head, looked away like he was trying to banish a memory. If it was a distraction, I was too far away from him to try anything now. I had officially passed beyond all hope.

'He would have made it slow,' he said. 'Emptied the whole damned gun, even though that's the stupidest fucking thing you can do. Make you get down on your knees, all that bullshit. Believe me, I've seen it. More than once. And each time it gets worse.'

Natalie's face. One more time. I had to see it. I closed my eyes and willed her to appear in my mind.

God damn it all, one more time. Please.

'You probably saved Harry's life. Hell, for all I know you saved my life, too. Despite everything else . . . '

Her eyes. Her hair. The scar on her chin.

'I mean, I figured you should get it clean. That much you deserve.'

He raised the gun and leveled it at my chest. I waited for the blast. I wondered how it would feel. Or if I'd feel anything at all. I didn't know how long I'd last, how many seconds my eyes would be open before it all went black. If I'd fall back down this little cliff, feeling the rocks on the way down or the cold water at the end.

He took dead aim at my heart. I could see the gun wavering in his hand. I stopped breathing.

'Fuck!' he said. He pulled the gun up until it was cocked next to his ear, stood there looking up at the trees. 'Son of a whore! Look at me!'

He turned around, looked behind him, then up at the trees again, then back at me.

'Cap enjoys this shit,' he said. 'He really does. What kind of a man enjoys this?'

He wheeled around one more time. He moved the gun slowly, down from his ear, back to the firing position.

'Maybe you don't want to do this,' I said.

'Shut up.'

'I'm pretty sure you don't.'

'Shut the fuck up.'

'You're not like Cap.'

Another breath. Seconds passing. The man with one eye shut now, holding the gun steady.

'Fuck's sake,' he finally said. 'Cover your ears.'

'What?'

'I said cover your ears!'

I covered them. He took a quick look behind him, then he pointed the gun straight up and fired it two times.

He shook his head like someone had just nailed him right on the chin. 'God, that's a loud one.'

'I don't get it,' I said.

'I can't do this. I don't know how I thought I could.'

'So what happens now?'

'What happens now is that you die. As far as

Cap knows, as far as Mr. Gray knows, you're dead and gone. You understand me? You go back home, you stay the fuck away from all of us. You keep your friend away, too.'

'If I do that, you've gotta stay away from the reservations.'

He shook his head. He almost smiled at me. 'You're talking like someone who's in a position to bargain.'

'It has to work both ways.'

'Don't worry. We'll be gone soon. I, for one, will never set foot in the Yoo fucking Pee again. You know summer's supposed to be a little warmer than this, right?'

He looked down at the gun. He wiped it down with his shirttail, looking past me, out at the water. When he was done, he dropped it on the ground.

'Give us a while,' he said. 'I don't know if Cap's gonna keep driving for a while, or turn around right here. Obviously, if he sees you on the road we both have a big problem.'

'I got it.'

'It's like Mr. Gray said. I can't do one fucking thing right.'

'Who is he?'

He was about to turn away from me. But that question stopped him in his tracks.

'You don't want to know,' he said. 'You don't want to know, you don't want to ask. And as of right now you don't even exist to him anymore, remember? So forget you ever saw him up here.'

'He seems like a hard man to forget.'

Brucie shook his head. 'You're fucking right

on that one. But do it anyway.'

Then he left. He walked to the road without looking back at me. A minute later, I heard the sound of the engine racing and then the tires spraying gravel. When that faded away there was nothing but the waves on the lake and rain falling softly on the leaves. I hadn't even heard it start, had no awareness of the rain or the chill in the air or anything else until this very moment. Me alone with a gun lying in the dirt and my life somehow given back to me. Whatever life I had left.

I sat down on the little cliff overlooking the lake. I watched the sailboat make slow progress, going east. The rain filtered through the leaves and came down on me in a fine mist, in no hurry. I had nowhere to go and a good reason to sit tight, so I did just that.

At one point I took out my cell phone, looked at the display. There was no signal to be found here. Digital signal, analog roam signal, smoke signal. I was on my own again, story of my life. I had the gun in my right hand now. I had to resist the urge to throw both the cell phone and the gun into the water below.

I stayed there a long time, maybe longer than I had ever sat in one goddamned place before. I kept watching the sailboat until it was gone and then I watched the clouds moving by and the waves hitting the shore one after another. The rain kept up until I could feel the drops running down my face. I was getting cold, but I had felt a lot colder.

I didn't want to move, because moving meant

161

going back home. And going back home meant calling Natalie and telling her we were done.

★ ★ ★

I had seen it so clearly while I was waiting to die. Things hadn't changed one bit just because I'd managed to live. I was holding on to her, trying to convince her that we could make this thing work across all this distance. This fantasy. This make-believe game between two very lonely people. Natalie working so hard to restart her career in a new city. Me back in Michigan, cleaning out my cabins, waiting by my phone . . .

Real couples wake up together and eat breakfast and make plans and get in each other's way. They might be apart for a few hours at a time, but they always find each other again, every night. Natalie and I had never had a day like that. Not once, ever, and sitting there on that cliff getting soaked to the bone I realized that we probably never would.

How did you ever, ever think for a moment, Alex, that this thing would really work?

So I sat there on the cliff getting slowly soaked to the bone, maybe hoping I could make it come out differently. Or just hoping I could avoid it a little longer if I just kept sitting there. Eventually, I had to stand up. Every ache I'd ever had in my body came back to me, along with a few new ones.

I walked slowly down the path, back to the road. When I got there, I had a new problem, because now I was wet and cold and miles away from my truck, and standing on one of the emptiest highways in the state of Michigan.

I started walking west, with the gun tucked in my waistband. I walked for twenty minutes, maybe thirty before I finally heard a car. It was coming from behind me. I turned and saw a black vehicle, and for one second I was sure it was Cap's Escalade and I was a dead man after all. But it turned out to be a Lincoln Navigator. I stood there and waited for it to slow to a stop beside me. I didn't even have to stick my thumb out. It was the Upper Peninsula, after all. This is what people do.

The window rolled down. 'Are you okay, sir?' It was a man in his seventies. I could see his wife sitting next to him.

'I could use a lift.'

'Hop on in.'

I got in the back seat. The woman turned around and looked at my wet clothes. 'What did you do, fall in the lake?'

'Something like that.'

The man asked me where I was headed. I was thinking if I was smart I'd go back up to Leon's house, have him take me back to my truck in the middle of the night. But I didn't feel like explaining things to him yet, and being smart wasn't usually an issue anyway. All I wanted to do was to get my own vehicle as soon as possible and to get the hell back home. So I asked him to drop me off in Hessel.

He didn't have any problem with that. He drove and his wife smiled at me and asked me if I needed a towel. She could unpack one from the bag in the back if I needed one. I told her no, thank you. Then I asked her how long they had been married. She said fifty-one years, with three kids and five grandkids.

The crazy thing was she looked a little like Natalie. Like Natalie would look when she was in her seventies, anyway.

'You ever play ball?' the man asked me.

'Baseball?'

'Yeah, you played, didn't you.'

'How did you know that?'

'I can always tell. I was a catcher myself. Way back when.'

'So was I.'

'Well, I'll be,' he said. 'Ain't that a kicker.'

If the couple had suddenly turned into space aliens, I don't think it would have fazed me at that point. It was a day when anything could happen.

Anything at all.

When we got to Hessel, I asked him to drop me off where the road down to Mr. Gray's house began. The man insisted on taking me all the way to my destination, out of his way or not. More true northern Michigan behavior. So I let him drive all the way down to where I had hidden my truck that morning. I kept watching for Cap's Escalade, but I never saw it.

'You have a house down here?' the man said.

'No, just visiting.' I indicated the driveway when we got to it. He pulled in and was headed all the way down to the house when I told him to stop. My truck was still there, pulled off in the bushes. If they thought it was odd to leave me

164

there, they didn't show it. I thanked them both a couple of times each. I told them to look me up in Paradise if they ever got up that way. Just stop at the Glasgow Inn.

The man backed his way out. I was alone again, this time not far away from the house where everything had turned to shit that day. I still had the gun in my waistband. I had the sudden urge to go back there and start all over again, but I knew Mr. Gray was gone now. And I figured I should keep my promise to Brucie, at least for one day.

I got in the truck and started it up, scraped my way through the heavy brush as I did a three-point turn and headed back out to the road. I checked my cell phone again. Even if I could get a signal here it was a moot point because now the phone was dead.

I drove home. I was shivering even with the heat on. I couldn't stop it.

I wondered if I'd have a message from Natalie when I got there, what I would say to her when I called her. What words would come to me, if any came at all.

I drove fast, taking the road through Rudyard and Trout Lake, through Eckerman Corner, up to Whitefish Bay, where I knew it would feel even colder. Where I'd be alone for the rest of the night. Then again tomorrow.

Alone. I would always be alone.

The sun was going down now. The whole day gone by. One more road, then the sign as you enter Paradise. 'Welcome to Paradise — we're glad you made it.'

Yeah, I'm glad I made it, all right. I'll check on Vinnie, see if both his eyes are open yet. Then I'll go bother Jackie until he makes me dinner.

I turned on my headlights when I hit the old logging road and the sudden darkness from the trees. I drove past Vinnie's place, saw that his truck was still there. To my cabin first for dry clothes.

My headlights swept across the Jeep parked in front of my cabin. I saw the Canadian plates. It took me a few seconds to believe what I was seeing.

I got out, went to my door. I opened it and saw her inside, waiting for me. She was wearing one of my sweatshirts.

'What are you doing here?' I said.

'What does it look like?' Natalie said, her arms wrapped around herself. 'I'm freezing my ass off.'

11

Everything I had been thinking about, this whole idea of how hopeless this thing with Natalie was, how breaking it off now would be the best thing for everybody . . . That was gone in about two seconds. Seeing her here in my cabin, waiting for me, that pretty much took care of everything right there.

'Natalie,' I said. I still couldn't quite believe it. 'I don't understand — '

'Are you going to say hello to me or not?'

She stood up and came over to me. My sweatshirt was three sizes too big for her. She looked tired. I put my hands on her shoulders, held her there in front of me.

'Hello, God damn it,' I said. Then I pulled her close to me. I kissed her and stroked her hair and remembered that this was the way she felt and the way she smelled.

'Why are you here?' I finally said.

She put her finger to my lips and led me to my bed without another word. She hesitated as we were starting to take our clothes off. I was shivering.

'Why are you all wet?' she said, feeling my shirt.

'It was raining.'

'Let me guess, you were working on the cabin.'

'Uh, no. Actually — '

'Never mind. Tell me later.' She fell back on

my bed and took me with her.

'Sorry this place is such a mess.'

'Will you shut up already?' She kissed me again and that was it for the talking. At least for a while.

I may have come home cold and miserable, but she changed all that in a hurry.

'So tell me,' I said later. My arms were around her and she was facing away from me. Her hair was in my face, her skin was touching mine, back to chest.

'Tell you what?'

'Why you're here. Did you make the bust?'

'Actually, no.'

'You didn't?'

'Not yet.'

'Not yet? So why aren't you still undercover.'

'Who says I'm not?'

'I don't get it.'

'We called a time-out,' she said. 'We had to back out for a couple of days.'

'Why? What happened?'

She took a long breath. 'God, Alex. You wouldn't believe it. After all the prep work with Rhapsody, all those meetings in the coffee shop every morning . . . We finally got the big meet set up. Antoine Laraque in a hotel room, ready to buy guns. Or so we thought.'

'So you thought?'

'We never got him to say it. We never got to the punch line. He and Rhapsody came to the room . . . Don and I were there . . . '

'Don Resnik, your partner.'

'Right. My supposed bodyguard. He had this

suit on, black sunglasses, the whole deal. I'm this woman with a connection in Michigan, somebody who wants to move guns across the border. A lot of guns. We've got it all set up, and then finally, they're both coming up to the room. Rhapsody comes in first. She's wearing this wild zebra suit. Zebra shoes, the works. And then Laraque comes in. The man himself . . . '

'Yeah?'

She didn't say anything.

'Was he wearing a zebra suit, too?'

'No,' she said. 'Laraque was not wearing a zebra suit.'

'So tell me about him.'

'I don't know how to say it. It's going to sound ridiculous.'

'Go ahead.'

'He wasn't that big, first of all. Don's like six foot five, remember. Laraque couldn't have been six feet tall. Maybe five ten, tops. He wasn't really built, either. I mean, he didn't look that strong. I'm sure Don could have thrown him through the window with no problem.'

'Okay . . . '

'He had short hair. A very high forehead. He was wearing glasses. Hell, I'm making him sound like an accountant.'

'So far.'

'That's just it, Alex. I can't describe what he was really like. You'd have to see him in person. You'd have to see him move around a room and shake your hand. And then sit down across from you and look at you . . . I mean, remember, I had cops in the room behind me, cops in the room in front of me. I had a cop out in the hall. I had a cop built like a football player *in the room with me*. All of them had guns. Even Don, standing right at my side. I was the safest woman in Toronto ... And yet, I have never felt more terrified in my entire life.'

'Why?'

'I don't know. Because he was there. This man. He just had this ... this power about him. I can't explain it. But I could feel it.'

I thought about it. 'Okay, so what happened to the bust?'

I still couldn't see her face. It was just her voice, and the tension in her body.

'I tried to get him around to the punch line. I even had some samples with me. Some handguns, a couple of small machine guns. I put them out on the table, told him I had a supplier in Michigan, asked him if he'd be interested in doing business. He said he'd like to know how I came to consider him for such an enterprise. That's what he called it. An enterprise. So I told him about running into Rhapsody, hearing all about her in prison. The whole story. Rhapsody was right there, but she didn't say a word. She just leaned back in her chair and took out a cigarette. I was getting a little rattled, so I actually told her it was a nonsmoking room, just to see if I could get back on top of things.'

'What did she say to that?'

'Nothing. She took out her lighter and lit up.'

'And then blew the smoke in your face?'

'Women don't do that. She blew it straight up in the air. With a little smile.'

'Very smooth.'

'No,' she said. 'Not really. I think she was just as terrified as I was.'

'What, being in the room with you guys?'

'Maybe. I'm not sure, exactly. But remember, this woman didn't just do hard time at Kingston, it sounds like she practically ran the place. This was the worst prison in Canada, before they shut it down.'

'Then how could she be so scared?'

'Well, at first I thought it was Laraque who was making her so nervous. But I'll tell you, all he had to do was touch her, just once, and she was fine. The same old Rhapsody I'd meet every day in the coffee shop. Totally cool. On top of the world. It was like he was recharging her, you know? Giving her energy. Or hell, like they were having really good sex, except it was just him reaching over and putting his hand on her arm. Two of his fingers on the back of her wrist. That was it.'

'Yeah?'

'I know it sounds crazy, but I saw it with my own eyes. I asked Don about it later, but he had no idea what I was talking about.'

'It wasn't obvious?'

'I guess not,' she said. 'Or maybe a woman would be more likely to pick up on it.'

'A woman who knows all about good sex, you mean.'

'Whatever you say, Alex.'

'No, seriously. So what happened next?'

'Well, that's when it got even crazier, because no matter what I said, Laraque refused to play along with us. He'd almost say something, like yes, he was interested in imports from the States. But that he had, what did he say, he said he had other offers to consider, different combinations of merchandise, different terms . . . He started talking about it like it was just another investment opportunity, and how there were cold markets and warm markets and hot markets, and how much he respected men down in the States who knew how to make money. He even quoted Warren Buffett, something like, how did it go . . . 'Be afraid when others are greedy, and greedy when others are afraid.' You ever hear that one?'

'No, I haven't. But it makes sense.'

'Yeah, it does. But the whole time he was going through all this . . . I mean, I didn't think he was even carrying, but it was like I kept expecting him to stop, and to reach over . . . and touch me. Except instead of making me feel better, like he was doing for Rhapsody, he would kill me. Just like that. One touch and I'm dead. It was like he had me hypnotized.'

It was hard to hear, but I wanted the whole story. Every detail. 'But you're saying he never made a real offer,' I said. 'He didn't give you something you could nail him on?'

'I swear, Alex. It was like he knew exactly what we were doing. The whole thing, the setup, the cops in the other rooms, recording him, listening to every word. He knew I was a fake, Don was a fake, everything was fake. And that one wrong word from him would bring it all crashing in on his head. But he didn't say it.

The whole time, he was just toying with us. And when he got tired of doing that, he stood up and he walked out.'

'Do you really think he knows you're a cop?'

'I don't see how he could. But deep down in my gut that's exactly what I was feeling when we were in that room. This guy can see right through me.'

'So what happens next?'

'He told us he wanted to meet again. He wanted me to go back to my contact and to have him send samples of other merchandise . . . Notice how he didn't say guns. The whole time, he never once said the word 'gun.' And when he said 'other merchandise,' if you took him literally, he could have been asking me to bring back samples of fabric. So he could make some nice suits or something. He also said he'd like us to come to his office next time, let him be the one extending the hospitality, because it was his city, after all.'

'You're not really going to his office next time . . . '

'I don't know, Alex. I have no idea what's going to happen next. They told me to disappear for two days, to make like I was really leaving town to confer with my connection. That makes you a gun dealer now, by the way.'

'Gee, thanks.'

'Don't mention it. Anyway, I need to call them tomorrow, to see what they're thinking. The leader of the task force wants to keep pursuing it, but my CO wants to pull me.'

'I'm with him. You can't go to his home turf.

173

What are you gonna do, walk in there wearing a wire?'

She turned on to her back and looked at me. 'It's not up to me,' she said. 'I'll see what they say.'

'You don't have to do it if you don't want to. You know that.'

She closed her eyes. 'You're not helping.'

'Why do you say that?'

'You're supposed to tell me I need to go back and finish the job. Get the bad guy and help shut down his operation.'

'I'm not thinking about that part,' I said. 'I admit it, I'm only thinking about you and keeping you safe.'

She pulled me closer to her. She held on tight. 'When I think about being in a room with Laraque again,' she said, 'all I can think about is how much I want to be with you. I've never felt this way before, Alex. About anybody. It really scares me. It's like I have a life now. You know what I mean? It sounds kind of corny, I know, but it's like I have something to live for.'

It killed me. What she was saying, it absolutely killed me. I knew I'd have to tell her my own story, about what had happened that very day, being led to the edge of the water and believing that my life was over, and how I thought about her and was glad that she would keep on living without me. That she would be better off in the long run.

It was always me pushing this, me trying to keep us together, when she had her own problems and it felt like she was never letting me

174

get too close to her. But now, on a day when we both faced our own deaths in different ways, it was Natalie who wanted to hold on to us. It was Natalie who wanted to keep on living so we could be together.

'So what do we do now?' I said. Suddenly, anything was possible.

'I don't know. But I do know two things for sure.'

'Yeah?'

'One is that I want to go to sleep right now.'

'And the other?'

She settled in next to me. It was cold outside. It was dark and colder than any summer night should ever be.

'I can't even say it . . . '

'What?'

'I've never walked away from anything in my life,' she said. 'Not because I was scared.'

'You don't want to go back?'

'Don't let me.'

'Are you serious?'

'Yes,' she said. 'Whatever you do, don't let me go back there.'

12

I woke up before she did. It was a Sunday morning, another day of cold mist hanging in the air. But today everything felt different. I stood there over the bed and watched her sleeping. 'Don't go away,' I said softly. Then I headed to Vinnie's house.

His truck was still where I had left it. I didn't imagine he had even noticed the cut battery cables yet. I slipped in through the open front door and found him asleep on his couch. His feet were propped up on the table. His face was every shade of red, purple, green, and blue. I knew he'd be looking worse for a few days before he started to look better, but this was one beaten-up face. He seemed to be sleeping all right, though. His breathing was even. So I left him there and promised myself I'd be back later to check on him.

I had one more thing to do before going back to Natalie. I had a reservation for one of the cabins, and as far as I knew, the family was still coming up from downstate. I had called them and left a message, giving them a chance to cancel, but they never did. What they'd do up here if they were still coming, I couldn't imagine. Who knows, maybe they wouldn't mind wet, chilly air that feels twenty degrees colder than it really is. Maybe just being away from home was enough to make them happy. If they were still coming, I was going to try to make them comfortable.

I threw some firewood in the truck bed and drove down to the fifth cabin. It was the nicest place left after my father's masterpiece was burned to the ground. I loaded up the wood stove and started it. I stacked the rest of the wood inside to keep it out of the wet air. By the time I was done, the place was already feeling cozy.

I wrote the family a note, told them to make themselves at home, told them I'd be down in the first cabin if they needed me. I didn't know exactly when they'd get here, but I assumed it wouldn't be for a while, unless they were already on their way and were driving most of the night.

When I got back to my cabin, I opened the door and smelled coffee. Natalie had a pot going, and was sitting on my bed looking at her cell phone. She was wearing my sweatshirt again. This time it didn't look like she was wearing anything else underneath it.

'You're right,' she said when I came in. 'Your cell phone reception sucks here.'

'We make up for it in other ways. Like the perfect summer weather.'

'Yeah, what's with that, anyway? I can't believe I have to go back to Canada to get warm.'

'I've heard some of the old-timers talk about it. Every twenty years or so, it's like summer just forgets to come.'

'I need to use your phone,' she said. 'This thing just isn't going to work.'

'Go ahead.'

I poured myself a cup of coffee while she called the Mounties' office. I could only hear her part of the conversation while she talked to the special operations commander. It was mostly a string of yeses and I understands. When she was done, she hung up the phone and stayed sitting on the bed.

'What's going on?' I said.

'There's some disagreement about whether we're going to pull the plug. As of now, we're still a go.'

'They can't be serious.'

'I need to go back, no matter which way they call it.'

'When?'

'Tomorrow morning.'

'So it's a pretty short visit.'

'Are you sorry I came out?' She had a hint of a smile on her face.

'Uh, no. I think I'll take it.'

'It'll be your turn to come out to Toronto.'

'Okay,' I said. 'I think I can find the place.'

'I need to call Don. Then we can go do something. You have any plans for today?'

'Lady's choice.'

She dialed my phone again. 'Don,' she said when it went through, 'where are you? Keller is looking for you.'

I waited for her to finish the conversation. It felt a little strange, hearing her talk to the man she was spending so much time with in a hotel room. I knew she wasn't alone with him. I knew it wouldn't matter even if she was. It was just a gut reaction that I couldn't quite stop.

'He sounds really weird today,' she said when she hung up. 'He must be feeling the stress, too.'

'You know, you made me promise you something last night.'

She looked at me. 'I know,' she said. 'But I have to go back. You know that. I was just a little freaked out last night.'

'Or maybe it was the voice.'

'Which voice.'

'You know. The cop voice. In your head. The one you should always listen to.'

'Come here.'

'Why?'

'You said it was lady's choice today. I just thought of the first thing I want to do.'

★ ★ ★

When we were finally dressed and on our feet, we headed down to the end of my road. I showed her the work Vinnie and I had been doing on the last cabin.

'This is going to be beautiful,' she said. She ran her hand along the staircase.

'I hope it's half as good as what it was before,' I said. 'That's all.'

'You're doing all this for your father, aren't you. You couldn't bear to see this place destroyed.'

'I don't know how far I would have gotten without Vinnie helping me.'

'Where is he today? I'd like to see him.'

I hesitated. 'Sure, if you want to . . . '

Vinnie had been with us from the beginning,

from the first time I had met her, up at the lake. Through the death of her partner. I knew she must have felt almost as close to him as I did.

'Is he at the casino?'

'No, he's home. I don't think he'll be going to work today.'

'What happened?'

'Well, you remember our little adventure the other night?'

'The one where you ended up in the jail?'

'That would be the one. Vinnie ended up running into those guys again. This time, it was one against two.'

'How bad is he?'

'If I told you he probably looks worse than he really is . . .'

'I'll be the judge of that. Let's go see him.'

We drove down to Vinnie's cabin, parked next to his truck. 'He's going to be surprised to see you,' I said as we went to the door.

I opened it. The couch was empty now, the blanket folded on one arm.

'Vinnie!' I said. 'You've got company.'

I went to the bathroom, expecting to find him with his face in the sink again. Or maybe taking a bath, trying to make himself feel better.

He wasn't there.

'Son of a bitch.'

'What's the matter?' Natalie said.

'He's not here.'

'That's his truck outside, isn't it?'

'Yeah, I disabled it yesterday. I didn't want him going anywhere.'

'Somebody else gave him a ride?'

I thought about it. 'His cousin Buck,' I said. 'Damn it, I bet Vinnie called him.'

'Where do you think they went?'

'I don't know exactly.' I didn't think he'd know where to find the vacation house down in Hessel. Unless he got Caroline to tell him. 'But I know a few places to start. Come on.'

We got in my truck and rumbled down to the main road. I was about to gun it through town, but at the last moment I pulled into Jackie's parking lot.

'Why are we stopping already?'

'I want to check here real quick, see if he stopped in. Jackie might know something.'

When we went inside the Glasgow, there was Vinnie sitting by the fireplace. He had a bag of ice pressed to his face. Before I could say a word, Jackie was all over me.

'Alex!' he said. 'What in goddamned hell is the matter with you?'

'Jackie . . . ,' I said. 'Vinnie . . . '

'Look at his face, Alex! Look at him! You left him all alone in his cabin all day yesterday, and all last night! You even cut the goddamned battery cables in his truck so he couldn't go anywhere! What were you thinking?'

'Listen — '

'Listen yourself, God damn it! What were you trying to do, starve him to death? What if he had to go see a doctor? Is this the way you take care of your friend, by leaving him stranded in his cabin? He had to walk all the way down here just to get something to eat and some more ice for his face! I'm waiting for an explanation, Alex. I really want to hear it, because this is the stupidest goddamned thing you've ever done. And believe me, that's saying something.'

'Jackie — '

'What, Alex? What are you going to say?'

'I want to introduce you to somebody.'

That stopped him cold. He finally noticed Natalie standing behind me.

'Hello,' she said. 'You must be the famous Jackie.'

'Hello,' he said, his voice suddenly throttled down about twelve notches. 'You must be the famous Natalie.'

'Where's Vinnie?' Natalie said. Then she saw him. 'Oh my God, what happened to you?'

He tried to get up from his chair.

'Sit down,' she said. 'Who did this?'

'I did. It's all my fault.'

'I'm serious, Vinnie. Who did this?'

Vinnie looked up at me for some help. 'Natalie,' he said, 'what are you doing here?'

'I came to see Alex, so I could kick his butt. How come he wasn't there to help you?'

'Hey,' I said.

'I told you,' Vinnie said. 'It's all on me. It's not Alex's fault.'

'We're supposed to look out for each other,' she said. She touched the side of his face. 'My God . . . '

'You scared the hell out of us,' I said. 'We were about to drive all over the U.P. looking for you.'

'What, you think I'd go back for more? Already? How stupid do you think I am?' He

182

tried to smile at Natalie. It was hard to do with a swollen upper lip.

'You should go to the hospital,' Natalie said.

'I'm feeling better already. Seriously. Come on, sit down, tell me what's going on.'

That's how we ended up spending the whole afternoon at the Glasgow Inn. Natalie got her chance to totally disarm Jackie and convince him that she was the best thing that ever happened to me. Vinnie kept icing his face and resting by the fire. I brought out some cold Molsons and gave her one, told her I knew which side of the border had all the good beer.

'At last,' she said to me, 'you get something right.'

As great as it was, I couldn't help feeling a little unsettled. Here was Natalie sitting in the Glasgow, pretty much owning the place already. But this was the one place I came to every single day of my life. I talked to Jackie here, I met up with Vinnie here, I watched a game on the television over the bar. Or I just sat here by the fire, all by myself. Now in one afternoon the place had changed. I'd never be able to come here again without thinking of Natalie.

And hell, what about my cabin? What about my bed? I spent the night sleeping beside her, waking up to listen to her, to touch her. To make myself believe that it was really happening. How will I ever sleep in that bed alone now?

If this thing with Natalie doesn't work out . . . everything will be different. Everything. It's like I'm putting all my chips on the table now, making this one last big bet with my whole life.

Happy with Natalie Reynaud. Or unhappily alone forever.

That's what I was thinking that cold July afternoon. But what the hell, right? It was about time.

*　*　*

Vinnie wanted to go back to his cabin, so we drove him up there. All three of us wedged in the front seat of my truck. We got him comfortable on his couch, got his bottle of ibuprofen, got his bag of ice.

'Are you sure you don't want us to stay?' Natalie said.

'I'm positive,' he said. 'Go out to dinner or something. Do something good.'

'We'll come back later,' she said. 'We'll stop by and check on you.'

'Just go. I mean it.'

'Okay,' she said. 'Okay.' She bent down and kissed him on his tired, beat-up face, this man who had once saved her life. And mine. 'You rest.'

'Alex,' he said, as we were leaving.

I went over to him.

'Life is smiling on one of us,' he said in a low voice.

'You got that right.'

'Do me a favor. Don't blow it.'

'I'll try not to.'

We left him there, closed the door, and went out into the evening. It was still light out, a cold gray light that looked just like November. But I

184

could not have been a happier man.

'Jackie makes a great beef stew,' I said. 'How about it?'

'Let's save that one. I've got another idea for dinner.'

I was suddenly picturing something in my cabin, dinner in bed perhaps. But she had something totally different in mind. She wanted to go to the last place on earth I ever would have thought of.

A few minutes later, we were speeding down M-28. 'You really want to go to the Freighters for dinner,' I said. 'At the Ojibway Hotel.'

'That's right.'

'Don't we both have some pretty bad memories of that place?'

'That's why I want to eat there. So we can banish them forever. If I'm going to be spending a lot of time over here, we can't go on avoiding one of the nicest restaurants in town just because something bad happened there once.'

'Your wish is my command.'

'Is that a cop behind us? What are you going, about ninety?'

'I'm not sure, actually. I think the speedometer is broken.'

I looked in the rearview mirror and saw the car gaining on us. It was one of the state guys. He closed to about a hundred yards before he slowed down and did a U-turn. In another few seconds, he was just a speck going the other way.

'How come he didn't ring you up?' she said.

'They all know me by now.'

'Must be nice. Special favors from the police.'

'Speaking of which . . . Well, we'll see about that later.'

'You're buying me dinner first. I'm not that easy.'

The sun was just starting to go down when we hit the Soo. I parked downtown on Portage Avenue, just a few doors from where Vinnie and I had found our friends in the bar a couple of nights before and gotten arrested. Yeah, there were great memories all around this part of town.

We went in through the hotel entrance and walked to the back of the place, where the restaurant overlooked the locks. We could see a freighter moving slowly through, maybe a seven-hundred-footer. We sat down at one of the tables along the window. In fact, it was the very same table we had had on that one fateful night, when a man who seemed to know us said some strange and horrible things to us, and then walked out and died in the snow.

'If a weird old man approaches us,' I said, 'I'm leaving.'

'Hey, isn't that . . . '

I turned to see who she was referring to, and looked right up into the smiling face of Chief Roy Maven.

'Constable Reynaud,' he said. 'What a great pleasure.'

He bent down and took her hand. For one second I thought he was going to get down on one knee and kiss it.

'Chief Maven,' she said. 'How have you been?'

'Just fine, thank you.' He gave me a quick nod. 'McKnight.'

'Evening, Chief.'

'You've been staying out of trouble, right? I don't want to come in tomorrow morning and find you in my jail again.' He turned back to Natalie. 'Did Alex tell you about that?'

'Yes, Chief.'

'Darn. That would have made my night if you hadn't heard yet.'

'Chief . . . ,' I said.

'Relax, McKnight. We're all out of uniform here. Those of us who still wear them, anyway. Can I introduce my wife?'

He brought the poor woman over, this woman who had married Roy Maven and conceived his children. She actually looked quite sane and even pleasant. Apparently, she had already heard about me, with Maven bringing home tales from the office, the latest trouble this McKnight character had gotten himself into. We all had some more fun at my expense, and then they excused themselves.

'It's always good to see you, Constable,' he said to Natalie. He gave me another nod and then they were off.

'Okay, now all I need is a big boat to come plowing through this window,' I said. 'That will make the evening complete.'

'I think you secretly like that man,' she said.

'If it's a secret, it's one I don't know about.'

'I think he's very charming in his own way.'

'You're just torturing me now. I hope you're enjoying yourself.'

'Absolutely.'

Later, after dinner, we walked through the Locks Park. It was getting darker and colder by the minute. We stopped at the fountain and threw pennies in for good luck. I kissed her.

When we were back in the truck, I asked her if I could make one more side trip before taking her home. That's how we ended up going down to Rosedale, to Leon's house.

'I have to give him back his gun,' I said. 'And I think this will raise my stock with his wife.'

'What do you mean?'

'Well, she thinks every time I come over, it's to drag Leon into something dangerous. So imagine if I'm just bringing you over to meet the family.'

'And returning his gun.'

'I won't let her see that part.'

The house looked empty when I pulled into the driveway. I had the sudden fear that Leon was out looking for trouble like everyone else in my life. But of course that was nonsense, a product of my overactive imagination. Besides, I thought, if he was really out doing that, he wouldn't have taken his whole family with him.

'I'll hold on to the gun,' I said. 'Maybe I'll see him tomorrow.'

'Tell him hello for me if you do.'

Because you won't be here tomorrow. That's the thought that was running through my head, all the way back to Paradise. It was totally dark now. The cold mist that was settling on us every night this summer was back again, dancing in my headlights, coming together in tendrils and then

188

drifting apart as we passed through it.

It was quiet for a long time. Finally I spoke up.

'You tired?'

'Little bit.'

Her profile in the faint glow of the dashboard. The little scar on her chin.

'You're really going back tomorrow?'

'I have to, yes.'

'Okay. But you don't have to go undercover again if you don't want to. No matter what anyone else says, that's your call.'

'They're going to shut everything down because I'm getting cold feet?'

'If it doesn't feel safe to you, you can't ignore that.'

'I'll go back,' she said. 'I'll see what they decide.'

'You can't do it.'

'Says who?'

'Natalie, you told me yourself you think Laraque can see right through it.'

'It was just the fear talking. I'll be all right.'

'No, you won't. You can't go.'

'It's not up to you, Alex.'

'You asked me not to let you go back,' I said. It came out with more of an edge than I wanted. 'I'm doing what you asked me to do.'

'Well, now I'm asking you to back off. You're not making this any easier.'

'Fine. I'll back off.'

'Alex, I'm sorry.'

'Yeah. Me, too.'

It hung there between us as I rounded the bay and headed up to Paradise. I wasn't sure what else to say. Or if it would do any good.

We passed Vinnie's place. There were no lights on. We didn't stop.

'I need to call the station one more time,' she said as I pulled in front of the cabin.

'Go on in. I'm gonna check on the family down the road. They should be here by now.'

I watched her get out and go inside my cabin. Then I closed my eyes and swore at myself a few times. I put the truck back in gear and drove up the road to the fifth cabin. The lights were on. There was a minivan parked outside. I got out and knocked on the front door.

The father answered. He might have been ten years younger than me. Maybe only five. But he had a couple of young kids. The boy looked about eight years old, the little girl about four. They were sitting with their mother by the wood stove.

'Listen,' I said. 'I know you reserved this place, but you didn't have to come up here. I can't imagine this is what you had in mind.'

'It's good to get away from everything, Mr. McKnight. No matter where you go.'

'Call me Alex. Please.'

'Hey, why is it so cold?' the boy asked.

'Sorry about that,' I said. 'I thought I ordered warm weather for you guys.'

'Don't be sorry,' the boy said. 'We love it!'

'Yeah,' the little girl said. 'Is it going to snow tonight?'

'Yeah, snow in July!' the boy said. 'How cool would that be?'

I ended up staying there for a little while,

getting to know the family. I told them all about Paradise, what they could go out and do the next day, starting with a trip up to the Shipwreck Museum. The boy showed me the remote control car he had brought up with him. The girl showed me her stuffed animals. When they were all settled in, I thanked the man again, wished them all a good night. I told them to come down to the first cabin if they needed anything.

When I was back outside, it hit me.

It could still happen.

I could have something like this. A wife, two kids, all of us happy to go away together, no matter what the weather was. As long as we were together.

It was something I had given up on long ago. Something that had passed me by, something I tried not to think about. But tonight anything seemed possible. Anything. Even this.

It wasn't too late.

God, Alex. Listen to you.

I got back in my truck. On the way back to my cabin, I practiced a few versions of my apology. I'm just so worried about you. I hate the thought of you being in harm's way. Sometimes I want to say things to you and they just come out all sideways.

Yeah, something like that, Alex. That'll do it. Too bad there aren't any twenty-four-hour florists in Paradise.

The last normal thought in my head, before everything slows down.

Trees.

More trees.

Fog.

I round the corner. The red glow of a vehicle's taillights. One glimpse and then they're gone.

Vinnie out, doing what?

But no, his truck is still grounded. It's not Vinnie.

Somebody else? Who could be here?

The cabin. Front door open. Light streaming out onto the ground, like something spilled.

The door can't be open. It does not make sense.

Stop the truck. Get out and move. Running now. Natalie. What on God's earth is going on? Natalie.

Through the open door. Squinting in the sudden bright light.

Phone on the floor. Cord curled around a table leg.

Natalie. Where are you?

Push the table away. Glass breaking. Water on the floor.

Something else. The bright color of it. The shock like something plugged into my spine.

The red. The blood.

Her face, her eyes open. Staring up at me.

My sweatshirt on her chest now. She had put it on again. I was going to give it to her. I was. It's dark now, stained and wet. Holes in the fabric.

One of them here.

Another here.

One more. Ruined.

Natalie.

On my knees, holding her. Lifting her from the floor, from the blood. Her arms hang. Her hair.

Hanging to the floor.

Natalie, please.

Grabbing for the phone, trying to remember how it works, which numbers to press. Somehow I have to keep her off the floor. I can't drop her. I can't let go.

Natalie. Hang on.

But there's nothing there. Nobody to hear me. Her eyes do not move.

The warmth of her gone, her life, herself. She is gone.

She is gone.

13

A sheriff's deputy, first on the scene. An ambulance. Natalie taken from me, pried out of my arms. Then three state police cars. Red lights spinning in the fog.

Questions. Voices. Did you hear anything?

No.

Did you see anything?

Lights.

What kind of lights?

A car. A truck.

You can't be more specific?

No.

Did anybody follow you home?

No.

We know this isn't easy, Alex.

No.

No, you don't know.

The sun comes up. The earth keeps spinning, for whatever reason. Time is obliterated. An hour passes or a minute or a day. There's no reference point anymore, because nothing ever changes. Everything is pain. Pain is all there is or ever will be. Pain so real it makes its own fog. I can't see anything else.

More questions.

I'm in the next cabin up the road. I can't be in my own place. A crime scene now. As if I could ever go back there anyway. I'm in the second cabin, the one my father built by himself, the summer after the first. The summer of the second cabin, the summer before the third cabin. Before the fourth then the fifth then the sixth and then he died. He's dead.

Name other dead people, Alex. Strange, strange thoughts coming to me now. I can't stop them. Go ahead, name some more dead people. My mother. My old partner. Who else?

No, don't say it. Don't you dare.

It's light out now. The sun rising on the world. It's still cold. Jackie comes to sit with me. He doesn't have much to say. He folds his hands together and presses them between his knees. He asks me what he can do for me.

Nothing.

He stays a long time. Vinnie comes to relieve him. I am apparently not to be left alone. Jackie on the way out, telling me he'll be back. Vinnie taking the chair, his face still a swollen mess.

Minutes pass, or hours, or days. He's not looking at me.

'Alex . . . ,' he finally says.

'Yes.'

'Alex, how did this happen?'

'I don't know.'

'Who did this?'

I say nothing.

'Alex, who did this?'

'I don't know yet.'

'You have an idea. You think it was them.'

'Them who?'

'You know who I'm talking about.'

I shake my head. The rage still on the upcurve, not all the way there yet. Not by a long shot.

'Alex, what are we going to do?'

'We can't bring her back,' I say. I haven't lost it yet. I can still say things like this. 'We can't bring her back, so it doesn't matter what we do.'

His hand on my shoulder, squeezing hard. 'Don't worry about it right now. We'll figure it out.'

'Yeah. We will. We, uh . . . '

Then I can't talk anymore. From one moment to the next, I lose the ability to make words. I'm rocking in my chair. Back and forth, back and forth.

If I had never gone up there on that New Year's Eve, this thing wouldn't have happened.

If she hadn't come out here from Toronto, this thing wouldn't have happened.

If I hadn't left her alone in the cabin, this thing wouldn't have happened.

Or at the very least, we'd both be dead now. That would have worked just fine. Much better than living in this black hole.

Then something happens. Time snaps back into place. The clock starts ticking again. I realize that twelve hours have passed since the thing happened.

That's the other important change. It's the thing now. For the rest of this day, it will be *the thing*. I'll feel the pain of it, but I'll know that the thing itself can be kept at bay, as long as I start moving, and stay moving. For a few hours, at least, I can keep the thing just far enough away to function.

Leon showed up. He stayed outside the cabin

for a minute, talking to Vinnie, their voices a low rumble in the wind.

'Guys,' I said. I could speak again.

They didn't hear me.

'Guys!'

They both came in at once.

'Give me a little time here, okay?'

'What do you mean?' Leon said.

'Give me an hour. Go down to Jackie's, get some breakfast.'

They didn't want to leave. They kept standing there.

'Come on. Please. I need to be by myself for one hour. Go get some breakfast. Vinnie, you must be starving.'

'The police will be coming back soon,' Leon said. 'They'll have some more questions.'

Meaning what, I wanted to say. Like that will do any good for anybody. 'I know,' I said. 'I know. I just need an hour to myself. Then I'll be ready.'

'We're not leaving you,' Vinnie said.

'Please. One hour.'

'You shouldn't be alone.'

'I need some food. You can bring me back something.'

'I'll stay. Leon can get you some breakfast.'

'That's a good idea,' Leon said. 'I'll do that. I'll be back soon.'

'Guys, please.'

But Leon was gone before I could say another word.

'Just go down there,' I told Vinnie. 'You don't have to stay here.'

'I don't have any choice, remember? You cut my battery cables.'

So take my truck . . . The next logical thing to say, right? I didn't say it.

'Okay,' I said. 'Okay.'

We sat there. I felt the thing coming closer. I had to move.

'Do me a favor,' I said. 'I need some aspirin. There's some in the bathroom.'

Vinnie got up. He went for the aspirin. As soon as he was out of sight, I stood up and went to the door. I tried to be quiet about it.

'I don't see it,' I heard him say. Whatever came next, I didn't catch it. I was out the door and in my truck.

And then I was flying.

★ ★ ★

I passed Jackie's place. Leon might have heard me roaring by, might have stuck his head out the door and caught my taillights vanishing down the road, but there was no way he was going to catch me. He didn't even know where I was going.

I went south, leaving Lake Superior, heading straight for the other lake. The sun was out today. I had to flip the visor down. If the sun was actually warming things up, I didn't notice. Leon's gun was still in the box under my seat.

It couldn't have been Laraque, I thought, or anyone else from Canada. They had no idea that Natalie was here.

No, I had another person in mind.

If he had found out that Brucie couldn't do the job, whether Brucie admitted it to him, or whether he just *knew* somehow . . . Either way, if Cap knew I was still alive, he would come for me. If I wasn't there, who the hell knows . . . Instead of waiting, instead of coming back . . .

God damn, why couldn't I have been there?

Or maybe he really did want to take her. Maybe that was his plan. Do that to me first, break me into little pieces, then come back later to finish up. From what Brucie had said about him . . .

I tightened up on the steering wheel, nearly lost my wheels for one sick moment, fought my way back. The road was empty.

I got off 1-75, took the two-lane road east, along the shore of Lake Huron. I drove into Hessel, took the secondary road that ran down the peninsula, took the smaller residential road off of that, turned the corner.

I saw the black Escalade on the road, saw the face behind the wheel. On pure impulse I swung hard, veering across the road. I felt the impact on the corner of my bumper, the Escalade sideswiping me and then running headlong into the ditch. I left the road on the opposite side, obliterated a mailbox, then a small tree. I was out the door before the truck had settled.

Cap came out of the Escalade, lost his footing, and had to put one hand on the ground to keep from falling on his face. He staggered back too far the other way, trying to find his feet, looking like a man who'd been spun in a blender. I was

199

on him before he even saw me.

I planted my right fist in his gut, felt all the wind leave his body. He tried to grab me. I hit him with my left hand, caught too much of the crown of his head, and felt my whole arm go numb. He went down.

I kicked him in the ribs, had the urge to keep doing that about twenty more times. Then I remembered the gun. It was still in the truck. I went back for it, looking up and down the road. My truck was off the road, but his back end was blocking half of it. If anyone came by, they'd have to slow down.

So they'd get a good view of me putting a bullet in his head, I thought. I grabbed the gun, went back to Cap. He was on his hands and knees trying to draw a breath. I kicked him again, flipping him over. There was a bloody scrape on his forehead.

I bent down over him. His eyes focused on me.

'McKnight,' he said. 'Fuck. You're alive?'

'Yes, I am. Surprised to see me?'

He was. It was unmistakable. Under the circumstances, I didn't see how he could be faking it. He was genuinely shocked to see me.

'Brucie killed you.'

'Obviously he didn't.'

'That pussy.'

I put the gun to his temple. I remembered the last time I had pointed this gun at him, the way he had taunted me for sounding like some kind of yooper hick. 'I'm going to kill you,' I said in a dead even voice. 'How's that sound?

Am I doing better this time? I'm going to blow your brains out, all over this road. They'll be picking parts of your head out of the bushes for a week.'

His eyes went wide. He tried to slide away from me.

'How am I doing?' I said. 'Do I sound convincing now?'

'What do you want?'

'Where's your partner?'

'I don't know.'

I hit him in the face with the butt of the gun. 'Where is he?' I said.

'I told you, I don't know.' He kept his face away from me while he spit out blood. 'Brucie disappeared. If you're alive, that might explain it.'

'What do you mean?'

'He knows what'll happen to him if Mr. Gray finds out.'

I thought about it. I could feel the flame inside me starting to burn out. I knew Brucie hadn't done it. He had already proven to me he wasn't a killer. And if Cap was truly this surprised to see me alive, then obviously it couldn't have been him, either.

What the hell was I doing here?

'Wait a minute,' I said. 'What would happen to me?'

'What are you talking about?'

'You said Brucie knows what would happen to him if Mr. Gray finds out I'm alive. What would happen to me?'

'Forget it. You'd be done.'

'Would he send somebody up here to do it?'

'Of course he would.'

'He wouldn't give you a call? Tell you to take care of me?'

Cap swallowed hard, like he was thinking about what life would be like if Mr. Gray decided he couldn't be trusted. 'I have a feeling I don't exactly work for him anymore,' he said. 'But he has other people.'

'What if I wasn't home? What if there was somebody else in my cabin?'

I felt dizzy, just saying the words. Cap didn't answer me. He spat out some more blood.

I grabbed him by the face, made him look up at me.

'If there was a woman in my cabin, God damn you . . . If Gray sent somebody up here to kill me . . . what would happen to her?'

He shook his head. 'If you knew him, you wouldn't even have to ask.'

I wanted to hit him again. I wanted to use the gun like a hammer and smash his face in until there was nothing left. Then I wanted to put the barrel of the gun in my own mouth and pull the trigger.

I didn't do it. Instead, I grabbed his shirt and pulled his face close to mine. 'Did he do it? God damn you, you stupid piece of shit. Did he do this thing? Tell me the truth.'

'If Brucie left you alive, there's no way he could keep it from Gray. There is no fucking way. Trust me, the next time he talked to him, it would all come out. Which can only mean one thing.'

202

I kept holding on to his shirt. My arms were shaking.

'Where does he live?' I said.

'Mr. Gray?'

'Yes, Mr. Gray. Where can I find him?'

'It's not a big secret, McKnight. You know where St. Clair Shores is?'

'Yes.' It was an affluent suburb, next to Detroit.

'The house is on Trombley Street, right on the water. But the place is a fortress, man. And he's got a bodyguard who could take you apart with one hand.'

'You've been to the house?'

'Yeah, a few times.'

'How do I get in?'

'Are you serious?'

'Tell me how I get in the house.'

'Don't go in the front door. Go around to the back. He has a study on that end of the house. There's a door by the pool.'

'Do you think he's home today?'

'What, you're gonna drive all the way down there right now?'

'Yes, I am.'

'Then I'll give you one more piece of advice.'

'What's that?'

'As soon as you see him, shoot him in the head. Don't wait one fucking second. Shoot him in the head and keep shooting until you run out of bullets.'

I wasn't sure what to say to that. After everything that had happened, he was being almost helpful.

'You never did pick up the drugs from Canada,' I said.

He looked up at me. 'Who are you, anyway? How the fuck do you know this stuff?'

'Is that why you were buying those Vicodin from Caroline? You needed a little fix until the big shipment came in?'

'Talk to Brucie. If you ever see him again. He's the one with the pill problem.'

'I meant what I said about staying away from her.'

'I told you, it was Brucie. You think I wanted to hang around with that skank?'

I took the gun out of my right hand and hit him with my fist. He didn't try to cover up. He shook his head and spit out some more blood.

'You'd better grow a set of balls before you get to Gray's house,' he said, 'and learn how to kill somebody. You try this little toughguy act on him and he'll rip your heart out of your chest.'

'If I learned how to kill somebody, I'd be just like you.'

'In your dreams, McKnight. But maybe you can manage it for one day.'

'You're alive on this earth,' I said as I got up. My right hand was throbbing. 'And she's gone. How fucked up is that?'

He stayed on the ground. He didn't say another word.

I got in my truck, backed it out onto the road, and turned it around. To the main road, to the highway, to the bridge to the Lower Peninsula.

To St. Clair Shores and the man they call Mr. Gray.

14

From where I was starting, it was over three hundred miles to Detroit. I crossed the Mackinac Bridge, hit the Lower Peninsula. I stopped for gas in Gaylord. An hour south and it already felt twenty degrees warmer. I got back in the truck and pointed it straight down 1-75, the lifeline of the state but just another lonely road up here, going through little towns like Grayling, West Branch, Pinconning. Around Bay City the traffic started getting heavier. I kept driving. No music, no radio. Hardly a thought in my head, beyond I'm here and I need to get there. Not even thinking yet about what I'd do when I arrived. Everything turned off but the driving muscles.

Except for the pain. I couldn't turn that off. I didn't see how I ever could.

The thing was still there. Not owning me yet. Somehow I was still keeping it just outside. As long as I kept moving . . .

Another hour and I was in Flint. The sun was out. I drove through Auburn Hills. I was getting close to Detroit now. My old hometown, the ring of suburbs on three sides, inching out farther and farther into the farmlands. All these sleepy little crossroads turned into boomtowns now, with all the new houses, the strip malls. I saw the places without recognizing them. Not that I was really looking. I kept my eyes on the road and ate up the miles.

When I was on the edge of the city, I took I-696 due east cutting through some of the older middle class suburbs, Warren, Center Line, Roseville. The highway ended: I got on 11 Mile Road, headed straight for the water, where the original old-money suburbs were strung along Lake St. Clair like pearls. Grosse Pointe, Grosse Pointe Park, Grosse Pointe Farms, Grosse Pointe Shores, where the automotive families had their big houses. As a Detroit cop, long ago, I knew exactly where Detroit ended and the Grosse Pointes began. I knew it to the inch, and so did the people who lived on either side of that line. Needless to say, the Grosse Pointe cops were better paid and better equipped. Their motivations were slightly different than ours. As long as the trouble stayed on our side, they were happy.

On the northern end of the Grosse Pointes was St. Clair Shores, always trying to keep up. Hell, maybe it had caught up by now. I had been away from the place for more years than I cared to count.

I hit Jefferson Street, the main thoroughfare, turned right, and went south into the heart of town. There were nice houses, nice little shops. At every block a cross street ran east to the water. There were so many peninsulas, so many boat channels. In a way, it was sort of like Hessel, but here there was so much more of everything. More houses, more people, more money. The traffic was heavy. I couldn't even remember the last time I had rolled my truck down a busy suburban street. I felt like a madman from the great white north, descended upon the big city.

I kept driving down Jefferson, looking at the street signs. Lakeland, Manor, Madison. All the old money names. Statler, Benjamin, Revere. I was starting to wonder if I'd missed it. I figured a few more blocks and I'd be in Grosse Pointe Shores.

Then I saw it. Trombley Street.

On the water, Cap had said. I took the left, drove down the peninsula. The houses got bigger. Lots of Tudors, the occasional Victorian. Seriously upscale houses. I wasn't surprised Mr. Gray lived here. I wondered if his neighbors knew he was a stone-cold killer.

At the end of the street, there was a big iron gate. An intricate script G was centered on either side. I had just been wondering how I'd find his house, how I'd have to pull up to some woman walking a poodle, roll down my window so she could see my unshaved face, ask her where the Gray house was. Like that would go over well.

But no, here it was. I was sure of it.

The gate was wide open.

I drove through. The driveway led up to a big white Mediterranean house. Columns, statues, the works. There was a yard big enough for a football game, with immaculately cut grass. A huge white tent was set up, like they were going to have a wedding here. Or just had one. Through the poles of the tent I could see down to the shoreline. A double-decker yacht sat next to the dock.

I couldn't see anybody anywhere.

I parked the truck near the tent and got out. This time I knew enough to put the gun in my waistband right away, save me from having to come back for it. They were actually having summer weather down here, so it was too warm for my jacket. But I left it on to cover the butt of the gun.

So now what? Do I just walk around to the back of the house?

Yes, Alex. That's exactly what you do. Walk right around the house like you belong here.

There were tables set up under the tent. Some of them had vases with cut flowers in them. From the looks of the flowers, the event had already happened, maybe a couple of days ago. I grabbed the biggest bouquet I could find, took out a few of the wilted flowers, and carried it toward the house.

I saw a pathway leading around to the back, flat circles of stone set in the grass. As I turned the corner, I saw the gate to the pool, between a statue of a man drawing a bow and arrow and a statue of a woman holding a big urn. The statues were blindingly white, like everything else around the place. It said something about the man who lived there, but I wasn't sure what. At this point, I didn't care.

I opened the gate and walked through. The area around the pool was all white marble. There were more white statues. White pool furniture. A high white fence all around the place. I was wondering when I'd see something that wasn't white when somebody hit me hard in the back of the neck.

I went down on the marble. The vase came out of my hands, shattering when it hit the floor. There were shards of glass everywhere, water, flowers. I was lying in the middle of it. Before I could get up, I felt somebody's foot on my back. I was pushed down hard on the marble. I could feel the glass cutting into my chest. Then something exactly like the barrel of a gun pressed against my back.

'Don't move,' a voice said. I didn't. He gave me a quick one-handed pat-down, taking the gun from my waistband.

'Up,' he said.

I stood up slowly, brushing off the glass, pulling a few shards out of my jacket and pants.

'This way.'

He was a big man, bigger than Brucie. He probably had the biggest hands I'd ever seen on anyone in my life, so big the automatic in his right hand looked like a water pistol. This had to be the man Cap had mentioned, the man who could take me apart without breaking a sweat. He was wearing a white track suit.

I walked ahead of him, as he gestured to the door leading into the house. He stopped me with one huge hand, opened the door, and ushered me inside. After all the white, this room was done up in dark wood. It was like stepping out of the sunlight into a cave.

There was a plasma screen television on one wall. Mr. Gray sat in one of several leather chairs, watching a soccer game. An immense field of green. For some reason that surprised me. From the one time I had seen the man, he didn't seem like someone who would watch television, or do anything a normal human being would do.

'Sit down,' he said to me. He glanced at me for all of one second, then turned his attention back to the game.

I sat down in one of the leather chairs. The man in the white track suit stood behind me. Nobody said anything for a while. Gray kept watching the game. I never cared much about soccer, and I was in no mood to pay attention to it today. The players on one team were passing the ball back and forth, looking for an opportunity to shoot. That much I could tell. This was the last result I could have predicted for myself that day, sitting in Gray's house while he watched soccer.

Somebody finally took a shot. It went a good thirty feet over the goal and into the crowd.

'When it doesn't bend,' Gray said, 'you just look foolish.' He hit the pause button on the television, freezing the goalie in the middle of his goal kick. Then he turned to face me. He was wearing a gray golf shirt. Gray pants.

He studied me for a few seconds. 'You were at the summerhouse. You were the man with the gun.'

I didn't answer him.

'Your name again?'

'Alex McKnight.'

'Apparently, Bruce couldn't close the deal with you,' he said, shaking his head. 'Yet another disappointment. What a team those two make.'

'I have another name for you.'

'Another name?'

'Natalie Reynaud.'

'Who would that be?'

'That's the woman who was killed in my cabin last night.'

'I don't understand what that has to do with me.'

'I have good reason to think you were responsible.'

'Why would you think I had something to do with that?'

'You wanted me dead,' I said. 'If you found out I was still alive . . . '

'You think that would concern me? I didn't want you dead per se, Mr. McKnight. I just wanted you gone. There was nothing personal involved.'

'You're a killer. You're a criminal who gets rid of people without a second thought.'

Gray looked up at the man standing behind me. I was expecting to feel his hands around my neck, or the gun pressed to the back of my head. It didn't happen.

'A man can be many things,' Gray said. 'A soccer fan. A father . . . '

'A gangster. A drug lord.'

He gave me a little smile. Not a warm one. 'Is that what you think I do? You think I sell crack to kids in Detroit?'

'You're not out on the corner yourself, no.'

'I make my living in imports and exports, Mr. McKnight. Imports and exports. I'm a business-man.'

'Uh-huh. What kind of 'import' are your men

up north working on?'

'They're not my men anymore. I can assure you of that. But let me ask you, do you know the difference between an illegal drug and a prescribed medicine?'

I thought about it, what the right answer would be. 'A doctor, for one thing.'

'Yes. A doctor tells you to take the prescribed medicine. He gives you permission to take it.'

'Meaning what?'

'Have you ever seen somebody die a slow, painful death?'

I didn't have to go far for that one. The darkest year of my childhood, watching my mother die. 'Yes,' I said. 'I have.'

'Have you seen someone lose their very sanity because of the pain they're in?'

'Let me guess. That's where you come in. You sell pills to people who need them. I bet you don't even make a profit.'

Gray looked up at the man behind me again. 'What do you make of our Mr. McKnight?'

The man didn't say anything. If he made some kind of gesture, like a shrug of his huge shoulders, I couldn't see it.

'When we last met,' he said, 'how come you didn't tell me I owed you a great debt?'

'I wasn't aware you did.'

'You saved my son's life.'

'I helped get him off the boat. That's all.'

'You're being modest. Harold was knocked out cold. He would have drowned.'

'I did what I could at the time. I wasn't the only one.'

'You're not making this very easy,' he said. He leaned forward in his chair and put his hands together in front of him. 'It's generally not in my nature to be forgiving. Aside from which, it's usually bad for business.'

'Did you send somebody to my cabin or not?'

'If I did?'

'Then I kill you,' I said. 'Or I die trying.'

He tapped his fingertips together. 'First of all, and please understand this . . . If I had indeed sent someone to your cabin, I would have sent him to kill you, not this woman you speak of, who I'm sure I've never even laid eyes on. And second, if I sent someone, you wouldn't be here right now talking to me. You would be in the ground. Are we clear on those two points?'

'We're clear.'

'This woman,' he said. 'She was close to you?'

'Yes.'

He shook his head. 'If Cap did this on his own . . . '

'He didn't.'

'You're sure about that.'

'I don't believe he knew I was alive.'

'You think you'd know if he was lying.'

'I don't think you can fake an immediate reaction like that. He was surprised that I was alive.'

'Okay, so you trust your gut on that one. I'm with you so far. But what did he say after that?'

'I don't remember every word. The bottom line was that if you found out I was still alive, you'd send somebody else. And if that person found Natalie instead of me in my cabin . . . '

213

'You believed that?'

'I had no reason not to.'

'At some point, did he actually suggest that you come down here and kill me?'

'He didn't have to,' I said. Although I was beginning to see the point. Shoot him in the head, he had told me. Don't wait for him to say a word. Just shoot him in the head.

'Look at it from his point of view. What's his biggest problem in the world right now?'

'That would probably be you.'

'I assure you, you can eliminate the word 'probably.''

'He told me which door to come in.'

'There you go. You wanted to believe it was me. So you did. Cap played you like a harp, Mr. McKnight.'

'Or else you're the one playing me right now.'

'I think it's time for you to use your gut again,' he said. 'Now that you're sitting here, who do you believe?'

I looked him in the eye. We both sat there for a long time. The television cast a an eerie green glow over everything in the room.

'If you did it,' I said, 'then you wouldn't be having this conversation with me. You'd just have your man here kill me and be done with it.'

'Actually, Mr. Stone doesn't do that kind of housekeeping for me. But yes, aside from that, you're exactly right. So what should we do now?'

'I don't know.'

'My daughter got married two days ago. We had three hundred people here.'

If I was supposed to congratulate him, I

missed the opportunity. I kept quiet.

'It was a beautiful day. Two days ago. You're telling me that the very next day, yesterday . . . someone took this woman from you.'

'Yes.'

'You loved her.'

'Yes.'

'Enough to do this, to come here. The very day after she died.'

'Yes.'

'I'm sorry, Mr. McKnight. That's all I can say. I know it's not much.'

It was a strange thing to hear from him, this man who would next have to decide if I'd get a bullet in the head.

'In your case, you lost her in a second. Like that.'

He snapped his fingers.

'For me,' he said, 'it was nineteen months of watching my wife die. If I could, I wonder if I'd trade places with you.'

He picked up the remote again. He weighed it in his hand.

'Thank you for helping my son,' he said. 'Please go now and do not come back here again. Mr. Stone will show you out.'

He hit a button and the soccer players came back to life. The ball was advancing to the other side of the field now. I didn't get the chance to see if they scored. Mr. Stone ushered me back to the front door. He followed me outside to my truck. When I was about to get in, he took my gun out of his pocket and gave it to me. He held it dangling between two

215

fingers, like you'd hold a dead rat.

I took it from him. He turned around and went back to the house without saying a word to me. I started the truck, turned around, and went back out the driveway. When I got back to the main intersection, I stopped. My hands were shaking.

Easy, Alex. Easy.

Okay, I can go left here. Or I can go right. Left or right. Which way do I go?

I wasn't lost. I knew exactly how to get back to 1–75, how to go back to the Upper Peninsula and everything that was waiting for me up there. But in that moment, sitting there in my truck in St. Clair Shores, waiting for my hands to stop shaking, I wasn't sure if I wanted to go home.

I didn't see the car pulling up behind me. When he honked his horn, I just about leaped out of my skin. I looked in the rearview mirror — it was a BMW convertible, some guy in sunglasses with both hands raised like I was the most helpless human being he ever had to wait behind. I was about to open the door and go after him, had my hand on the door handle in fact. I thought better of that idea, took the left turn, and headed down toward Detroit. I wasn't sure what I would do there. I just couldn't think of anywhere else to go.

I drove through the Grosse Pointes. It was funny how Jefferson Avenue meant one thing here, then all of a sudden you hit the Detroit city limit and the same street became something else entirely. It took me downtown, past Woodward Avenue, where I had been shot, where Franklin had died. How many years had that been the black hole in my life? I was free of it now. It was ancient history, utterly surpassed by this new thing.

I was so tired now. But I had to keep moving. I could feel the thing right behind me, waiting for me to slow down.

No. Not yet. Keep moving.

I drove by the old precinct house. I could walk in there now and not a soul would know me. The way I looked right now, they'd think I was a crazy person. An EDP, as they still probably call it. Emotionally disturbed person. Sure, you used to work here, they'd say to me. Sure, you were once a cop.

I almost stopped at a bar. From somewhere inside me a little voice told me that would be the worst possible thing to do right now. The exact opposite of 'keep moving.' Besides, they wouldn't have Canadian beer.

I could go to Windsor to get some. It was right across the river, just a few minutes away.

No, not that either. Not Canada.

I drove by Comerica Park, where the Tigers played now. Next to it was Ford Field, the new park for the Lions. For old time's sake, I drove by the old Tiger Stadium. The great gray battleship. What next? My old high school? The house in Redford? From out of nowhere I remembered a day in my life, a million years ago when I was a sixteen-year-old sophomore playing on the varsity baseball team. My first game in the uniform. First at-bat, I walked. Second at-bat I nailed one over the center-field wall. It was a

3–0 count. I even remember that. I didn't take the pitch. I always hated to take a pitch. I swung and I crushed it.

Why do I remember that right now? Why does it come back to me like it just happened? Everything about that day.

It was an away game. In Dearborn. I had to go see that ball field. Before I faced anything else, I had to go see where that day happened.

Dearborn is right next to Detroit. Home of the Ford Motor Company, where my father had put in so many years. I took Michigan Avenue to Telegraph. Took that north, over the Rouge River. Where was that ball field again? I needed to find it. I was afraid to stop and ask somebody. I was afraid they'd have no idea what I was talking about, or if it was an old-timer, that they'd tell me the field had been turned into something else a long, long time ago. No more center-field fence, just a parking lot or a row of houses or whatever the hell else.

When I got to Warren Avenue, I started to wonder if I'd gone too far. There had been a hardware store here when I was a kid. Tela-Warren Hardware, that was its name. All this stuff coming back to me today. Where was it coming from?

I was starting to see double. I almost sideswiped somebody and pulled over while two or three cars honked at me. There was a big salt dump here now, where the hardware store had been. A big building full of salt and sand for the trucks to spread on the road during the winter. It was a lonely place now, a place out of season. I stopped the truck in front of it. I'll be no bother to anybody here, unless I'm still here in a few months when the snow starts falling.

I put my head back. I closed my eyes. After being in motion all day long, it felt strange to be still now. Who'd have thought this is where I'd end up? Next to a big pile of salt in Dearborn, Michigan.

I don't want to sleep now. I just want to rest my eyes.

Just rest my eyes. Yes. That's all . . .

The banging woke me up. I had no idea how long I'd been out, but it was dark outside now. How the hell did that happen? And who the hell —

Somebody was banging on my side window. A beam of light came stabbing into the truck, blinding me. A flashlight. I rolled down the window.

'Excuse me, Mr. McKnight?'

'What? How do you know my name?'

'I called in your plate, sir. They told me the Michigan State Police are looking for you.'

That didn't sound good. Next he'll say they need to speak to me, that I need to come with him, the whole routine. Not that I cared anymore.

'They're very worried about you,' he said. 'I understand you lost your, um . . . '

I finally looked up at his face. It was a local Dearborn cop. He looked like he was about fourteen years old.

'That you lost your companion, sir. I'm sorry to hear of your loss.'

Companion. An odd word. An odd thing to say to me. And yet it sounded about right. That's what Natalie was. After a life of being lonely, she was my companion.

'Thank you,' I said. 'I appreciate it.'

'If you'd like, I can find a place for you to stay tonight.'

'No, thanks. I should head home. What time is it?'

'It's about nine thirty. Would you like me to call the state guys? Get you a ride back up there?'

'No. I'll be all right.'

'Okay, then. Please drive carefully.'

'I will,' I said. 'I will. Thank you.'

When he was gone, I pulled out onto Telegraph, heading north. The sleep had given me a little energy boost. I felt like I could make it all the way if I really wanted to.

I stopped for gas again. A million insects buzzed in the bright lights above my head as I filled up the tank. I got a big mug of coffee and hit the road.

I spent the next four hours driving. Straight up 1–75. I had the vent open so the fresh air would hit me in the face. The air getting colder and colder as I drove.

By the time I hit the Mackinac Bridge, it felt like November again. Just a few hours on the road and I was back in the land with no summer. It was a stolen season.

My right headlight started to flicker. Finally, it went out. It must have been damaged when I ran Cap off the road. Hard to believe it was just this morning. Hard to believe, as it hit midnight, that the world had made one complete revolution since the thing happened.

The thing.

Another hour on the road until I hit Paradise. The last town on the edge of the earth, it felt like. Lights on in the Glasgow Inn. I kept going, turned onto my road. Drove up past Vinnie's place. His truck there, the lights out. Past my cabin. Where the thing happened.

The thing. The thing.

I went to the second cabin, my new base of operations. My new home, if I had to have one. I went inside, turned the lights on. I put some wood in the stove. Then I finally took off my jacket, heard the rattle in my pocket. I put my hand in, pulled out the bottle of pills.

It took me a moment to remember how I'd gotten them. It was the day I went to the house in Hessel, back when I was stupid enough to think I could point a gun at those guys and scare them away. There had been two empty pill bottles on the kitchen counter, and this one, half full. The prescription was for a woman named Roseanne Felise. I was figuring Vinnie could take these, show them to Ms. Felise, and ask her why she sold them. That's what I was thinking when I took them. But now . . .

I sat down at the table with the bottle in my hand. I opened it. I turned it over and watched the pills scatter out onto the table. I counted them. Twenty-three pills. Twenty-three perfect little Vicodins.

I thought back to what Mr. Gray had told me.

About painkillers, about how some people need them and can't get them. How much he was really motivated by that, I couldn't say, but I did know one thing. When you really need them, these pills do the job. I knew that all too well.

A couple of these and I could close my eyes tonight. I could keep the thing away from me, not have to deal with it until the next day.

Unless I took a couple more of these tomorrow morning.

Or hell, if I took them all right now . . . I'd never have to deal with the thing at all.

I sat there for a long time, looking at the pills, making up my mind.

That's when Vinnie came in the door. He didn't knock. He came in and saw me sitting there looking at the pills on the table.

'What are those?' he said. One eye still swollen now, the other almost normal.

'Vinnie . . . '

'Alex, what are those pills?'

'Vinnie, she's dead.'

He came over and tried to sweep the pills off the table. I grabbed his arm.

'Let me have them,' he said. He tried to hold me with one hand, going for the pills with the other. We were in a wrestling match now. I pulled at his shirt, got hold of his ponytail and tried to throw him to the ground. He put his shoulder into me and the whole table got turned over, the pills rolling off along the floor in every direction.

The thing was breaking through now. I couldn't hold it off any longer.

'She's dead, Vinnie. She's dead. Do you hear me?'

'Yes,' he said, still holding on to me. 'Yes.'

I had him by the collar now. I could have wrapped my hands around his neck and strangled him.

'Natalie is dead,' I said, my face just a few inches from his. 'Somebody killed her.'

'I know, Alex. I know.'

I grabbed Vinnie's shoulders. He put his hand behind my neck.

'Somebody killed her,' I said. The thing was all over me now, pouring through the broken ramparts. The rout was on.

'She's dead, Vinnie. She's dead.'

15

I slept. From complete and total physical exhaustion I fell into a deep sleep, with no dreams. Thank God for a night with no dreams, but the cold fact of what had happened was waiting for me when I woke up. I had to face it. I opened my eyes and saw that I was in a strange bed. The second cabin. Yes. Vinnie there on the couch, still asleep.

Through the window I could see the gray sky and the long needles of a white pine. I could hear Vinnie breathing, a light wind outside, a bird calling to another. I could hear the last piece of wood burning down in the stove.

Then a loud knock on the door. It startled me, and woke up Vinnie. He looked around, disoriented for a moment, then saw me. The bag of ice he had pressed to his face the night before was now a bag of water. There was another knock on the door.

I got out of bed, still in my clothes from the day before. I opened the door. I was expecting Jackie. Maybe Leon. Maybe the state police detective catching up with me again. Instead I saw the last person I ever would have expected at my door.

It was Chief Roy Maven.

'Chief,' I said. 'What the hell.'

'Can I come in?'

I stood aside and let him in. He took off his hat.

'What are you doing here?' I said.

'Did the state police reach you yesterday?'

'No, I was gone most of the day. I got back late.'

'You know they were looking for you?'

'I'm sure they'll find me sometime today. Why do you ask?'

'You didn't hear the news, then. The Mounties found Natalie's partner yesterday. He'd been dead for at least twenty-four hours.'

'What? Her partner's dead, too? Don something.'

'Don Resnik. They believe he was killed a few hours before Natalie.'

I stood there holding on to the door.

'Umm,' Maven started to say. 'I guess I don't know what to say. I'm sorry about what happened.'

'Thank you. But how was Resnik killed? Was he shot?'

'Yes. Twice.'

'Do they think it was the same gun?'

'They don't know that yet for sure. Maybe later today they will.'

'I don't understand,' I said. Everything was starting to look different now. 'I thought this was about me. I thought it was someone here in Michigan . . . Not from Canada.'

'They don't know anything for sure yet.'

'Why did you come all the way out here? The state guys could have told me about Resnik.'

'I'm doing this as a personal favor to Staff

Sergeant Moreland.'

'Moreland? Isn't that Natalie's commanding officer?'

'Yes. That's him.'

'I don't get it. Why would he want you to tell me about Natalie's partner?'

'That's not why I came here.'

'Then why?'

'I came here to take you to Canada. Please go get cleaned up.'

'*You're* taking me to Canada?'

'Yes,' Maven said. 'That's what Moreland asked me to do. So come on, go take a shower, shave, put yourself together. It's a long way to Sudbury.'

'Why are we going to Sudbury?'

'Because, McKnight — ' He was about to lay into me, like I'd seen him do at least a dozen times in the past. Force of habit, I guess. But he stopped himself just in time. 'Alex . . . we're going to Sudbury because they're going to have a service for Natalie there. Okay? Moreland asked me to bring you there.'

A service for Natalie. I had to let that one sink in for a while.

'Why Sudbury?' I finally said.

'There'll be officers there from her old Hearst detachment. Some of the officers from Toronto. Some of the Mounties. Sudbury's sort of right in the middle.'

'Can Vinnie come, too?'

'No, I don't think so,' he said. He gave Vinnie a look, then did a double take when he saw the state of Vinnie's face. 'Did you get in another fight or something?'

'Who, me?' Vinnie said. 'Why do you say that?'

'I probably don't want to know. Anyway, I'm sorry, I think he just wants you there for the service . . . Then he wants to speak to you for a while afterward.'

'It's okay,' Vinnie said. 'You go for both of us.'

'My suit,' I said. 'It's in my cabin.' It was the last place I wanted to be, even for a second.

'I'll get it,' Vinnie said. 'You go get cleaned up. You haven't shaved in two days.'

Thirty minutes later, I was wearing my only suit, my neck scraped raw by a dull razor. I was sitting in the passenger's seat of Chief Roy Maven's unmarked squad car. He was barreling down M-28 at a speed that would have made even me look like the minister's mother on her way to the euchre club. He hadn't said another word to me since we left Paradise.

'What, is it about two hundred miles to Sudbury?' I said.

'Not quite that.'

'When did Moreland call you?'

'Yesterday.'

I knew that Maven and Moreland had talked to each other in the past. They had already bonded over the one thing they had in common — a certain man from Paradise who kept showing up in the general vicinity of trouble. I wasn't sure that Moreland had ever stopped blaming me for at least some of it. With Maven, I didn't have to wonder.

'What else did he say?' I asked.

'He didn't say much else to me. I think he's

saving that for you.'

Maven came up behind a camper, pulled into the left lane, and left it in the dust. He hit I-75, took that north to the International Bridge. When we got to Canadian customs, things got a little interesting. The woman in the booth wasn't accustomed to police officers from the States telling her why she could save her questions. Eventually, Maven had to step out of the car, go into the little shack to speak to someone else in charge. When he got back behind the wheel, he was ready to tear someone's head off.

'Moreland left specific goddamned instructions to let us through without delay,' he said as he gunned it back to full speed. 'How the hell that could be so hard to understand is beyond me.'

He looked at his watch as he hit the traffic in Soo, Ontario. He swore at a few drivers before he finally turned his flashers on. It's funny how an unmarked car suddenly makes you pay attention when the headlights and all the hidden auxiliary lights start dancing back and forth.

'Technically not kosher for me to do this in Canada,' he said, 'but I'd like to see them try to stop me.'

I would have felt sorry for anyone who did. Soon we were out of the city and on the King's Highway, heading due east. We passed through the Garden River First Nation. I had come to a healing ceremony here with Vinnie, once upon a time. We drove through Bruce Mines and Thessalon, and as we got closer to Blind River I could feel the lump in my throat. This was the way to Natalie's house, the way I had driven so many times, back and forth. When the relationship was young and we were both feeling our way through it. God damn, all the hours on this very road, looking forward to seeing her again. Coming home happy. Or coming home wondering if this thing would ever work out.

We passed the turnoff for McKnight Road. It had always felt like a lucky charm to me, seeing that sign. If Maven noticed the name, he didn't say anything.

Through Iron Bridge, over the Mississagi River. This was getting harder for me. I wanted to close my eyes and not see these places again.

Finally, we drove through Blind River. The house was a mile east of town.

'You all right?' he said. It must have been pretty obvious.

'This was her town.'

'I'm sorry. There's no other way to get there.'

'I know. It's all right.'

I couldn't help watching for her driveway, looking through the trees, just to see the house one more time. When we were past it, I looked out the window in the opposite direction. I watched the North Channel rolling by us, the green water under the dull gray sky.

Algoma Mills, Serpent River, Cutler, Sheddon Township, Walford, Victoria. A string of small Canadian towns, with miles and miles of empty road between them. The trees got heavier as we left the water and headed toward Sudbury. We'd been on the road almost four hours now, with Maven driving like a speed demon. Finally, we could see the Superstack rising high above the horizon, which could only mean that Sudbury was just ahead.

We started to see the nickel mines, the desolate piles of white ore that made the place look like something on the face of the moon. As we got closer, the Superstack loomed over a thousand feet above us, this giant chimney that fed the sulfur gases to the winds. There was supposedly a lot of environmental reclamation going on around here, a lot of great places to live now, especially around Lake Ramsey, but I was in no mood to forgive the place today. It just seemed like the strangest place in the world to say goodbye to Natalie.

'You realize she's not going to be here,' Maven said, as if he were reading my mind. 'I mean to say . . . with the investigation still underway . . . '

'Her body, you mean.'

'Yes.'

'Then why are they doing this today?'

'Well, they're not exactly sure when they'll be able to put her to rest. With an open case like this, not to mention having two different countries involved . . . it could take weeks. So they decided to go ahead and have the service.'

'I understand.'

'They're going to take her back to Hearst, eventually. They'll bury her there.'

'Okay.'

'Like I said, though . . . Sudbury's the one place everybody can get to today.'

'Why are you doing this?' I said.

'I told you. Moreland asked me.'

230

'No matter what he said, you could have said no. I could have come up here by myself.'

'He seemed to think that would be a bad idea. He wanted me with you.'

It still wasn't adding up for me, but I let it go. I kept my mouth shut while Maven drove through town, looking for wherever we were supposed to be. He was about ready to blow a gasket for the second time that day when we finally found it. It was a funeral chapel on the east side of town, just past the rail yards.

A funeral chapel. Where they had funerals, although this one would be with no coffin. Yet one more thing to hit me between the eyes, just when I felt like I might be on top of things. From one second to the next, I wasn't sure I could do this. I wasn't sure that I could even get out of the car and walk into this place.

There were dozens of police vehicles parked outside, from both the Ontario Provincial Police and the Royal Canadian Mounted. Maven parked the car. We got out.

'Are you ready?' Maven said to me.

'No.'

'Would you like to stay out here for a moment, get some air?'

'Yes, one minute.'

I turned away. I walked to the far side of the lot, stood there looking out past a row of houses at the trains in the yard. Nothing was moving.

Okay, I told myself. Go do this. Do it for Natalie.

I went back to Maven, gave him a nod.

231

Nothing else. He went to the front door and opened it for me.

When we stepped inside, I saw fifty, maybe sixty uniforms. Mostly men, a few women. They were all in full dress, the OPP in their blues, the Mounties in their reds. Shoes shined bright, white gloves. Some of them were wearing their Stetsons, others held them in their hands. I couldn't see one other person who wasn't wearing a uniform. Me in my black suit that should have taken a trip to the dry cleaner's before I put it on . . . I wouldn't have felt more out of place if I had been wearing a pink tutu.

Somewhere you're sharing in the joke, Natalie. Somewhere you're laughing. That's the thought I held on to, the only thing that got me through that first five minutes.

I saw Staff Sergeant Moreland across the room. He was a tall man with a full head of white hair. He could pass for a kindly old grandfather until he decided he was unhappy with you. I knew that all too well.

He gave me a long look, then a nod. He saved the grim smile for Maven.

We had to stand around like that for a few more minutes. I could feel the mood of the room changing, as everybody became aware of my presence. Things got quieter. Finally, people started to sit down in the pews. Maven and I sat alone in the last row.

That's when I saw her picture. It was sitting on a table, with a blue flag folded up next to it. Next to that was her hat, and next to that was a black velvet pillow with what looked like medals resting on top of it.

There were roses, lilies, a big bouquet of what looked like wildflowers. Either somebody knew that she loved wildflowers, or it was just a lucky guess.

A clergyman stepped up to the podium. Finally, another man in a dark suit. He said some words about Natalie Reynaud. About duty and honor and serving her country. It was obvious he had never met her. The words could have been about anyone.

Then Sergeant Moreland went up to the podium, walking as slowly as any man could. He started out talking about Natalie growing up in Blind River, how she came to his detachment when she was only twenty-three years old. He had to stop then. He closed his eyes and breathed out hard. He swayed so far that three of the men in the front row got to their feet, as if they'd need to catch him. Moreland fought through it, told everyone what a great officer Natalie was, what a great person. How she was like the daughter he never had. That seemed to shut him down again. I was sitting there in the last row, feeling the burning in my stomach.

'We have a man here named Alex McKnight,' he said, regaining some of his composure. 'He's the man in the suit. In the back row. He was closer to Natalie than anybody else, so I hope you'll take a moment to give him your best wishes. Thank you.'

The clergyman got back up and asked if anyone else would like to say anything. None of the other officers stood up. They probably didn't want to follow Moreland. Or maybe, in the end, none of them had really gotten to know her well enough. The only partner she had for more than a few months was a Senior Constable named Claude DeMers. And he was dead.

I asked myself if I wanted to stand up, if there was anything I could tell these people. I decided that I couldn't. Whether that made me a weak person, or a wise person, I'll never know for sure.

When the service was over, everyone stood up and filed slowly past the table. Maven and I waited until the room was almost empty, then we stood up for our turn. I took a long look at the picture. Natalie in her blue uniform, hair pinned up, wearing her Stetson. Her expression all business. I couldn't help but smile at it. The one smile I would manage all day.

I touched her hat. 'Goodbye,' I said. 'I love you.'

When I turned around, I saw a few of her fellow officers watching me. I couldn't help but wonder how much they knew about me. I couldn't imagine Natalie talking about me too much. Their only other source of information would have been Sergeant Moreland, and beyond whatever he may have told them about me, they all had to know she was in my cabin when she was killed.

Three of the men approached us, all of them dressed in OPP blue.

'Mr. McKnight,' one of them said. I saw something in his eyes before he reached for my hand, got myself ready just in time. His grip was hard enough to break bones. I didn't flinch.

The second man shook my hand, just as hard as the first.

The third man didn't extend his hand at all.

'Sergeant Moreland tells me you were a cop once,' he said.

'Yes.'

'Nice of you to show up for her today, Mr. McKnight. Of course, she could have used you a few nights ago.'

'Excuse me?'

He grabbed me by the lapels. I didn't try to stop him.

'Let go of him,' Maven said.

'This doesn't concern you, old man. And that badge doesn't mean shit here.'

'Let go of him now or I'll put my boot up your ass, so help me God. Right here in the chapel.'

The other two officers were trying to pull him off me now. I couldn't think of one thing to say to the man. There was a part of me that couldn't help but agree with him.

The spell was broken by the sound of the bagpipes. The three men left us there. I straightened my suit and then Maven and I went outside. Everyone was standing around in the parking lot, talking in small groups. After a few minutes, it was obvious that nobody really knew what to do. There was no coffin to put in a hearse. No procession of cars to the cemetery.

Sergeant Moreland finally came up to me. His eyes were still red. He shook my hand, then Maven's. He thanked Maven for bringing me out.

235

I thanked him for thinking of me, for making it possible for me to be here.

'I'm sure Chief Maven told you,' he said to me, 'that I'd like to have a few words before you go back.'

'Of course.'

'The local detachment is just down the road,' he said. My first clue that this might be more than just a polite chat. 'I've already arranged an interview room for us.'

'An interview room?'

'Yes, Alex.' He looked me in the eye. 'There are a few things I need to know.'

16

The Sudbury detachment was a single-story brick building in the middle of town. It had about as much charm as Maven's building back home. Moreland was waiting at the front door for us. He led us both to an interview room. It happened to look exactly like an interview room in the States, or probably any interview room in any police station anywhere in the world. A single table, a few chairs. A mirror on one wall.

'Would you like Chief Maven to stay?' Moreland asked me. 'Or would you prefer to do this one-on-one?'

'I'm not exactly sure what it is we're doing,' I said. 'But the chief brought me all the way out here. I don't see why he can't stay in the room.'

'Very well.' He sat down at the table and asked me to sit across from him. Maven took a third chair and sat at the end, as if he were the referee in a chess match.

'As I indicated before, I'd like to ask you some questions,' Moreland said to me. He took out a legal pad and a pen. 'Some for our investigation. Some for myself.'

'Go ahead.'

'First of all, tell me everything that happened, from the moment Natalie came out to your place.'

I thought back for a few moments, then I gave him the full rundown. Natalie showing up at night. The two of us spending the next day together, going to the Glasgow, going into town, even the quick side trip to see if Leon was home. Everything I could think of. Then going back to my cabin . . .

'You left her there alone,' he said. 'For the first time all day?'

'Yes. Things were getting a little tense between us. We both needed a few minutes to cool off. Plus I had to go take care of some people in one of the other cabins.'

'Why were things getting tense?'

'Because I didn't want her to go back to Toronto. I could tell she was scared.'

'Did she say that to you?'

'Yes. She described the meeting with Laraque and the woman.'

'Rhapsody.'

'Rhapsody, yes. She had been spending a lot of time with her. I already knew that part. But this was the first time she had met Laraque in person. From the way she described him . . . '

'Yes?'

'She told me that she had a gut feeling Laraque had seen through the whole trap. That he was just playing with her. With everyone.'

Moreland was busy taking notes. Perhaps this was helping him. Doing this police business, writing things down like I'm sure he'd done a thousand times before.

'She also told me,' I went on, 'that you didn't like the idea of her going undercover in the first place.'

He looked up at me. 'She told you that?'

238

'Yes, she did. I guess you could say that you and I were both in complete agreement on that point.'

He looked down at his pad. He wasn't writing anything now. He was just staring at the words.

'So you left her at your cabin,' he finally said. 'How long were you gone?'

'Fifteen minutes. Maybe twenty.'

'You live in a pretty isolated place, don't you?'

'Yes.'

'When you came back, you saw a vehicle?'

'I saw taillights. That's all.'

'You can't tell us anything else about the vehicle?'

'No, I'm sorry. It was a little foggy.'

'It was foggy.'

'Yes.'

'So you were gone for fifteen or twenty minutes. And when you came back . . . '

He looked down at the paper again.

'I didn't hear anything,' I said. 'I know that's the next question. The cabin was close enough for me to hear a gunshot.'

'So whoever this was, he used a suppressor.'

'It would seem.'

'You heard about Don Resnik. We estimate he was killed about six hours before Natalie, although he wasn't found until the next day. Someone shot him in his apartment. His body was right by the door. So they figure he answered the door and got it right then. Whether he looked through his peephole or not . . . Well, in any case, he still had his wallet. Nothing else looked out of place. So it wasn't a random robbery.'

'Was it the same gun that killed him?'

'No, it wasn't. The ammunition was similar, but it was definitely two different guns.'

'But it still could have been the same person,' I said. 'He could have made it from Toronto to Paradise in six hours.'

'Yes, although he probably would have had to take a plane. Which would explain a change of guns. We're checking on that angle right now. Everyone who flew into Chippewa Airport. Or Pelston. Or Soo, Canada. Any airport that would have gotten him to your place in time.'

'So what about Laraque? Does anyone know where he was all day?'

'The folks in Toronto tell me he was seen several times that day. They were definitely keeping an eye on him.'

'It could have been somebody working for him.'

'It could have been, yes. But how did this person know to find Natalie in your cabin? That's the question I keep coming back to.'

'I don't know the answer. I really don't.'

'Why would Laraque have two police officers killed, anyway? If you look at it objectively, it's probably the dumbest thing he could ever do.'

'Why?' I said. 'Because it would turn up the heat on him? If he knew he was getting set up, how much more heat could he feel? Maybe this was a message to you and to those guys in Toronto, and to every other law enforcement officer in the country.'

'You're assuming he considers himself untouchable then.'

'If he does,' I said, 'I'd like the chance to prove him wrong.'

'Meaning what? If you knew for sure that it was him — '

'What would I want to do to him? Once again, Sergeant, I think we'd be in total agreement.'

'What I'd want to do is build a good case against him and put him away forever.'

'You're speaking like a police officer now,' I said. 'But as a man . . . as a friend who loved her . . . I think you'd have a different idea.'

'I understand what you're saying. That's why we follow the law instead of our own personal motives.'

'I was a cop for eight years, Sergeant Moreland. I know all about what the law can do. And what it can't do. There's knowing something without any doubt, and there's being able to prove it in a courtroom. It's not always the same thing.'

He put the pen down and sat back in his chair. 'You see, this is where we run into a real problem, Mr. McKnight.' He looked over at Maven, who had been sitting there as still as a wax replica the whole time. 'What do you think, Chief?'

'I can understand what McKnight is saying,' Maven said. 'I'd have the same thoughts myself. But ultimately . . . '

'The phone,' I said.

They both looked at me.

'When they found Resnik, you said he still had his wallet, right?'

'Yes.'

'Did he have his cell phone?'

'I honestly don't know. Why do you ask?'

'Natalie called him that day. First she called the Mounties' office to check in. Then she called Resnik to see how he was doing.'

'But if she used *her* cell phone . . . '

'She didn't. She used my phone. A regular landline.'

'Why would she do that?'

'Because she wasn't getting a signal. Cell phones never work very well in Paradise.'

'So if she called Resnik on your phone . . . ,' Moreland said. 'It wouldn't be too hard to trace it back to you. The number's right there on the phone, in the caller history. You have a listed number?'

'Yes.'

'They look it up in a reverse directory. Hell, they could have gone to the Internet, looked you up in three seconds. They've got your name, your address . . . '

'Six hours later . . . ,' I said. Suddenly, I was feeling sick to my stomach.

Moreland picked up his pen again and started writing.

'I can't do any more of this right now,' he finally said. He sounded tired. He sounded like he'd be gone from this job in a matter of days. 'I do have something to give you, though.'

He stood up and left the room. When he came back, he had a folded-up blue flag in his arms. There was a small wooden box on top of the flag, and on top of the box was a hat. I recognized it immediately.

'Her medals are in this box,' Moreland said, 'along with her badge and her warrant card. Ordinarily, all of these items go to the nearest member of her immediate family. As you know, Natalie's family is all pretty much gone. So I figured, in her mind anyway, you'd be as close to family as anyone else.'

He put everything down on the table.

'I'll be honest, Mr. McKnight. I often thought that you were the worst thing that ever happened to her. Whenever there was trouble in her life, you seemed to be right there in the middle of it. But maybe I was wrong about that. I don't know. Maybe you were her last chance at being happy.'

He put his hand on the hat for a moment, lightly.

'I know I've asked you before not to come back to Canada,' he said. 'That was just me talking, you understand. Just looking out for Natalie. Well, now I have the chance to make it official. The people in Toronto have asked me to formally exclude you from entry into this country, for the foreseeable future.'

'What are you talking about?'

'It means you go home today, and you stay there. Your name is on a list now. If you try to cross the border, *anywhere* along the border, you'll be detained. Is that understood?'

'No. It is not understood. Why are you doing this?'

'I told you, this comes from Toronto,' he said. 'Although I don't necessarily disagree with it. We're going to work with the Michigan State Police and the FBI to solve two murders. One in each country. Your particular talent for getting in the way of things is not going to be helpful.'

'Sergeant Moreland — '

'Good day, Mr. McKnight. Chief Maven. I'm glad you could be here. Have a safe trip home.'

Those were his last words to us. He left the room. He was walking even more slowly now, like he didn't have much left, like the day had taken just about everything from him.

There was nothing else for us to do except leave. We went out to Maven's car and started the long journey home.

'That's why you're here,' I said. We weren't even out of Sudbury yet. 'To make sure I go right back to Michigan.'

'If you think that's the only reason,' he said, 'then I don't know what to say to you.'

Three hours later, we hadn't said another word to each other. I sat with the flag and box in my lap, Natalie's hat in my hands. I kept turning the hat around and around while I thought about everything Sergeant Moreland had said. Especially about Antoine Laraque.

Three hours to think about that while the trees rushed by, and then the flat, wide open fields as we got closer to the lake. Then the lake itself. We drove through Blind River again. As we got close to the bridge, I finally cleared my throat and said something.

'About what I said back there . . . '

'Forget it,' Maven said.

'Seriously, I appreciate what you did today. I guess I'm not used to you giving me any kind of break.'

'I said forget it.'

'Okay.'

We crossed the bridge. Maven drove to Paradise. The sun was going down now. Eight hours in the car, a couple of hours in Sudbury. It had been a hell of a day.

'I'll buy you a drink,' I said as we got close to the Glasgow.

'I'm gonna get home to dinner.'

'Okay, good enough.'

'Moreland was right, by the way.'

'About what?'

'About everything,' he said. 'First of all, when he said you were Natalie's last chance to be happy. I saw the two of you together in that restaurant. She was a happy woman. I hope you'll remember that.'

I wasn't sure what to make of that one. How much more could Maven do for me in one day?

'He was also right about you staying the hell away from there,' Maven went on, suddenly sounding a lot more like the man I knew. 'So help me God, if I find out you're sticking your nose in this thing . . . '

'Somebody took her life away from her,' I said, 'and that person is walking around on this earth *right now*.'

'I'll make sure they tell me what's going on,' he said. We had come to the second cabin now. He pulled over and put the car in park. 'Every step of the way, until they nail this guy. I'll call you every goddamned day if you want. Just don't go and mess this up, McKnight. Do you hear me? Will you listen to me for once in your life? If you do something stupid, then your life will be over, too. Do you think Natalie would have wanted that?'

I didn't have an answer for that one. I couldn't tell him the truth, that I didn't care what happened to me. That I truly, honestly did not care. I could only care about one thing.

'Thank you again, Chief.' I got out of the car.

'McKnight, God damn it.'

'Thank you. I mean it.' I shut the door and walked away. I didn't hear him leave until I was inside.

★ ★ ★

I hadn't eaten anything all day, and there sure as hell wasn't any food here in the second cabin. I didn't feel much like being sociable, even with Jackie, but I didn't have much choice. I went down to the Glasgow, told Jackie about the service, had some of his beef stew. I had a cold Canadian, held the bottle in my hand for a long time, thinking about what Natalie had said. You think Canadian beer is better than American beer . . . For once you get something right.

I couldn't stay long. I said good night to Jackie, went back up to the cabin. It was dark now. As I pulled in, I saw Vinnie's truck parked there. He must have spent at least part of the day fixing his battery cables. Now he was inside waiting for me.

I went through the whole day again. With Vinnie, I went a little deeper into what Moreland had told me. Everything about Laraque, and how the killer probably tracked down Natalie to my cabin. Vinnie listened carefully to everything I said. When I was done, he told me he was taking me somewhere.

'I really don't feel like going anywhere else today,' I said.

'Everything's ready,' he said. 'You have to come.'

'What are you talking about?'

'Let's go, Alex. It's time.'

Anyone else I might have kept arguing. I figured I owed Vinnie the benefit of the doubt. So I let him drive me over to the reservation, past the casino, to his cousin Buck's house. He parked his truck and took me out behind the house. I had been here once before, and now it looked like I was back for the same reason.

Buck had built a sweat lodge in his back yard, a half circle about ten feet in diameter. He had lashed some saplings together and then covered them with canvas and every old rug he could get his hands on. From the outside, it looked like something in the middle of a garbage dump. But on the inside, it was something pretty amazing.

Buck was there with three other men from the Bay Mills tribe. They all nodded to me solemnly, without a word spoken. Wide faces with dark, careful eyes. Long hair down every back. They had a fire going, and they were heating rocks in the middle of it. As soon as he saw me, one man started to lift the rocks with a long shovel and take them into the sweat lodge.

The other men started to undress. I knew the drill, so I did the same. Soon we were all

247

standing there in our underwear. It was cold enough to start me shivering in three seconds, even though the calendar still claimed it was July.

The men went into the sweat lodge. I followed them. The steam was already overpowering. Buck dipped a great iron ladle into a bucket of water and poured it on the hot rocks. Then he put a few sprigs of sage on the rocks. One of the four medicines. The last time I had been here, the medicine had been for Vinnie. His brother had been murdered. Today the medicine was for me.

I sat there in the dark, and as I did I felt my muscles begin to relax. All the tension in my body, since that one horrible moment, me sitting on the floor, holding on to Natalie. It was slowly leaving me. Buck put more water on the rocks. I was sweating. The steam filled my lungs. It was inside me and all around me and now it felt like I was floating in it.

It was dark. There was a faint glow from the rocks and nothing else. Vinnie had told me once that he saw things in the steam, that that was part of the experience, part of why the Ojibwa treasured this. I had believed him only as far as you can believe something you'll never see with your own eyes. But on this night, as the steam grew so thick it seemed to be something you could hold in your hand, I looked into it and I saw Natalie. God help me, I saw her standing there right in front of me. She was in her uniform. Her hair was pinned up. She wasn't wearing her hat. She smiled at me and reached out her hand like she would touch my chest.

Then she was gone.

If I was imagining it ... If my mind was using the blank slate of the steam to create this picture ... I don't know. I don't really care. I saw her and she was as real to me as anything else. When I came back out of the sweat lodge into the sudden shock of the cold air, I felt like I had been plugged into something powerful and been recharged. My heart didn't hurt any less, but at least I had some life in me now. I felt like I was ready to face anything. Or anybody.

'You look good,' Vinnie said to me. 'You look much better.'

'Thank you. How did you know I needed that?'

'You're my blood brother, remember?'

'I might need your help,' I said. 'I have some things to do now.'

He looked at me. In the dim light from the house I could see the bruises on his face, the raccoon-like shiners around his eyes. 'I won't help you destroy yourself. This thing will devour you if you let it. You know that.'

'Vinnie, do you remember when we went up to find your brother? Everything that happened by that lake?'

'Yes, of course.'

I grabbed his right hand. 'You took these two fingers right here,' I said. 'You took these two fingers and you dipped them in your own blood, and you painted two stripes on each side of my face. Do you remember that?'

'Yes, Alex.'

'You painted my face and you said it was time to go to war.'

'Yes. I did that.'

'Natalie was my family,' I said, letting go of his hand. 'You know what she meant to me.'

'Yes.'

'So it's my blood now,' I said. 'And it's my war.'

17

I woke up in a strange bed again, everything coming back to me at once like it probably would every morning for the rest of my life. I couldn't imagine how it could ever feel normal. I didn't *want* it to feel normal, because that would mean I had accepted things the way they were, had even gotten over it as well as I was going to and had moved on with the rest of my life.

The thought was an obscenity to me. I promised myself that morning that I'd never let it slip away from me. As much as it hurt, I never wanted to stop feeling like her death had just happened.

Vinnie was in the kitchen, making coffee. He had insisted on staying with me again. He said he'd keep doing it until he felt I was ready to be alone. He said it wasn't up to me to decide that. I didn't fight him too hard. Truth was, it was good to have him around.

I got out of bed and sat at the table. Vinnie brought over a cup of coffee and put it down in front of me. He didn't try to say good morning, or ask me how I slept or, God forbid, ask me how I was doing. He put his own cup down and sat across from me. His face was about halfway back to normal now, both eyes open, the swelling down, the darker bruises beginning to fade. But he still looked like a man who should give up fighting two men by himself.

251

'Let's just say,' I began, 'that I needed a boat . . .'

He took a sip of his coffee, didn't say anything.

'A good boat, say. Fast, with a long range.'

Another sip.

'A depth finder. And GPS, of course.'

He didn't look at me.

'I'm just thinking out loud here,' I said. 'If I were to ask you, do you think you could find one?'

'That would depend.'

'On what?'

'On whether you'd be using it to get yourself killed.'

'That can't happen.'

'Why do you say that?'

'Because I'm already dead.'

He put his cup down. 'You've been to an Ojibwa funeral,' he said.

'Yeah?'

'How long did it last?'

'What are you talking about?'

'When we buried my brother, how long did the funeral last?'

'I don't remember exactly. A few days.'

'Four days. And that was short. I've seen them go seven or eight.'

'What does that have to do with me?'

'This happened, what, three days ago? You've barely begun to deal with it.'

'Vinnie . . .'

'I'll do anything you ask,' he said. 'You know that. But you have to give yourself some time first. You don't even know for sure that this man was responsible.'

'Two cops were setting up a sting on this guy. They both end up dead, on the same day.'

'If it's that obvious to you, then it'll be that obvious to everyone else. This guy will go down for it eventually.'

'I don't think I ever told you this story,' I said. 'In fact, I'm sure I didn't. I haven't thought about it in years. There was this cop in Detroit named Jim Romano. He was a detective. An old-timer. He was just about ready to retire when I was a rookie. I think I only met the man one time. Anyway, he got it in his head that he was going to take down this big shot, Paulie Masalsky, who was the biggest bookmaker on the whole west side. He owned a bar on Michigan Avenue. He used to have runners going all over the place, bringing slips to a room he had upstairs. He had a buzzer behind the bar in case a cop ever came in. Just press the button and they'd burn the slips real quick. If they were on flash paper, it would only take one second and they'd be gone. Or else they'd flush them, whatever. Standard operating procedure for a bookie.'

Vinnie picked up his cup again. He started into it while I kept telling the story.

'There was a rumor that Romano's brother had gotten into some trouble with Masalsky,' I said. 'You know, he ran up a big debt, and Romano was gonna see if he could get Masalsky to back off. Either that, or he really just wanted to run the guy out of business. Either way, he got it in his head that he was going to spend his last year on the force making Masalsky's life miserable. He'd go in the bar all the time, and of course whoever was behind the bar, they'd have to hit that button and the guys upstairs would scramble around, burning up the slips or flushing them. Romano would come to the bar and have one drink, ask where Paulie was, tell the guy to give him his best regards, something like that. Three, four times a week. If he thought the bartender was getting lax on the buzzer, he'd actually tell him he was going to go up the stairs to see if Paulie was up there. Whatever it took to make sure those guys were dumping the slips. This goes on about three months. Everybody on the force knows about it. It's almost a running joke. Then one morning Jimmy Romano's found dead in the trunk of his car.'

'Let me guess.'

'You don't have to. Everybody knew who did it. Like I said, I was just a rookie, but I'd hear guys talking about it in the precinct. They had a police funeral for the guy and Masalsky actually sent over some flowers. It was this big arrangement, one of those horseshoe things. It said something like 'Sincere Condolences' on it, but it might as well have said 'Sincerely Fuck Every Last One of You.' I was out drinking with some of the cops after the funeral, and they were all talking about what they were going to do with the flowers. You know, like take them over to Masalsky's bar and shove them down his throat one by one.'

'I probably know the answer to this,' Vinnie said, 'but did they ever arrest him?'

'Of course not. He was in his bar all night, had about sixteen alibis lined up. The man who actually pulled the trigger, hell, he was found in the Detroit River a couple of months later. They recovered the gun and everything. But there was no way to pin it on Masalsky. Absolutely no way. For years after that, whenever I was out with some other cops after work, inevitably the story about Romano and Masalsky would come up. It would always be like, 'Who's going to take a run at this guy? Who's going to take him out? The rest of us, we've got you covered. It'll never come back to you.' Stuff like that. But it was just talk. It never really happened. You know why?'

'Why?'

'Because all those guys had something to lose. They had families. They had careers. When it comes right down to it, it's one thing to talk about going over the line. It's another thing to put your whole life at risk and to really do it.'

He shook his head slowly. 'That was a long time ago. A totally different situation.'

'It's the same idea. Some people are untouchable. It's just the way it is. Only now, I've got nothing to lose by going after him. Nothing at all.'

'Alex, I understand why you're saying that. Believe me. But you had a life before Natalie came along. You had other people who needed you. They still do.'

'I'm sorry,' I said. 'I don't mean that to sound like a reflection on you. Or anybody else.'

'You can't go around thinking your time on earth is over because you lost somebody. You think Natalie would want that?'

I finished my coffee. Then I stood up and headed to the shower. 'If I need your help . . . ,' I said. 'I won't ask you for anything else. Ever. Now I'm going to go get dressed. I've got some things to do today.'

★　★　★

It was a sunny day. Actual, bright sunlight, with a temperature that bordered on warm. It was the first almost-summer day of that July. It would also be the last.

Not that it mattered to me.

I got in the truck and drove out to Leon's house. I figured he wasn't back to work at the motor shop yet. I knew I was right when I saw his car in the driveway. I parked, went up to his door, and rang the bell. Eleanor answered. Of all the times I had come to this door, she had never looked so horrified to see me.

'I just want to talk to Leon,' I said. 'I'm not dragging him into anything, I promise.'

'Alex,' she said, opening the door. 'Oh my God, you look so . . . '

I braced for the impact. She wrapped both arms around me and squeezed.

'I am so sorry about what happened, Alex. I am so, so sorry.'

'Thank you,' I said, trying to breathe. 'I'll be all right. Really. Is Leon here?'

She didn't let go. As much as it hurt, I had to admit, there were worse things for me on that particular day than a huge bear hug. I relaxed for a moment, put my right arm around her. I closed my eyes and felt her start to cry on my shoulder. When Leon showed up, she finally broke away from me.

'I'm sorry,' she said, brushing my shoulder. 'I'm getting you all wet here.'

'Don't worry about it.'

'Let us know if we can do anything. Okay? Will you do that?'

'Yes, of course. Thank you.'

She put her hand on my cheek. Then she went back inside.

'Alex,' Leon said. 'What can I do for you?'

'I just wanted to talk to you.'

'Sure, come on. Let's walk a little bit. Can you believe the sun's out today?'

That's how we ended up walking through his neighborhood. There were more houses, about the same size as his. Not much else. You had to drive up to the Soo to buy food, or gas, or just about anything.

'The man's name is Antoine Laraque,' I told him. 'I was hoping you could check him out on your computer.'

'What do you know about him?'

'Not much. He lives in Toronto. He apparently buys guns from America and sells them to gang members. Or probably anyone else who has enough money. He spends time with a career criminal named Rhapsody something. I'll have to try to remember her last name. Anyway, Natalie finally got to meet Laraque in person a few days ago. She said she's never been around a more frightening person in her life.'

'Frightening in what way?'

'Not in the sense of being big and imposing. She said he just had this . . . power. It was hard for her to describe.'

'Aside from dealing in guns, no other idea about what he does? Some business front he might have?'

'No idea.'

'You don't know where he lives in Toronto?'

'No. Probably in a big house somewhere. I'm just guessing.'

We kept walking. I could tell Leon was thinking about it. He was thinking hard.

'There's not much to go on,' he finally said.

'I realize that.'

'There's a good chance we won't be able to dig up much information at all. A guy like that, he probably makes a point of staying mostly invisible. For all you know, Laraque isn't even his real name.'

'I suppose that's possible,' I said. 'But that name comes right from the police. They've been watching him for quite a while.'

'Are they still watching him now?'

'I'm sure they are, yes.'

'You don't want to leave this to them?'

'They have it right now. If they can put together a case, then great.'

'I take it you don't think they can.'

I didn't feel like going through the whole thing again. 'Let's just say that as a former cop,' I said, 'I know how hard it can be.'

'As a general rule, yes, but — '

'I just want to know more about him. That's

all I want right now.'

We kept walking. The sun had gone behind a cloud for a minute. Now it came back out and made everything bright. It felt warm on my face.

'I'm worried about you,' Leon finally said. 'I think you're still in shock over what happened. Rightly so.'

'You sound like Vinnie now.'

'Are you going to listen to either of us?'

'Whenever I have a problem,' I said, 'I come to you and you think of at least five different ideas. One of them is going to be completely insane, but that's the one that usually works. I can't tell you how much I've appreciated all the help over the years, Leon. I mean that.'

'I'd do it all again, Alex. We're a good team.'

'I just need your help one more time. That's all I'm asking. Just one more time.'

'I understand. But so far, all I can see is you walking up and down the street in Toronto, calling out his name.'

'You'll look him up on your computer, right? You'll see what you can find.'

'Yes, I'll do that much. In the meantime, any chance of you giving me my gun back?'

'Why, do you need it?'

'I think I'd just feel better if I held on to it for a few days.'

'You're the one who's always telling me a gun should be my best friend.'

'Maybe right now you need a different kind of friend. I'm just saying — '

'I'd like to keep it for a while,' I said. 'If that's all right.'

He didn't answer me. We kept walking. We went back to his house. He promised me he'd find out everything he could about Laraque. I promised him I'd tell him before I did anything stupid.

I'm not sure either of us was telling the truth.

18

I didn't know where to go next, so I drove up through the Soo. Without really thinking about it, I found myself on Portage Avenue, seeing all the people out enjoying the sunshine. I parked the truck, got out and walked through the Locks Park. I'm not sure why I was doing this, why I would go look at the fountain, the last place I had kissed her. Maybe I needed to refuel myself, remind myself of what was gone from my life. Because whatever I was going to do next, it was starting to look more and more like I'd be doing it alone.

Story of my life. And even more, of Natalie's. The fact that she died alone, too. That was the worst part. Her whole life, first as a young girl in Blind River, with everything that happened with her stepfather. Then later, as a cop, posted way the hell up in Hearst, on the last road in Canada. Me finding her, living by herself in that big house, so alone there she made me look like a socialite.

She lived her whole life alone and now she died alone. Before I could stop myself I imagined her body in a metal drawer somewhere, waiting to be put in the ground.

No, Alex. Keep moving.

I went down to the water and looked out at the St. Marys River. Ontario was right there on the other side. Maybe, what, a half a mile away?

A long time ago, I could have swum that with no problem. I had a sudden urge to climb the fence and dive right in. I could practically feel the cold water on my skin. I'd swim for Canada, and either I'd make it all the way, or else I'd drown somewhere in the middle. Either way, I couldn't see a downside.

All right, I thought, time to get your head on straight. Go do the next thing you can do. Then the next. You're living for one thing now. After that, well . . . You can deal with everything else when you're done.

I walked back past the fountain. A brilliant move on my part, I said to myself, to come here today, to remember how she looked that night. I can barely stand up straight it hurts so much. Yeah, Alex, this was genius.

I got back in the truck, closed my eyes until I could breathe again. I headed toward home, flipping the visor down against the sun. On a whim, I detoured north through Brimley. I passed the old abandoned railroad car, all boarded up and sitting there on a forgotten corner of the road, looking like it should be full of ghosts. A couple miles later, I turned off on the road that looped along Waishkey Bay.

I was thinking maybe Tyler could help me out. He was a Coast Guard auxiliarist, after all, although he obviously did things his own way. He knew all about boats, and about the local waterways. Beyond that, he seemed like the kind of guy you could trust, the kind of guy who'd understand a big problem.

I parked the truck in front of his house and

rang the doorbell. Nobody answered. I rang again and waited. Then I walked around to the back of the house.

I saw the boat out on the water, about a hundred yards from shore. Tyler and Liz were both on board, sitting in deck chairs with their backs to me. They seemed to be looking out at the bay. I stood on the shoreline, watching them. It felt strange to be here again, remembering that night, how cold it had been, how impenetrable the fog. Now, on a bright and sunny day, the whole scene looked so much different.

Tyler and Liz probably did this every day, I thought. Every nice day, at least. Drift out in their boat, sit on the water with nowhere to go. Just be together.

I didn't want to disturb them, didn't want to make them bring the boat in. There was a rowboat there by the dock. I thought, what the hell, I'll go out and talk to them.

I stepped down into the boat, feeling it rock under my weight. I sat down slowly and then grabbed the oars. I started rowing, skimming the water on the first stroke and banging the oars into the metal sides of the boat. I got the hang of it on the second stroke. Another thing I hadn't done in a million years.

I made my way out to them, moving backward, looking over my shoulder every few strokes to make sure I was heading in the right direction. As I got closer, Liz turned around and spotted me. She was confused for a moment, then she broke out in that big smile of hers. For one second I thought maybe she hadn't even heard, as impossible as that would be in a place like this where everybody knows everything about everybody. The smile melted in an instant.

She nudged Tyler, who turned around and went through his own version of the same reaction. Confusion to recognition to that mixture of feelings you experience around someone who's suffered a tragedy. Empathy and sorrow, yes. Also discomfort, a nervous unease. I wondered how long I'd be evoking this in every single person I ran into.

'Alex!' Liz said. 'You don't have to row out here! We would have come in.'

'You guys looked so peaceful out here,' I said. 'I'm sorry to interrupt.'

I should have just turned around and left, I thought to myself. Did I really need to talk to Tyler this much?

He came over and threw me a line. I tied off the rowboat and climbed aboard. As soon as I had my feet on deck, Tyler took my right hand. He held it with a firm grip and looked me in the eye, his free hand on my shoulder. He started to say something, stopped himself, gave me a tight smile.

'I can't imagine what brings you here,' he finally said. 'But if there's anything we can do for you . . . ' I could tell he meant it. I could have asked him for anything. That's the kind of people they were, both of them.

These are real Yoopers, I thought to myself. These are the people who make this place what it is.

'I don't mean to intrude,' I said. 'I was just driving by, thought I'd stop in.'

'I'm glad you did,' Tyler said. 'Would you like some coffee?'

'Yes. I could use some right now.'

Liz poured me a cup while Tyler unfolded another deck chair. He set it up so I was sitting in the middle.

'We do this a lot,' Liz said. 'It's the best part of living here.'

'I don't blame you,' I said. 'I can't imagine a better spot to have a cup of coffee.' I looked out at the bay, at the shifting colors in the water as the clouds moved through the sunlight. Today, you could see all the way across the bay. The line of trees on the far side was the Canadian shore.

'Actually, I wanted to ask you something,' I said. 'About getting over there.'

'To Canada?' Tyler said. 'What's the problem?'

'Well, it's like this . . . '

I let out a breath and looked out over the water. Natalie would have loved this day, I thought, the first day that even remotely resembled summer around here. The fresh air out here on the water, the sunlight, the way the boat was rocking gently on the waves.

What are you going to tell these good people, Alex? That you want them to smuggle you over the border? So you can do what? Hitchhike to Toronto? Then what? What's your plan? Leon was right. You might as well walk up and down the streets, calling out his name.

'Alex,' Liz said, 'are you okay?'

265

'What do you want to ask us?' Tyler said.

'I don't know what I'm doing anymore,' I said. 'I'm sorry.'

'That's okay,' Tyler said. 'You know, Liz and I lost somebody once. You never get over it. Some days you live with it better than others. But it never goes away.'

'That's right,' Liz said. 'It never does.'

'Just sit here with us,' Tyler said. 'See if you can enjoy the day, at least for a little while. Maybe that's all you can do right now.'

I sat back in my chair, feeling like everything had been drained right out of me. I didn't want to agree with him, didn't want to accept what he was saying, but in the bright light of day with the wind coming in across the water, I couldn't argue with him. I couldn't think of one thing to say.

We sat there for a long time. Eventually, I closed my eyes. The rocking of the boat would have lulled me to sleep, but then I heard Liz get up and go to the edge of the deck. When I opened my eyes, she was leaning over the gunwale, staring down into the water.

'Hey, Tyler,' she said.

'Hmm?' He was half asleep, too.

'Remember how we were out here the other day, looking for that thing?'

'Yeah?'

'This is the first sunny day we've had in so long . . . You can see a lot better now.'

He got up and looked over the gunwale. I followed them, looked over the edge, saw the sunlight penetrating the water. I saw the silvery flash of a fish below the surface, a good four feet deep.

'Hot damn,' Tyler said. 'You're right.'

'What are you waiting for? Let's go look again.'

'What are we talking about here?' I said.

'You remember the boat wreck, of course . . . '

'How could I forget?'

'Remember how those guys came back the next day, looking for that box?'

'Yeah. Are you telling me — '

'Let's go,' Liz said. 'Before we lose the light.'

Tyler pulled up the anchor and started the boat. In another few seconds we were headed out to the old bridge pilings.

'We came out here a couple of times,' Liz told me. 'But you know what the weather's been like. No sun, plus the water's been so choppy. We couldn't see a thing down there.'

'Do you remember where the wreck was?' I said. I looked out at the pilings. Two parallel rows, at least twelve on each side. They all looked exactly the same to me.

'They left their mark,' Liz said. 'You'll see.'

It didn't take long to get out there. Tyler came in close as slowly as he could. Then he cut the engine and grabbed a long metal hook. He reached over the side and dug it into the soft wood of the nearest piling, bringing the boat to a dead stop.

'What do you carry that thing for?' I said.

'I use it when I'm doing my Coast Guard rounds,' he said. 'In case I have to latch on to a boat, or try to pull somebody out of the water.'

'The boat hit that one right there,' Liz said, pointing to the piling on the opposite row. 'You can just see the mark on the side there.'

'I see it.' It looked like somebody had tried to cut into the piling with a dull ax.

'If that box sank,' Tyler said, 'it's gotta be right around here somewhere.'

'It was yellow,' Liz said. 'Isn't that what they said?'

'I thought it was orange.'

'Either way, we should be able to see it.'

We spent the next few minutes leaning over the gunwale. If someone had been watching us, they'd have to wonder just what the hell we were doing out there.

'I'm not seeing it,' Liz said. 'How deep is it here?'

'Depth finder says eight feet,' Tyler said.

'That might be too deep. Even with this light, I don't think we'll be able to see down that far.'

'You may be right. Let me just pull us over here a little bit . . . '

He worked the hook into the wooden piling again, moving us into the center of the double rows.

I looked into the water, but the sunlight seemed to reach about four or five feet into the water, no more.

'I can't see anything,' Tyler said.

'There,' Liz said. 'Right there.'

'Where? I can't see.'

'Let me have that,' she said. She took the hook from Tyler and extended it down into the water. The hook disappeared into the depths.

'You've got better eyes than I do. Can you feel anything down there?'

She didn't answer. She was concentrating hard on what she was doing, feeling along the bottom of the lake with the metal hook.

'I don't want to stir things up too much,' she said. 'We'll never find it again . . .'

'Do you have it?'

'No. Wait . . . No . . . Yes!'

'There's gotta be a handle or something, right?'

'I hope so,' she said. She kept working the pole, then she tried pulling. 'I think I might have it hooked now. But I can't lift it.'

'Here, let me try,' he said. He took the pole from her.

'Careful. Don't lose it.'

'I'll try not to.' He pulled up on the pole. It seemed to come up about two inches. 'Okay, this is heavy. This is officially very heavy.'

'Can I help you?' I asked. I moved next to him and put my hands on the pole.

'I think we have to keep it at this angle. Otherwise it might come off the hook.'

'Got it,' I said. I started to put some muscle into it. 'I'll try to work with you here.'

'Okay, let's give it some power now. Nice and smooth.'

We both pulled together. I could feel my back starting to complain. My arms were already burning.

'Just keep going,' he said. 'It might get easier once we get it off the bottom.'

It didn't get easier. We had to lug the pole up

out of the water, inch by inch. When we had made enough progress, whoever had the top hand was able to switch it to the bottom.

'I'm seeing it now,' Liz said. 'I was right. It's yellow.'

The yellow got brighter and brighter as the box came closer to the surface. My arms felt like they were shot now, but we were so close. The box was almost up to the surface. We both gave the pole another strong tug, a little too much this time. I could see the hook jerking at the handle. Then slipping.

'We're losing it!' Tyler said.

I reached down and grabbed for it, felt my fingers wrapping under the handle. But the box was beginning to sink again. I held on tight, leaning over so far now that it would surely pull me right into the water. Or else pull my arm right out of the socket.

'Get the pole down here again,' I said. 'See if you can get the handle. I can't hold this much longer.'

'I don't want to catch your fingers,' he said, working the pole back into position.

'Don't worry. Just give it a try.'

I felt the pole brush against my little finger.

'Are you clear?' he said.

'Go for it.'

He pulled hard. I could feel the box coming up again. I gave it one more good yank. Now the box was half out of the water. Tyler tried to help me get it over the gunwale, but there was no way that was going to happen. We didn't have the leverage.

'Liz,' he said. 'Start the boat and take us to shore. If we can just get to shallow water . . . '

She was on it. I could hear the propeller churning against the water. Soon, we were moving. Tyler and I each had a hand on the handle. It was all we could do to keep the box against the side of the boat.

A long minute later, Liz had pulled the boat parallel to the shoreline. She cut the engine and let the boat drift even closer, until the hull made contact with the bottom.

'Okay,' Tyler said. 'We can let go.'

We both did at the same time. The box went straight down, sending a plume of water right into our faces. We both had to sit there rubbing our right arms for a while before we could speak.

'What the hell is so heavy in that thing?' he finally said.

'Good question,' I said.

'Let's get it to shore.'

He jumped over the gunwale and landed in water up to his knees. He pushed the boat toward the dock, so Liz could tie it up. I got out and came around to where Tyler was standing. I waded out into the water and helped him drag the box onto the shore.

It was a large scuba box, mostly yellow with a black watertight seal running all around the top. I bent down and saw the damage to one side of it. There was a large dent in the plastic, and the seal had obviously been compromised.

Tyler lifted the padlock on the front latch. 'Whatever's in here is so heavy,' he said. 'It's a wonder this thing ever floated.'

I thought about it. 'Maybe floating was never a consideration,' I said. 'They weren't thinking about crashing the boat. They just wanted to keep something locked up tight.'

'I wonder what's in it?'

I looked at him. 'You work on cars, right?'

'Yeah?'

'So you must have quite an assortment of tools.'

'We can't open this.'

'I think we probably can.'

'We need to turn this over to the police.'

'We will,' I said. 'Right after we open it.'

'I don't know, Alex . . . '

I was standing there, soaking wet from the knees down. If I had been wavering in my reasons for coming here to see Tyler in the first place, here was a small mystery I could at least solve. This box those men had wanted to find so badly . . . I had assumed all along that it was filled with cash, brought along in the boat to give to someone in Canada in exchange for a large amount of prescription drugs.

But money didn't weigh this much, not unless it was solid gold.

'Tyler, I can't even tell you what I've been through in the last few days. What I've lost. I have nothing else to lose now, so I'm going to open up this box. You can help me or you can stand aside.'

He looked at Liz, then at me. 'Sounds like if I want to stop you, I'll have to go get one of the shotguns.'

'That's probably what it'll take, yes.'

272

'In that case, I'll be right back.'

I watched him walk to the garage. He emerged a few seconds later. For one second I thought I saw the shotgun in his hands. But no, it was a long crowbar.

'Here you go,' he said as he handed it to me. 'I'll tell the police this is how we found it, that it must have gotten damaged in the wreck. If they look close enough to see crowbar marks, you're on your own.'

'Thank you, Tyler. I owe you a drink.'

The front latch looked solid, so I started in on the side that was already damaged. I slipped the crowbar in through the cracked seal, working it back and forth until the opening got bigger. Some dark water came seeping out. I kept working the crowbar, bending back the lid. The plastic started to give way. I saw Liz flinch when a large piece came off with a violent cracking noise. Looking inside, I saw another box. This one was made of wood. It was stained dark from the intruding water.

I had to keep working hard on the lid until I could get the inner box out. At this point, there was no way it would look like damage from the crash, but I didn't care. I pulled at the wooden box. It slid out. There was another box underneath it. More beside it. There had to be a dozen of them.

I held the wooden box in my hands for a moment. I had a gut feeling I already knew what was in it. I opened the box and saw that I was right.

It was a gun. Some kind of small machine

pistol, like a miniature Uzi. There was black felt inside the box, molding perfectly to the gun and showing it off like it was some kind of exotic jewel.

I put the box down, took out another. When I opened it, I saw a pistol. A Colt .45. Things were coming together in my mind now. I felt a cold, sick wave flowing right through me.

'This is some serious hardware,' Tyler said. 'It explains the lock, I guess.'

'If they got stopped by somebody,' I said, 'the box couldn't be opened without a warrant. That's enough reason right there.'

'How much do you think these are worth?'

I shook my head. 'I'm sure these are worth something. But you know . . . I mean, how much can a dozen guns go for these days? A few thousand dollars, tops?'

'Those guys acted like they really, really needed to get this box back,' Tyler said. 'I was expecting to see a lot of money. Or diamonds. You're telling me it's just a few thousand dollars worth of guns?'

'I bet the dollar value wasn't the point,' I said. 'They wanted to find this box so nobody else would. They didn't want anybody to make the connection, to figure out what these guys were really up to.'

'They were selling guns, you mean. So these guns here . . . Hell, these were — '

'Samples,' I said. 'These were samples.'

'Just like salesmen. God damn, Liz, those guys were selling guns.'

'No,' I said. 'No. They weren't selling guns.'

274

I was already moving. Tyler called after me, but I didn't even turn around. After almost losing my steam, now I had a new mission. I ran to my truck, sprayed gravel as I spun out of his driveway and hit the road.

They weren't selling guns.

They were trading them.

19

Guns for drugs. It made a terrible kind of sense. God knows, America had enough guns, in every shape and size. Legal, borderline legal, or way over the line illegal, America had them. Of course, there was no shortage of hunting rifles in Canada. But handguns, concealable weapons, little submachine guns you can tuck into your jacket . . . that was a different matter. If you wanted to buy something like that in Canada, you were out of luck.

What Canada did have in abundance was drugs. Especially painkillers. Hell, you could walk into any drugstore in Canada and buy Tylenol with a low dose of codeine right over the counter. The stronger stuff, the serious opiates like Vicodin, Oxycontin, sure, you'd need a prescription. But nowadays, how many Americans were doing mail-order business with Canadian pharmacies? It was a gray area in United States law, whether it was legal to fill your prescriptions in Canada. But as long as the different federal agencies were bickering about it, the gates were wide open. That meant lots of drugs being made in Canada, lots of drugs being moved around from one place to another. Some of them getting lost, maybe. Some of them not quite reaching their intended destinations.

Certain people in one country, with access to lots of drugs, needing a certain kind of gun.

Certain people in another country, with access to lots of guns, needing a certain kind of drug. Both countries right next to each other, with a long, mostly open border.

Imports and exports, like Mr. Gray had said to me.

Imports and exports.

That's what was ringing in my head as I drove down to Hessel. As badly as my first two visits to Mr. Gray's summerhouse had gone, something told me I needed to make one more trip. Cap was probably long gone by now, but hell, maybe Brucie would still be there, hanging on to the hope that he was still working for Mr. Gray. I didn't imagine he'd be terribly happy to see me, but that would be the least of his problems.

It was starting to get cloudy again, the sun retreating already after just a few hours of bright light, of warmth. Saying, this is all there is. See you next year if you're lucky. I kept driving as the lead-colored sky took over again and the temperature dropped. I could feel the air itself changing.

I turned off the highway, found the road that ran down the peninsula to Mr. Gray's summerhouse. My third trip there . . . The first I had parked at the neighbors' so I could sneak up on the place. The second time I didn't even make it to the house at all, catching Cap on his way out of Dodge and beating him half to death right there on the roadside. Now, finally, I drove my truck down the driveway like a regular human being and parked it in front of the house. Cap's Escalade was long gone. The red Viper and the silver Mercedes were both there. I had to think back for a moment, remembering that Mr. Gray had taken his son with him, and had left Harry's car here. The other car must have been Brucie's, although I couldn't picture him driving a Mercedes. He seemed more the kind of guy who'd drive a shiny new Hummer.

I stuck the gun in my belt again, just in case. For all I knew, Brucie had gotten over his little hang-up about shooting people. I went to the front door and knocked. Nobody answered. I knocked again. Nothing.

Two cars here, but no people? It didn't make sense. I tried opening the front door. It was locked. Then I remembered how I'd gotten in the first time.

I went around to the back. Everything looked exactly the same. A horseshoe pit. Beer bottles. An empty dock. I tried the patio door. Just like last time, it was unlocked.

One step into the house and I knew something was seriously wrong. There was a sickly sweet smell hanging in the air. One part death and one part something else, probably just as evil. The primitive part of my brain started hitting the evacuation button — the red alert, just-get-the-hell-out-of-here-right-now button. But I wanted to take one quick look through the house first.

I walked through the main room. The whole place had gone from a mess to a disaster. There weren't just beer bottles all over the place now. There were pizza boxes, ice cream cartons, the remains of three or four frozen dinners. Lots of cigarettes. Mr. Gray would have been sincerely disturbed to see his place looking like this. And I knew it was about to get much worse.

The smell got stronger as I went up the stairs. For a moment, I wasn't sure I'd be able to take it. Then the wave of nausea passed and I kept going. The first bedroom was cleaned out now. This must have been where Cap had slept. The second room was pretty much the same story. Harry's room, I was guessing. The third room was where everything had gone straight to hell.

There were more empty beer bottles, at least thirty of them all over the floor, the bed, the dresser. There were overflowing ashtrays. More food containers. That's where some of the smell was coming from. Mixed with that was the unmistakable aroma of marijuana smoke. The rest of it had to be Brucie, or what was left of him. But I didn't see him anywhere.

I looked on the other side of the bed. He wasn't there. I knew he was a big man, so there weren't many places left to hide. Then I saw the closet door.

When I slid it open, the smell washed over me like a hot wind. I thought I'd lose it right there. I had to cover my face to stop from retching all over the place. He was curled up on the floor of the closet, drawn into himself in this tight little space like some kind of sick animal. Typical junkie behavior. His eyes were open, all white, as the pupils seemed to be rolled back in his head. I saw a couple of needles on the floor next to him. A belt he had obviously used to tie off. A spoon. Matches.

I remembered what Cap had told me, the last

time I saw him. Brucie was the one with the pill problem. He wasn't lying about that one, I said to myself. Brucie was the one stupid enough to dip into the merchandise and get himself hooked.

Then the conversation with Terry LaFleur, the woman from the clinic, came back to me. I replayed everything she had said, me and Vinnie on one side of the table, in the restaurant at the Kewadin, Terry on the other side. She was ratting out Caroline and her little scam, getting those prescription painkillers and selling them. The big danger, Terry had said, was that the pills went outside of the clinic's control, and whoever took them did so with no supervision, no safety net. Once they got hooked, if the pills stopped coming . . . that's when things got really dangerous. Because someone hooked on Vicodin will do anything to hold on to that feeling, even if it means going to something else. Something more dangerous. Something deadly.

Just like this.

I knew there was heroin up here now. Vinnie would talk about it now and then, having heard about it from some of the younger guys on the rez. From the poppy fields in Afghanistan or wherever else they were growing it these days, I couldn't imagine a farther trip for a bag of the stuff to make. But here it was right in front of me, having stopped the heart of a man stronger than an ox. It must have been one hell of a hit.

I couldn't think of one thing to do about it. Call the police, tell them I found an OD, tell them they should come get him out of here? No rush on that one. He wasn't going anywhere. Right now I had other things to do.

I worked my way back through the house, looking in each room, then down the stairs. When I was in the kitchen I could almost breathe again without gagging.

What are you looking for, Alex? What do you think you're going to find?

The map was still laid out on the kitchen table. All the major waterways, all around the Les Cheneaux Islands, Lake Huron, around Drummond Island. I bent down to the map, examining it closely, trying to see if someone had made a mark somewhere. A little X to mark the spot. If they had, I couldn't see it.

Imports and exports. Guns for drugs. I stood up straight, looking around the rest of the kitchen. The last time I was here . . . There were some pill bottles there on the counter. Beer bottles, trash. What else? I had seen something else before I was interrupted, before they came back in and I had to hide.

Before they came back in.

All three of them. Cap, Brucie, Harry. I had assumed that morning that they had gone into town, that they were out eating breakfast or something. That they had just come back while I was standing there. Like the three bears returning home . . .

But there were three vehicles outside that day. The two that were still out there now, plus Cap's Escalade. Three people, three cars. If they had been in town, how did they get there?

Unless they hadn't been in town. Unless they

hadn't driven anywhere at all. Which would explain why I hadn't heard a vehicle when they came back. All of a sudden, there they were at the front door.

They couldn't have been in the boat. The boat was wrecked. The dock was empty.

Boat keys. There was another set of boat keys sitting here on the counter. I had assumed they were just duplicates for the wooden boat. Although if you had a duplicate set, why would you leave them lying around on the counter?

I looked on the counter. I opened the drawers. There were no keys here now. Did Brucie have them? Would I have to go back upstairs and search his clothes? That was the last thing in the world I wanted to do.

You're getting ahead of yourself, I thought. First go see if there's another boat out there. Then worry about the keys.

I went out the back door, stood on the porch for a moment, sucking in the cold, fresh air until I was dizzy. Then I went down to the edge of the water. There was a heavy mist forming on the surface now, the relative heat of the day giving way to the cool evening. I went out on the dock, looked down the shoreline in both directions. There was a big willow tree, its long leaves touching the water on one side. Some tall weeds standing in the shallows. But no boats.

I looked across the channel. I could barely see another dock on the far side. It was just as empty as the one I was standing on. All these summer homes here on the channels, most of them empty at the moment, with no summer, no reason for anyone to come all the way up here.

An idea. All these other houses ... Most of them empty.

I went back through the yard, looking for some kind of path, some break in the trees and the high tangles of sumac, wild raspberry, poison ivy, whatever the hell else. I found a path of sorts, followed it, the brambles cutting into my arms. From the next yard, I looked down at the water. There was a canoe overturned on the shore, nothing tied to the dock. So much for this one.

I worked my way back through the brush, fought through the opposite side of the yard until I was standing on yet another shoreline. Another empty house. Another empty dock.

Now what?

Now you use your head for once. They had come in through the front door, not the back. Instead of fighting my way back to the yard, I went up the driveway. I walked down the street until I was at the front of Gray's property. I hadn't seen a driveway on the other side of the street yet. Until ... Over there. Down a hundred yards more.

I went to the driveway, walked all the way down to the house. It looked like one of the older houses on the peninsula. It might have been one of the first, built way back when, before Les Cheneaux turned into a hot property. A one-story cottage, everything you'd need in a summerhouse without any of the fancy architecture. No strange angles on the roof, no soaring windows.

The house looked dark inside. There were no cars parked outside. Nothing going on here at all. Then I walked around to the backyard and saw something interesting.

Down by the shore, there was a boathouse, the kind they used to build right on the water, after dredging a channel underneath. You don't see a lot of them anymore. Maybe they're too hard to maintain. Or maybe if you have a big enough boat, you dry-dock at a marina. No matter the reason, here was one of the originals, and even though the paint was peeling and the whole thing was starting to lean to the right, it was at least forty feet long and another twenty feet high. It could obviously hold a lot of boat.

I walked down and looked through the little window in the door. I could see a big cabin cruiser inside. It had to be at least a thirty-footer.

I tried the door. It was locked. The only other way in was the big overhead door leading out to the water. The door probably came down right to the surface, maybe with a couple of inches to spare. If I really wanted to, I thought, I could dive into the channel, swim underwater, and come up inside the boathouse. Yeah, sure, I could do that.

I took a quick look around, picked up a rock the size of a softball and broke the window. I reached inside and fumbled around with the doorknob. The door swung open.

The boat had been parked nose out. The lettering on the back read *Ruth's Revenge*. I walked around the gangplanks on all three sides, looking her over. The boat was wrapped up tight, like it hadn't been taken out in weeks. But of course that may have been a deliberate ruse. One other thing I did notice — either this boat was built to ride low in the water, or else it was holding a very heavy load.

As I unsnapped the cover on the starboard gunwale, I remembered another boat, about this size, owned by a man who was now very much dead. He had used it to smuggle high-end kitchen appliances into Canada without paying the tariffs. At the time, it had seemed like some major-league criminal activity to me. But if this boat here was holding what I thought it was, it would make the appliance scheme look like kid's stuff.

When I had unsnapped enough buttons, I stepped down inside the boat. There was a little table on the rear deck with four chairs around it. There was an ashtray still overflowing with butts. A cooler filled with empty beer bottles. A short ladder led up to the top deck, but I wasn't interested in going up there. Instead, I opened the door to the cabin and looked inside.

When my eyes adjusted to the darkness, I saw the crates. They were stacked in the cabin, as many crates as you could possibly fit in there. I grabbed one and pulled it down, slid it back to the rear deck so I'd have a little more light. It was made of rough wood, about four feet long, two feet wide, two feet deep. Like a miniature coffin. I didn't think I even had to open it, but I did anyway, just to confirm what I already knew.

I pulled off the top of the box, moved the

loose packing material, and saw the dull gray metal inside.

⋆　⋆　⋆

One web, one spider. That's the way it works. Or so I thought.

I thought I was caught in one web myself, the spider a man named Gray. I thought Natalie was in another web entirely, the spider a man named Laraque. Kneeling beside this crate, in this boat, inside this boathouse, on this peninsula fifty miles south of Paradise, I came to know, finally, that there was only one web after all. One web with two spiders on opposite ends.

All those Mounties and OPP's and American ATF agents helping out on the task force . . . I wondered if any of them had any idea this was going on. That this was at least one major source for Laraque's guns. A key piece to their puzzle was sitting right here in this lonely boathouse, in a pleasure boat seemingly abandoned for the summer.

Not that they could use it. I was sure Gray knew exactly what he was doing here. A boat that belonged to someone else, sitting in a boathouse across the street from his summer-house. Purely a coincidence, he'd say. Without a hard link, they couldn't lay a glove on him. Like Laraque, Gray had enough money and power to make himself untouchable.

In any case, I still didn't believe Gray had anything to do with Natalie's death. Not directly. She was no threat to his end of the web. No, everything was pointing in the other direction. More and more each day.

But now, instead of having to go find Laraque . . . I had a new idea.

I climbed out of the boat, left the shore and came back up to the house. I peered in one of the back windows, saw no signs of life whatsoever. I tried the back door. It was locked. Once again, a delicate lock-picking operation was called for, so I found another rock and broke the window on the door, reached in, and opened it. I went to the kitchen and started looking in the drawers. I knew there had to be another key here, somewhere.

It felt strange to be in this house, but it was better than the alternative. The last thing I wanted to do was to go back across the street, have that smell hit me again, maybe even have to go upstairs looking for the key. I went through every drawer, was about to try the next room, when I saw the hooks on the wall. They were right above a poster showing every species of fish in the Great Lakes. On one ring there were two keys attached to a float. I grabbed them and left.

I went back down to the boathouse, found the switch for the overhead door, and hit it. It was like a big garage door opening, except instead of a driveway there was water. It was late afternoon now, and the low sunlight came streaming in as the door opened.

I untied the boat, took the cover off, got in and climbed up to the top deck. I put the key in and started it, remembering a second later that you're supposed to let a boat air out for a while if it's been in such a confined space. But what the hell. The engine came to life and nothing exploded. I inched the throttle forward and the boat started to move.

I kept it straight as it cleared the boathouse, then I turned the boat to the right, toward the open water. I knew how treacherous the channels were around here. With all the little islands, all the sudden shallow areas where you could so easily grind the propeller into the rocks . . . I was going to need some help.

I turned on the GPS. The screen looked blank at first, then I saw a line start to form, drawn from the top of the screen toward the center. At the bottom there were several sets of numbers. One pair had to be my latitude and longitude. The other number, it was getting smaller . . . twenty then fifteen then eight . . .

It's the depth, you idiot! I looked out at the water, and even in the fog I could see the large rock jutting up past the surface. I swung the boat hard to the left. When I looked back at the screen, the line had taken a turn, as well. The depth crept back up over twenty feet.

It's drawing my route, I thought, every inch of the way. But how's that going to help me? Then I saw a thick band appear on the edge of the screen. It got closer and closer to the central line. As I looked closer, I could see that the band was actually a thick accumulation of many thin lines, woven together like a rope. It was a history of every route this boat had taken. As long as I stayed in the band, I'd be retracing a safe passage.

I let out a long breath. This definitely made my life easier, at least for a while. I watched the depth hover in the twenties as I passed one small island after another, the rocks and trees floating by in a fog that was getting thicker by the minute. How anyone could have ever found his way through this maze without help, I couldn't even imagine.

At first, I was thinking I'd need to find a hiding place for the boat, a dead-end channel maybe. But that idea didn't last long. I could hardly see where I was going, for one thing. Even if I found a spot I could get to, I'd have no idea if the boat was really hidden. Not to mention the fact that I'd have to find my way back to Vinnie's truck.

The next idea was to find a secluded island, somehow get the crates off the boat, one by one, like a pirate hiding his treasure. Then take the boat back empty.

Another totally stupid idea, I thought. You'll never get close enough to the shore. What are you going to do, swim back and forth with the crates on your back?

I kept going. It took me about thirty minutes to clear the last island. The depth started dropping quickly, until a few minutes later it was over a hundred feet to the bottom of Lake Huron. Nothing like Superior, which can go down over a thousand feet, but more than enough for what I was about to do. The final idea, the one I had in the back of my mind the whole time.

I cut the engine and let the boat drift. Then I

started grabbing the crates from the cabin. One by one, I dragged them out to the rear deck. I wasn't sure why I felt I needed to open them, whether it was some kind of morbid fascination, or maybe just a confirmation of exactly what I was sending to the bottom of the lake. The first few crates all contained handguns. In the faint glow of the boat's running lights, it was hard to say exactly what kind of guns these were, but I was pretty sure I was seeing some Colt automatics, some Brownings, some Smith & Wessons. Good solid, concealable handguns, with the ammo packed right inside each box — from .22 through .380, .45, nine-millimeter. Everything you needed to start your own little war.

Each gun hit the water with a muffled splash and disappeared in an instant. It was hard work throwing the guns overboard, dragging out the next crate, opening it. Eventually I got into the more exotic weapons, the machine pistols and the mini-assault rifles, all with several magazines apiece. Some of them looked like toys they were so compact, and I knew from experience they'd sound no louder than a sewing machine.

I had taken three slugs from a gun just like this one, I thought as I threw it over the side. I put a little something extra on the throw, heard it splash somewhere out of sight. A hell of a world this is, that men would make these machines, and with such loving care. Little pieces of metal sent flying faster than the eye can see — perfect, smooth little projectiles that part the skin and destroy everything beneath it.

What a goddamned world, I thought. What a hopeless goddamned world.

When I dragged out the next box, I opened it and pulled out a small .22 caliber pistol. The front sight had been removed, and threads cut into the muzzle end of the barrel. I reached in and pulled out the suppressor. It was a cylinder, about eight inches long, much thicker than the barrel of the gun. I screwed it on tight, held the thing in my hand and looked it at for a long time.

I had never heard the gunshots, I thought. I was just down the road. When I came back, she was already gone. Whoever did it, he had a gun like this. Small caliber, low velocity. A good enough suppressor to damp down the sound to almost nothing.

Yes. He had a gun that looked just like this one.

I threw it as far as I could, felt the sudden stab of pain in my right shoulder. I picked up the rest of the crate and heaved the whole thing at once. I went back to the cabin, grabbed the next crate, my back straining with the effort, my shoulder throbbing with a dull ache now. I threw that crate into the water without opening it. Then the next crate and the next. I didn't want to see any more guns. I didn't want to feel the light coating of gun oil on my fingers. I wanted every last one of these crates on the bottom of the lake as quickly as possible, every last gun sunk a hundred feet in black water, every last round gone forever.

I had no idea how many guns I threw

overboard, how much ammo. There had to be a good seven hundred cubic feet of storage space on the boat. If I had sat down, I could have figured it out. How many hundreds of guns, enough to outfit a small army. How many hundreds of thousands of dollars in street value. All I knew was that none of these guns would ever make it to Toronto, would never kill a human being, would never do to somebody else what had been done to me.

If nothing else, this was one good thing I could do on this one day of what was left of my life.

When I thought I was done, I went down on one knee, breathing hard and rubbing my shoulder. I went back into the cabin to double-check, saw one more crate in the dark corner. When I dragged it out, I noticed it felt a little lighter than the others. Instead of throwing it right overboard, I opened it.

Something a little different, I thought. Just for variety. I reached in and pulled out a small .380 stainless steel pistol, with a barrel that couldn't have been more than two and a half inches long. Something for a lady to put in her purse, maybe. But no, what's this?

I pulled out an ankle holster. The gun fit right into it. This could come in handy, I thought. I grabbed a box of .380 shells, put everything in the pocket of my jacket.

I looked to see what else was in the crate, pulled out a black plastic box. I opened it. It took me a moment to realize what I was looking at. It was a Taser, the kind with the two electrodes that shoot out under air power and deliver a fifty-thousand-volt shock to whoever's unlucky enough to be standing in front of you. They were just starting to talk about these when I left the police force. I never got the chance to use one myself. Now maybe I would.

I still had Leon's gun tucked in my waistband. Add to that a backup gun hidden in an ankle holster and a Taser. It may have been a complete illusion, but I felt like my chances had just gotten a little better.

I threw the rest of the last box into the water and watched it go down. I looked out at the fog. It had erased everything, like nothing else in the world had ever existed at all. Just me and an empty boat, drifting to nowhere. That's all there was.

I wanted to stay out there. I wanted the fog to erase the memory, too, to make me believe it had never happened.

No such luck, Alex. You've played this card, now you've got to see the next.

I went back to the wheel, looked at the GPS and saw absolutely nothing. There was just me on the tip of a pencil-thin line, with no other history, like maybe the fog *had* erased everything else. Then I figured I had probably been drifting south, and if I was turned to the east now . . .

I started the motor and swung her around to the northwest. In a few minutes, I saw the old routes reappear at the top of the screen. I followed the band back through the maze of islands and peninsulas, another half hour on the water with the rocks and the trees slipping in and out of sight. It was getting darker now.

As I got closer to the boathouse, I had just enough light to center the nose in the open doorway. I felt the whole boat rock as I bumped into the back gangplanks a little harder than I wanted. It occurred to me that I had found the boat parked nose out, and now it was nose in. To whoever found it, this would be a clue that someone else had been here. This plus the broken window in the door and the fact that every last one of the guns had disappeared.

Before I left the place, I found a clipboard with paper and pen tucked in next to the driver's console. I thought hard about what message I wanted to leave. It was Laraque I wanted, but I figured somebody working for Gray would probably find this first. No matter. If both spiders are on the web, all you do is pull hard enough to make them both feel it.

'I have your merchandise,' I wrote. A lie I regretted for all of two seconds. 'I know you're shorthanded right now, so have Mr. L contact me and I'll be happy to make the delivery myself. I'll talk to him and only him.'

I underlined the 'only.' Then I signed my name. I knew that's all I needed.

I knew they'd know where to find him.

And where to find me.

* * *

When I got back to Paradise, it hit me. I needed to be in my own cabin in case they came looking for me. I needed to stay next to my phone in case they tried to call me. I pulled up in front, got out of the truck, and went to the door. No use hanging around outside thinking about it. I just opened the door and stepped inside.

Someone had done me a great favor. Whether it was one of the county deputies or one of the state guys, someone had cleaned up the place, had put everything as right as they could make it, had even tried to clean the floor.

The floor. The spot where Natalie died. I could still see it. God help me, I could still see where it had happened.

I can't do this, I told myself. I can't stay here.

But I have to. I have no choice.

I was so tired. I went to the bed, took off my clothes, left them where they dropped. I climbed into the bed, hoping to sleep, thinking maybe I'd have one more night when I didn't have to start watching for whoever might come after me. But as soon as I was in the bed I smelled her scent there. In one second it was all over me and inside me. Like she was right there next to me.

Everything I had done that day, it all caught up to me at that one moment. I wanted it to be over. I wanted Laraque to call me, or to come here himself so he could deal with me in person. Anything to see him face-to-face, so I could ask him if he had killed Natalie, and if he had, then why.

I wanted it to happen so bad. I didn't want to wait any longer.

I wanted violence. I wanted blood. It was the

only thing that made sense to me now.

Violence. Blood.

Little did I know how soon my wish would come true.

20

I spent a good part of the next day doing something I hadn't done in years. I took some empty cans to a secluded spot in the woods behind my cabin and practiced shooting, first with Leon's gun, then with the little .380 I had taken from the boat. I put the ankle holster on my left leg, practiced bending over and picking up the pant leg with my left hand, drawing the weapon with my right, coming up shooting. The miniature pistol had a surprising kick to it. After a few rounds, my right hand was starting to get numb. At least I had the sense to wear the earmuffs I kept around for whenever I ran my chain saw.

The Taser looked like a toy, especially when I loaded it up with eight double-A batteries. It was hard to imagine this thing emitting a charge strong enough to knock a grown man senseless and keep him down for several minutes, but that's what it was built to do. The nasty part was the pair of probes on the ends of the wires. They looked like long fish hooks, with barbs on the ends to keep them stuck inside the skin. According to the little booklet that came with the gun, the nitrogen canister would shoot the probes at a hundred and twenty miles per hour, with enough force to penetrate two inches of clothing. As long as both probes made contact with the skin, the electric charge would completely shut down the target's muscle control, sending the man down to the ground like he was having some kind of seizure.

Yeah, I can see how useful this would be, I thought. Put a man on the ground without killing him. This thing could definitely make the starting lineup, despite the fact that citizen use is illegal in Michigan.

I was still reading when I heard the footsteps. I dropped the booklet, took the gun out of my waistband.

'It's me,' Vinnie said as he stepped out from behind a tree. 'I heard gunshots.'

'I'm just practicing,' I said.

'For what?'

'So I'm ready if somebody comes after me. I have the right to defend myself, don't I?'

He came closer to me. He looked at the black box on the ground, picked up the instruction booklet for the Taser and scanned through it.

'I'm trying to help you,' he said. 'I'm trying to be your brother.'

'I know that.'

'If you go after him, you won't come back.'

'I'm not going to Canada.'

'Yesterday you wanted me to find you a boat.'

'It was a bad idea. I know that.'

'So then what's with the artillery here?'

'He knows where I live,' I said. 'He sent somebody to kill Natalie. If I had been there with her, I'd be dead now, too.'

He thought about it. Then he nodded slowly.

'So if somebody comes to finish the job,' I said, 'I'll be ready.'

He looked in my eyes, like he was trying to read something there. 'Have you eaten anything today?'

'I don't want to go down there,' I said. 'I'm not ready to deal with people yet. Not even Jackie.'

'I can bring you something.'

'That would be good. I appreciate it.'

He stayed there for a long moment, measuring me.

'I'll be back soon,' he finally said. 'Don't go away.'

'I won't.'

I went back to the cabin. There were no new messages on the machine. I brought the phone over as close to the front door as I could go. Then I set up two folding chairs outside and sat down on one of them.

Vinnie came back a few minutes later. He was carrying a plate of food and a Molson.

'Why did you move back to this cabin?' he said. He sat down in the other chair.

'I need to stay by the phone. If there's a break in the case, I want to hear about it.'

'You could install a phone in the second cabin.'

'I could. It would take some time.'

'Alex, there's something you're not telling me.'

I ate my dinner. It was beef stew, my favorite back when I could still taste food. I didn't drink any of the beer.

'Tell me what's going on,' he said.

Strength, I thought. Energy. I need to make myself eat. At least twice a day.

'You're not making this easy,' he said.

'Would it surprise you to know that I don't want you to get killed, either?'

'You think that's likely to happen?'

'If you stay too close to me, yes.'

'Do you think you're cursed?' he said. 'Anybody close to you ends up dead?'

'Not exactly.'

'Then why do you say that?'

The phone rang. I put the plate on the ground and stood up.

'I have to get that,' I said.

'Go ahead.'

Second ring.

'I need to take this call alone.'

'Who is it?'

Third ring.

'I'll tell you later. Just let me get this, all right?'

He didn't move.

Fourth ring.

'I'm sorry,' I said. I went inside the cabin and shut the door.

The answering machine was kicking in, the recording just starting when I picked up the receiver. The answering machine cut off. I looked at the caller ID. It read 'Unknown Caller.' I would have bet anything the call was coming from an untraceable cell phone.

'Hello,' I said.

'Is this Alex?' A woman's voice.

'Yes.'

'Can you guess who I am?'

'Is your name Rhapsody?'

'Well done.'

'That was fast. Mr. Gray contacted you already?'

'Never mind who contacted me. You know why I'm calling.'

'Is Laraque there?'

'He's not here at the moment. I'm calling to do you a big favor.'

'If you want to do me a favor,' I said, 'then tell Laraque to call me.'

I hung up the phone. It rang again about fifteen seconds later.

'Alex, that was not very nice.'

'You'll have to forgive me. I haven't been myself lately.'

'I understand you've suffered a loss,' she said. 'I know I wasn't as close to her as you were . . . '

'What did you just say?'

'I was her friend, Alex. At least I thought I was. Didn't she ever mention me?'

'What are you talking about?'

'We used to meet every morning for coffee. Antoine and I were really looking forward to doing business with her. Until, well . . . Until what happened. It was such a horrible thing.'

'Until she was gunned down in cold blood, you mean.'

'Alex, I don't know how much this will mean to you, but I'm very, very sorry about what happened. I can only imagine how you're feeling.'

'You're sorry.'

'Yes, I am. Under the circumstances . . . I mean, I know you want to lash out at *somebody*. But I think you've made a very big mistake.'

'Who did he send to kill her?' I said. 'Was it the same guy who killed her partner? Or was it a different man?'

'Antoine had nothing to do with Natalie's death. You need to understand that, Alex. The sooner you understand that, the better it'll be for everyone.'

'I want to hear it from him,' I said. 'I want to see him, face-to-face.'

'That's not possible.'

'Call me back when it is.'

I hung up again. It took a good thirty seconds for it to ring this time. I considered not picking it up, then thought, what the hell. Maybe it's him.

It wasn't.

'I'm trying to be understanding here,' she said. 'But you're not making it easy. Do you have any idea who you're dealing with now? I'm serious. Do you have any idea what he'll do to you?'

'He can't do anything else to me.'

'Use your head, Alex. Why would he kill two police officers? It doesn't make any sense.'

'If he didn't do it, why not tell me that himself? How come I get the errand girl?'

'Okay, number one, you can go fuck yourself with the errand girl. Number two, he doesn't even know I'm calling. Like I've been trying to tell you before you keep hanging up on me, I'm doing you a favor. If you tell me where the stuff is *right now*, I might be able to convince him to let you live. Do you understand what I'm saying, Alex? You've got one chance to avoid a very painful death. On account of how bad I feel about Natalie, I'm giving you that one chance.'

'That's very considerate of you.'

'Where's the merchandise?'

'Tell Laraque to call me. I'll discuss it with him.'

I hung up again, thinking it was time to ice them a little while, now that I had their attention. I was already out the front door when the phone started ringing again. Vinnie was still there, sitting on one of the folding chairs.

'Who was on the phone?' he said.

'Telemarketer,' I said. 'Pain in the ass.'

'Your phone's still ringing.'

'I know. They'll stop eventually. Come on, let's take Jackie's plate back.'

'I thought you said you didn't want to go down there.'

'I changed my mind. He's probably worried about me. I should go see him.'

'What are you trying to pull?' he said. 'You're gonna sneak off again.'

I raised my hands in surrender. 'You drive. We go together.'

That's how I ended up spending a couple of hours at the Glasgow that day. Jackie was surprised. He seemed a little unsure about how to treat me. He knew he couldn't abuse me like usual, but that didn't leave him many options. He was like a pitcher who can only throw one pitch.

He made me an omelet, even though the sun was going down. My first real breakfast in days. I had one beer. One more cold Canadian. I held the bottle and looked at it, wondering if it would be the last beer of my life.

It felt strange to be there. This place that was as much a home to me as my own cabin. I knew it would never be the same again.

I asked Vinnie to take me back up to the cabin. He didn't want to leave me there alone. Beyond that, I could tell he was worried I'd go running off somewhere. I could see him eyeing my truck like it was a bottle of gin he needed to keep away from an alcoholic. I promised him I wasn't going anywhere that night. That much I knew I could say and be telling the truth.

When he was gone, I went into the cabin. The phone was ringing. I picked it up.

'I tried to do this the easy way,' she said. Her voice had an edge now, sharp enough to cut glass. 'Now you're really going to be sorry.'

'Where's Laraque?'

'You're talking to me now, McKnight. I'm giving you one more chance.'

'Tell him I want to talk to him.'

'He *is* talking to you. Right now. He's doing it through me. I'm the agent here. I'm the mouthpiece. You talk to me, you talk to him. You got it? So tell me what you want.'

'You know what I want.'

'What's the bottom line, McKnight? We get the hardware back when what happens? Fill in the blank. I'm trying to work with you.'

'Do you know where the boat is right now?'

'The boat that had the merchandise on it? Yes. Unless you've moved it.'

'I haven't moved it. It's in the boathouse. Did they tell you where that is?'

'I know where it is, yes.'

'Tomorrow,' I said. 'I'll meet Laraque at the boathouse. Let's say eight P.M. That'll give him plenty of time to get over here.'

'You know that's not possible. He's got cops watching him now. He can't take a step outside without everybody knowing it.'

'Something tells me he's a pretty resourceful man. If it's important enough, he'll be there.'

'I told you, it's not going to happen.'

'If you really need to come, too, I guess I can't stop you. Personally, I'd recommend that you stay home.'

'If you hang up,' she said, 'so help me God, I will send somebody over there right now to kill you.'

'Yeah, I know that's how you guys do things. But this time, it would be a mistake. I'm the only one who knows where your guns are, remember?'

'You're the one making the mistake, McKnight. You have no idea.'

'Story of my life,' I said. 'Tell your man I'll see him tomorrow night.'

21

The moon was out. A miracle in itself after so many clouds, so much thick fog and blacked-out nights. The light came pouring through my windows, turning everything different shades of silver. It seemed to make the floor itself glow, so bright I could make out the stains there, the vague shadows that would always be there to remind me.

I could still smell her scent in my bed, just like the night before. If anything, the scent was stronger tonight. Impossible, but somehow it was.

I couldn't take it. I got up and went to the couch, wrapped the blanket around my shoulders as the wind picked up outside. I rocked back and forth, my eyes closed to the moon and the wind and the horrible cold hours of the middle of the night.

I was leaning half sideways when I opened my eyes, early morning sun coming through the windows now. My neck was stiff. I got up and took a shower, trying to loosen up under the hot water. I got dressed, had a cup of coffee. It felt like it was burning right through my stomach.

Vinnie wasn't here last night, I thought. He's not here now. For all his talk about not leaving me alone . . . But I know I've been pretty miserable to be around lately. I've been trying as hard as I can to drive him away. I should write the man a note, try to tell him why I'm doing this.

No, what the hell. He'll know why. If I don't live through another night, he'll have no problem figuring it out.

I wasn't sure what to do with myself for the rest of the day. Eight P.M. was a long haul. I didn't want to use up any more ammunition practicing, and I didn't want to go into town to buy any more. I didn't want to just sit here, watching the minutes go by. I didn't want to be around anybody else, either.

I finally took Natalie's picture outside with me, sat on my folding chair in front of the cabin and looked at her face for a long time. She was so serious in the picture — I had to try hard to remember her smile. I tried to remember that one look she'd give me, when she'd say something smart and she'd give me a little sideways glance to see if I'd caught it. Or the look she'd give me when she was done fighting with me. When she was finally ready to let me get close to her. Her eyes focused on me, almost nearsighted it seemed, like suddenly I was the only person in the world.

I sat outside and held the picture, felt the cold frame in my hands. The sun tried to warm the day. I went inside and ate the rest of the leftover beef stew from the night before. I didn't put ketchup on it, my own final touch, always over Jackie's objections. I didn't even heat it up. I couldn't taste anything, couldn't enjoy anything. I was a machine now, all wires and solder inside. On the outside metal and plastic.

Still no Vinnie. The day slowly ticking by and not a sign of him. Had he finally given up on me? It didn't seem possible.

Two in the afternoon. I was still alone. Four o'clock. Five. I ate again, whatever I could find in the cabin. Vinnie wasn't there to bring me anything else. At six o'clock I started to think about when I should be on the road.

Six thirty. It was about time. I should get there early, I thought. Take a good look around the place. I gathered up my supplies. Leon's Ruger in the right pocket of my jacket. The Taser in the left pocket. The backup pistol strapped to my ankle. I was ready.

Still no Vinnie. I should have been relieved that I wouldn't have to fight my way past him, but all I could do was wonder what the hell he was up to.

I found out as soon as I got into my truck and tried to start it.

I didn't even have to look under the hood. I knew what he had done.

'Son of a bitch,' I said as I got out. 'You have got to be kidding me.'

I walked the quarter mile down to his cabin. His truck was parked out front. I went to his front door and opened it without knocking.

He was standing at his sink, filling up another plastic bag with ice. He didn't say a word when I walked into the kitchen. He didn't move.

'Why did you cut my battery cables?' I said.

'Same reason you cut mine.'

'I don't have time for this. I need your truck.'

'You're not getting it.'

'Vinnie, God damn it. Don't even start this. I'm serious. Give me your keys.'

'You're not driving my truck, Alex. If you have someplace to go, I'm taking you there.'

'You're not coming with me. Give me your keys.'

'I'm coming with you,' he said. 'Period.'

'Vinnie . . . ' I closed my eyes for a moment, rubbed them, tried to think of the right words to say. Meanwhile, the time was slipping away from me. All day to wait and now I was suddenly racing the clock.

'You have to trust me,' I said. 'I need to go somewhere, and I need to go there now. Alone. You have to give me your keys.'

'You think this has been easy? You think I like you fighting me every step of the way?'

'Vinnie . . . '

'No, let me finish. I'm trying to understand what you're going through the last few days. I know it's not exactly the same as what I had to deal with, but I think I've got the general idea. I've been trying to be your friend, Alex. Your blood brother. I've been trying to be there for you, just like you were for me. But instead of letting me help you, you've been sneaking away whenever I turn my back. You've been driving around, all over the place, looking for a way to get yourself killed. And now tonight . . . God knows what you've got planned. God knows. You really think I'm going to let you just drive off and do this by yourself?'

'You have to.'

'It's not happening. I'm going with you, no

309

matter what. You'd do exactly the same thing if the situation was reversed. You know that. Hell, you've done it.'

'This is different,' I said, sneaking a look at my watch.

'It's not. It's exactly the same.'

'Give me the keys.'

'No.'

'Where are they?'

I looked around the place, spotted his keychain on the counter.

'Don't even try,' he said. 'You'll have to kill me to get them.'

He stood there, his hands at his sides. I knew I couldn't take the keys from him. There was no way I could overpower him. And there was no way I could let him come with me. I'd want him on any other trip, but not this one.

Not if I honestly didn't think I'd be coming back.

'I'm sorry,' I said. 'You don't leave me any choice.'

I reached into my jacket pocket and took out the Taser. Before he knew what was happening, I did the unthinkable. I pulled the trigger. The front cap exploded with a dull pop as the two wires shot toward him. I didn't have to do anything else. It was all automatic. The voltage was already moving as the wires hit his chest. Even after I dropped the Taser, the charge kept running through him for several seconds, doubling him up, putting him right on the floor like a tied-up calf in a rodeo.

I went to the counter and grabbed the keys.

Then I bent down and put my hand on his head. He was trying to speak, trying to move.

'You'll be okay in a couple of minutes,' I said. 'It's totally harmless. I promise.'

Cheap words from a man who'd do this to his best friend. I couldn't quite believe I had just done this.

This is what you've come to, Alex. This is what losing Natalie has done to you.

I touched his head one more time. He stayed there on his kitchen floor as I walked past him. The Taser had released a spray of confetti all over the place. I knew each little piece of paper had a unique serial number printed on it. It was all part of the weapon's design — incapacitate your man, but leave a trail of markers on the ground for full disclosure. In this case, I didn't think it would be an issue.

'I'm sorry,' I said to him as I opened the door. My hands were shaking. 'But it's not your day to die.'

⋆ ⋆ ⋆

The sun was just starting to go down as I drove Vinnie's truck out of Paradise, the lights from the Glasgow Inn in the rearview mirror. I took the same roads south, the same fifty miles, crossing the entire Upper Peninsula to Hessel, from the shores of one lake to another. I left the highway, drove down the peninsula to the summerhouse. My fourth time there now, and the road looked just as deserted.

I parked Vinnie's truck at Gray's house. I

didn't see any reason to hide it. I got out of the truck and walked up the driveway. The gun felt heavy in my jacket pocket. The small pistol strapped to my ankle brought back a sensory memory from long ago, the way the shin guards felt when I was working behind home plate.

It was almost eight o'clock now. I walked across the road and down the neighbor's driveway. When I got to the house, I saw that everything was exactly as I had left it. The back-door window was still broken, the rock I had used to break it still there on the ground. The boathouse door in the same state. I looked through and saw the boat still sitting there, nose in. It was riding a lot higher in the water now that its cargo was resting on the bottom of Lake Huron.

I wonder how long I'll have to wait, I thought. Hell, maybe Laraque is already here. Maybe he's watching me right now.

I looked all around me. Behind me the empty canal. The backyard, two rows of trees on either side of me, the darkness under the branches growing with each passing minute. Ahead of me the house. The driveway. The whole place seemingly abandoned to the ghosts of summer.

He'll be here, I said to myself. He has to be.

I stood there for a while. A half hour snuck by in the absolute silence. The sky got darker. Finally, I heard a vehicle up on the road. Two headlights appeared, turned onto the driveway, came closer, pointing right at me. I had to look away.

The vehicle stopped. The headlights turned

off. My eyes took a moment to adjust, then I saw two figures, one on either side of the car. It was a red Jaguar, one of the new, smaller models with the round front grill. I heard the two doors shutting, almost at the same time. The two figures started walking down toward me. I stood my ground next to the boathouse.

I looked from one to the other as they got closer. The woman was on my left, the man on my right. He had been driving. They walked slowly, the woman stepping carefully on the uneven ground.

They were both dressed in black. The woman in black raincoat, knee-high black boots, black stockings. A black bag hanging from her shoulder. The man in a long black trench coat, black leather shoes. He was wearing dark glasses, even now with the sun long gone.

They came closer.

'Alex,' the woman said. Her voice giving nothing away. No emotion at all.

'You're Rhapsody,' I said. She was a lovely woman, no question about it. She had the killer eyes. The dark eyebrows. A model's face, and yet something wasn't quite right. There was a sharpness in her features that would have put me on edge, even under innocent circumstances.

Like Natalie had said about her, she looked like a younger, sexier Cruella De Vill.

And Laraque . . . What I could see of his face behind the dark glasses . . . Natalie had told me he wasn't a tall man. He wasn't muscular. He wasn't physically imposing in any way. Yet the unspoken power that emanated from him . . .

This was him. I clenched my fists. This was him.

'You have no idea what we went through to get here,' Rhapsody said. 'I hope you're ready to make it worth our trouble.'

The bag around her shoulder was unzipped, in perfect position for her right hand to reach into it. I had no doubt about what was inside.

'Remember one thing,' I said. 'If you shoot me now, you don't get your guns back.'

'Who said anything about shooting you, Alex? We came here to talk.'

I looked at Laraque. He hadn't said a word yet.

'So talk,' I said. 'I'm going to ask you something. I want the truth.'

He didn't say anything. He didn't move.

'Please take the sunglasses off,' I said.

Nothing. He was a statue.

'He doesn't wish to take them off,' Rhapsody said.

'I'm not talking to you,' I said, without looking at her. 'I want to ask you one question, and I want to see your eyes when you answer me.'

Another long moment. Something flew over our heads. Either a bird out late or a bat out early.

'Take them off,' I said.

A movement, finally. He lowered his head a fraction of an inch. Then he reached up with his right hand and took off his glasses. He put them in his coat pocket.

As I stepped closer to him, I could sense Rhapsody shifting the bag around her shoulder. I was one second away from dying.

I didn't care.

'Natalie Reynaud was one of the police officers who met with you in the hotel room,' I said.

He looked me in the eyes. There was just enough light left to see his face clearly.

'She and her partner were both shot dead. I want to know if you were responsible for that.'

His eyes, a greenish shade of brown. Hazel, they call it. Although in the dying light it looked more like a dull shade of gold.

'Did you have them killed, Laraque? Tell me.'

He blinked once. Twice. Slowly, he shook his head.

You clear your mind. You ask the question. You listen, you watch. Your gut tells you if it's the truth.

'Tell me,' I said. 'Say it. Did you have them killed?'

'No,' he said. 'No, I didn't.'

I watched him. I remembered what Natalie had said about him, about the fear she felt just being in the same room with him.

Something happened then. His eyes moved. He started to look over at Rhapsody. Then he stopped.

It happened that quickly. But it was all wrong.

Forget if he was lying or telling the truth. In that instant, I knew something even more important. Natalie Reynaud would never be afraid of this man.

'You're not Laraque,' I said.

If there was any doubt, his reaction was all I

needed. The eyes went wide before he tried to regain control. 'What are you talking about?'

'You're not Laraque. What's going on here?'

The gun came out of Rhapsody's bag. It was just like some of the guns I had seen on the boat, an automatic with a suppressor fixed to the barrel. The damned thing was so long, it was a wonder she could get it out of the bag so fast.

'Okay, enough of this,' she said. 'Just tell us where the merchandise is.'

'Where's Laraque?'

'Never mind him. You need to deal with me now.'

'I told you I wouldn't talk to anybody else.'

'You don't understand what I'm trying to tell you. Laraque is out of the game. You can't talk to him.'

'First thing you can do, you can take Mr. Dress-Up here back to Canada. Was this Laraque's idea, by the way? Send a stooge over here to take his place? Is that the kind of man he is?'

'Alex, listen to me . . . '

'Second thing, you tell the real Laraque he has twenty-four more hours to get his ass over here.'

'You see, that'll be hard to do, on account of his being very dead right now. Unless you'd care to join him. Maybe you can talk to him on the other side. I don't know.'

'What are you talking about? Who killed him?'

'Who do you think, genius?'

'You did? Why would you do that?'

She shook her head. 'I know you're a man, so I'll try to talk slow here. I killed the boss so I could take over the operation. You understand me?'

'That's not a good enough reason,' I said. 'Not compared to mine.'

'Whatever you say, Alex. Just get over it, because we're not joking around here. Why don't you wise up and tell us where the stuff is right now, before we really hurt you?'

'Who's we? You and your caddy here?'

'No, not him. Jacques is my driver. He's quite harmless.'

'Then who are you talking about?'

'And just for the record, this whole fake Laraque thing, it wasn't my idea. I thought it was a little over the top myself.'

'Whose idea was it? Who are you talking about?'

'I think that's your cue, Babe,' she said. She raised her chin, said it loud enough for anyone else to hear, anyone who might be waiting in the trees.

I heard the footsteps. I turned and saw the man. I recognized him in a second.

It was Cap.

22

He had a gun just like Rhapsody's, with the same long suppressor screwed onto the end of the barrel. He walked over to me with a smile, like he was renewing his acquaintance with a long-lost friend.

'Alex and I have come to an agreement,' Rhapsody said. 'Your idea was ridiculous.'

'Is that right?' He moved closer to me, never taking his eyes from mine. He put his gun in his back pocket for a moment, just long enough to pat me down and to take Leon's gun out of my jacket pocket. I waited for him to go down each of my legs, to find the ankle holster.

But he didn't.

'Alex saw right through it,' she said. 'Jacques never had a chance.'

'The man wanted Laraque,' Cap said. He transferred Leon's gun to his right hand and threw it in a high arc. It splashed in the middle of the channel. Then he started to walk around me in a slow circle. 'So we gave him Laraque. I thought it would be easier this way.'

The fake Laraque put his hands up. 'Hey,' he said, 'you didn't tell me this guy would be here.'

'Shut up, Jacques,' she said.

'No, this guy's crazy. I didn't sign up for this.'

'Just shut the fuck up.'

'Seriously. I'll let you guys work this out. I'll be right over here.'

318

'You're not going anywhere.'

'The hell I'm not. I just quit.'

Cap turned from me and shot him twice in the throat. *Shoomp shoomp*, two muffled shots like the sound a nail gun would make. Me on the roof of my cabin, nailing down a shingle. That was the exact sound.

At first, the man showed nothing but surprise. He tried to speak, but couldn't make a sound, his vocal cords obliterated with everything else as the blood rushed down the front of his coat. He went to his knees, looking at the ground like he still couldn't quite fathom what had happened to him. He tried to speak again. Then he pitched sideways and spent the next few seconds staring up at both of us.

'Was that necessary?' she said.

'You told me he wasn't even a good driver.'

I watched the man die on the ground. It occurred to me, maybe this was one of his reasons for shooting him in front of me, so I'd know exactly what he was capable of.

'I thought you were long gone,' I said to him. 'After you tried to trick me into going after Mr. Gray.'

'What's this?' she said. 'This sounds interesting.'

'Never mind,' he said. He kept circling me. 'It was just an idea, a spur of the moment thing.'

'I thought you weren't afraid of Gray,' she said.

'I just put a bullet in his head two days ago. Does that sound like somebody who's afraid of anybody?'

'You killed Gray?' I said.

He stopped in front of me. 'Yes, I did. Now tell me where the guns are, or you'll get the same deal. I promise you.'

'I think he was afraid of you, too,' she said to me. 'I think that's why he came up with this idea.'

'Rhapsody . . . '

''Get Jacques to pretend,'' she said, imitating him, exaggerating the swagger in his voice. ''McKnight won't know any better. If he ends up killing him, so what?''

'What do you think?' he said to me. 'Do you think I'm afraid of you?'

'I think you talk pretty big,' I said, 'when your woman has your back.'

He made like he was going to turn away, then surprised me with a punch right in my gut. It folded me in two. I went with it, going all the way to the ground, feeling for the mini automatic under my pant leg. Lift and fire, if I do it fast enough . . .

No. Not yet. Either one of them would mow me down in a second.

'Okay, enough chit-chat,' Cap said. 'Where are the guns?'

Play this out, I thought. Buy some time, figure out what the hell is going on.

'They're out there,' I said, pointing to the water. I was struggling to get my wind back. Laraque was dead. Gray was dead. I couldn't believe it was all coming down to these two.

'What are you talking about, McKnight? Out there where?'

'I have to take you to them.'

'What did you do, hide them on some island like a pirate?'

'That's exactly what I did, yes.'

'He leaned down closer to me. 'Do you have any idea how much you've fucked up my life already? Do you?'

'The man says he's going to take us to the merchandise,' Rhapsody said. 'So let him do it.'

'You actually believe him?'

'He looks like a smart man. He knows if he gives everything back, we'll let him walk away.'

He grabbed me by the back of the collar. 'Where are they, McKnight?'

'He said he'd take us to them,' she said. 'Are you deaf?'

'I'm not falling for it,' he said. 'I swear to God . . . '

'You got a better idea?'

'Yeah, I do.'

He put the gun against my temple.

'That would be smart,' she said. 'We'd definitely get the guns back that way.'

He made a long muffled sound in his throat as he let go of me. I was starting to see the way things were between them. They obviously had a long history together.

'We need to clean up here first,' she said. 'Why don't you drag Jacques into the boathouse?'

'We can take him on the boat,' he said. 'Dump him in the water.'

'I'm not riding in the boat with him. Just put him in the boathouse for now. You take him back out and dump him later.'

'McKnight can do that.' He kicked me. 'On your feet.'

'He's still recovering from your little cheap shot, Cap. Just shut the fuck up and drag Jacques's ass into the boathouse, will you?'

'Rhapsody, I'm going to say this once. We're partners now. That means you don't get to talk to me that way anymore.'

'Pardon me. Will you please relocate Jacques to the boathouse? Is that better?'

He stared her down for a while, then he finally hooked his wrists under the dead man's underarms and started dragging him.

'Let's go,' she said to me. She waved me forward with her gun, careful not to step in the blood. 'Cap, you better hose this all off when we're done, too.'

He spat sideways and kept dragging. When we got to the door, he dropped the man for a moment and rummaged around in his pockets for the key to the door.

'Do you really need a key?' she said.

'I suppose not,' he said. 'On account of our friend breaking into the place. Real smooth, McKnight. Did you use a sledgehammer?'

'I thought your pal Brucie was watching over things,' she said. 'Where is he?'

'We can go see him if you like. But I don't think he's in any state to receive visitors.'

'Just open the door,' she said. 'It'll be dark by the time we get out there.'

He did as he was told. Then he dragged the dead man in and left him on the gangway.

'How far are we going, McKnight?' Cap

jumped into the boat and turned around, the gun pointed at my chest.

'It's not far,' I said. 'I'll take the wheel.'

'Like hell you will. You're going to sit there and you're going to tell me where to go.'

I got in and sat down on one of the chairs. Rhapsody sat across from me, a good six feet away. Cap climbed up to the captain's chair and started the engine. A minute later, we were pulling out into the channel.

'Which way?' Cap said, his voice raised enough for me to hear him over the engine. 'To the right?'

'Yes,' I said. 'Go all the way out to the lake.'

He turned around and looked at me, then at Rhapsody.

'You heard the man,' she said. 'Go to the lake.'

He shook his head and swung the wheel to the right, flipping on the GPS to follow the safe route, same as I had done. I sat there and thought about what was happening, and what my options were. With Laraque gone . . . Hell, it just wasn't making any sense to me.

'Did you really kill him?' I said to Rhapsody. 'I can't see you doing that.'

'Is that a compliment or an insult?'

'Now you're trying to collect his guns. You really are taking over.'

'That's the idea.'

'And if Cap here really took out Mr. Gray, then I'm looking at both ends of the deal now. You've got the Canadian side and Cap has the U.S. side.'

She looked out the boat at where we were

going, then back at me.

'I hope you can trust him,' I said. 'He seems a little psychotic to me.'

Cap looked back down at us. 'Just tell us where to go,' he said. 'Other than that, you can keep quiet.'

'I'm just making an observation,' I said. 'The two of you don't seem to get along so well.'

I was fishing now. I was trying to find any kind of leverage I could, or anything I could use to distract them, even for a moment.

'We get along fine,' she said. 'When we have to.'

'Whatever you say. It's not my business. I'd just be a little worried about having a partner who's so unstable.'

'Cap and I go way back, Alex. We're the ones who hooked up Laraque and Gray to begin with.'

'You had this planned all along? Wait for the right moment and then take over?'

She smiled at me. I wasn't getting anywhere. I needed something else, something to throw them off course.

'How far are we going?' Cap said. 'Do I stay in this channel?'

'All the way out,' I said.

'Then what?'

'I'll remember when we get there.'

He took both hands off the wheel for a moment to tighten the suppressor on his gun. He looked down at me as he did it.

'You're not messing with us here,' Rhapsody said. 'Are you? Because I'd be really disappointed.'

'Would I do that?'

'You don't want me to be disappointed, Alex. Believe me.'

'I understand.'

She had her gun in her lap now, her right hand still gripping the handle. There has to be something, I thought. What would Leon do?

'Things must be kind of hot right now,' I said. 'Maybe killing two cops wasn't such a great idea.'

'Yeah,' Cap said without turning around, 'maybe that wasn't such a great idea.'

'Don't start,' she said.

'Start what?'

'Did you hear me? Don't even go there now. It was an unavoidable mistake.'

'You still don't think I would have figured it out before shooting the guy?'

'How could you?'

'Well, let's see . . . If I went to his apartment . . . Yeah, maybe I would have noticed something first. His badge on the table, maybe? His official Mountie coffee mug? His diploma from the police academy on the fucking wall?'

He stopped himself, closed his eyes for a few seconds, like he was counting to three. When he finally looked back at the GPS, he had to jerk the boat hard to the left to get back on course. Rhapsody almost fell out of her chair. I had a sudden vision of her gun falling out of her hand, me making my move. But the moment passed.

'Nice driving,' she said. 'Is there anything you don't do well?'

'Go fuck yourself,' he said. 'And ask your

buddy where we're going here. We're almost out in the lake.'

'Keep going straight for a while,' I said. 'Hold the same direction.'

She killed Natalie's partner, I thought. Probably with that very gun. But over here in Michigan . . . There was no way Cap could have killed Natalie. Unless . . .

Wait a minute, why would they even kill them at all? If they didn't even know they were cops until afterward . . .

'McKnight,' Cap said. 'I'm starting to think you're just stalling here.'

'A few more miles,' I said. 'Hold your course.'

If they didn't know they were cops . . . then they must have thought they were real gun dealers.

'I don't remember any islands out here,' Cap said. 'You're taking us right out into the middle of fucking Lake Huron.'

If they thought they were real gun dealers . . .

God damn it. They thought they were competitors. They had this takeover all set up, until these new players arrived on the scene. Hell, that's probably why Cap and Brucie were stuck here for a few days. Maybe it wasn't the weather. Maybe it was Laraque trying to play the two U.S. angles off each other, work a better deal.

'McKnight, you'd better say something. Or I swear to God I'll kill you right now.'

Natalie and her partner didn't die because their cover was blown.

They died because their cover *wasn't* blown.

'McKnight?'

She killed Resnik, picked up his cell phone, and got my number. Gave that to Cap. Hell, that might have been a big surprise to him. Or maybe not at all. Maybe it explained a lot, why me and Vinnie were trying to drive him away. It would have all made perfect sense if he thought I was part of Natalie's supply chain.

So he came over to my cabin . . . thinking I was already dead, of course. But so what? Nobody else would have known that. I would just be missing at that point. He came to my cabin and he saw Natalie's Jeep there. Not my truck. Again, which would have made sense to him. I was just down the road, but he didn't know that.

He opened the door and found Natalie inside. He must have figured she had come there looking for me, and when I wasn't there, she had just settled in to wait for me.

Did he tell her she was waiting for a dead man? Did he say one word to her before he gunned her down in cold blood and then left?

Cap cut the engine and let the boat drift. He came down the stairs.

'Start talking,' he said, leveling the gun at my head. 'Where are they?'

'You killed her,' I said. 'You killed Natalie.'

'Yeah, no kidding. That's what I do, remember?'

I wanted to go for my gun right then. I wanted to empty every round into his body. Then take his own gun from him and do it all over again.

'Cap, just cool it,' Rhapsody said. 'Let me do this.'

'You've done enough,' he said. 'Look at where it got us.'

'What's that supposed to mean?'

'Look at us,' he said, gesturing in every direction. 'You don't think this is strange?'

'It's strange, yes.'

'Are you sure?'

'Yes, Cap. It's strange.'

'And yet you seem to be going along with it just fine. Take the boat out to the middle of the fucking lake. No problem.'

'I'm just playing it out,' she said. 'I'm taking Alex at his word.'

'Of course. Why wouldn't you?'

'What else are we supposed to do?'

'Nothing. You're right. Everything's going great. As soon as Alex gives us the guns back, wherever the hell they are we go and make the switch. The other boat's not even that far from here, eh? St. Joseph Island's right across the lake.'

They're distracted, I thought. They're totally focused on each other right now. This will buy me another second.

'That's the plan,' she said. 'If you'll let us get on with it.'

'We just zoom right over there. Your guys are waiting for us?'

'Yes, Cap. For God's sake . . . '

Right hand to pant leg, lift, remove the gun. Fire. How quickly can I do this?

'Oh, after we take Alex back and let him go,'

Cap said. 'I almost forgot that part.'

'Are you trying to ruin everything here? Because you're doing a great job.'

She looked at me, just as I was starting to lean forward. I stopped.

'I'm just getting it clear in my head,' Cap said. 'We're not going to shoot Alex and dump his body in the lake.'

'Of course not.' She looked at me again. I wasn't going to get my chance if she kept doing that.

'And you weren't thinking of shooting me and dumping me in the lake, either,' Cap said. 'I mean, once you have the guns and you don't need me anymore.'

'What are you talking about?

'I'm just saying, you went along with this pretty quickly. This whole crazy boat trip.'

Yes, I thought. Keep fighting with each other. I can use this.

'Stop it,' she said. 'We're partners now.'

'So I thought.'

'We are. And this is just the first deal, remember? We took care of business and now we're running the show.'

Think, Alex. There's a little fire here. How can you pour on some gasoline?

'Yeah,' Cap said. 'I guess we did. We killed the bosses and took over.'

Wait a minute, I thought. Something's not right here. What did Natalie say about that meeting in the hotel room? Rhapsody and Laraque together, the way she described them . . .

'We did it,' Rhapsody said. 'We can own the world now. Both of us.'

Every word coming back to me now. How scared Rhapsody had seemed, until he touched her. The power dynamic that only Natalie could see.

'Yeah,' Cap said, his eyes narrowed now. He was thinking hard. 'Both of us.'

There's no way, I thought. I knew it was a lie. She couldn't have killed him. She couldn't do any of this on her own, without him. It felt like Natalie was right there next to me now, giving me this one last card to play.

'How did you kill him?' I said.

They both looked at me.

'I'm talking to you, Rhapsody. How did you kill Laraque?'

'Shut up.'

'Just tell me. I'm sure Cap wants to know, too. How did you kill him?'

'I said shut the fuck up.'

'Tell him how you did it,' Cap said. 'Go ahead.'

'Knock it off. I'm serious.'

'Tell him,' he said. He was with me now. I had him on the hook. 'Tell the man how you killed Antoine.'

'I shot him. You know that.'

'Where did you shoot him?' Cap said.

'In the head.'

'No, where was he when you shot him?'

She let out a long breath. 'In the tub.'

'In the tub, right. In the bathroom.'

'No, his tub's actually in the kitchen.'

330

'Did he see it coming?'

'I'm not going to do this now,' she said. 'I told you to knock it off.'

'That's a pretty hardcore thing to do, Rhapsody. I'm impressed. It must have made a real mess. His brains all over the bathroom tiles?'

'Stop it.'

'But that's what it takes, right? That's what you have to do to get to the top.'

She didn't answer him.

'You know what would be a real shame?' he said. 'If you didn't actually kill him. If you just said you did.'

'Don't do this.'

'Because that would mean, what, that the two of you are already thinking about double-crossing me? Cutting me out of the deal and finding a new American partner? Now that Gray is gone?'

'Cap, I mean it.'

'After all, who wants a partner who's unstable?'

'That was Alex's word, not mine.'

She looked at me one more time. I saw her right hand tighten on the gun. Cap saw it, too.

He shot her in the stomach. *Shoomp*, the same muffled noise.

Rhapsody let out a low moan, dropped her shoulder bag to the deck, brought one hand to her stomach and leaned over like she was going to be sick. 'Cap,' she said. 'Cap, God damn. What are you doing?'

'I'll tell Laraque you had a little accident on the boat. I'm sure he'll get over it. Especially if he hasn't gotten his delivery yet.'

She wobbled like she was about to go down. Then she raised her gun. Cap shot her again, *shoomp*, this time in the chest. She stumbled backward and collapsed against the gunwale, her gun falling overboard into the water. The blood soaked her blouse, turning it an even darker shade of black.

I slipped my right hand down, against my left knee. Lift the pant leg, remove the gun, fire. Just like that.

He turned to me. I froze.

'Okay, now you,' he said. His eyes were wide open and he was looking at me like I was the one who just shot her. 'It's your turn. You are going to tell me where the guns are.'

'If I don't?'

It was all so simple now. All that was left was me and the man who killed Natalie, alone on a boat, in the middle of the lake.

'You even have to ask that question?'

Just turn away one more time, I thought. Give me two seconds.

'You kill me,' I said. 'I get it. So what if I don't care?'

I honestly didn't. Forget the gun on my leg now. If I had a bomb, I'd blow the boat up right there, without hesitation. Take him down with me.

'I've got a new deal for you,' Cap said. 'Something else for you to think about. If you don't tell me where the guns are, not only do I kill you, I go right back to shore, get in my car, and I go kill everybody else you care about. Your

Indian friend. Your other friends, on the lake . . . What were their names, Tyler and Liz? That fat guy, Leon. Hell, might as well take out his fat wife while I'm at it. That old guy at the bar. Am I leaving anybody out?'

A bomb, I thought. Blow the boat up right now. I'd take that deal in a second.

'I'll do them all tonight,' he said. 'Do you doubt me anymore? You don't think I'll do it? By the time the sun comes up, every single one of them will be dead. You've got three seconds.'

A bomb.

'You want to know where the guns are?' I said. I slowly got to my feet.

'What, are you deaf and dumb? Yes, McKnight. Yes, I want to know where the guns are.'

'I think we're above them,' I said. 'Right about now.'

'What are you saying? Are you saying they're in the lake?'

'Yes.'

'Are you saying that the fucking guns are in the fucking lake?'

'Yes, they're in the fucking lake. About a hundred fucking feet down.'

He stood there for a moment. If nothing else, I got the man to finally stop talking.

'Of course, it doesn't matter anymore,' I said. 'Because the bomb will go off in about one minute.'

I took a quick glance at my watch. Somewhere, Leon was smiling.

'What are you talking about?'

'This is why I wanted to meet you at the boathouse at eight o'clock. I knew I'd have you out here by nine. Right in the middle of the lake, too. Which is perfect. I wouldn't want to blow up anything else. Just us.'

'You're not serious.' He took a step closer to me.

That's right, I thought. Get closer. Another step.

'It's the last thing I need out of life,' I said. 'If I take you down with me, I'm happy.'

'No way, McKnight. There's no way.'

One step closer. Come on.

'Even if you turned around right now,' I said, 'we'd never make it to shore. It's a done deal.'

'Nice try. I'm not buying it.'

He took another step.

'I was at the boathouse a long time before you got there. You think I just sat there waiting?'

He didn't say anything this time.

'I put it right under the deck,' I said. 'Right there.' I pointed to a spot on the deck behind him.

In the same motion, I reached for the barrel of his gun. I felt it tingle in my hand as he fired it again. I pushed the gun upward, tried to get it over our heads so I could get a clean shot at him with my free hand. I swung him around as hard as I could, driving my left elbow into his chin. He kicked at me, tried to knee me in the groin, tried to swing the gun back around toward my head.

I went with his motion, ducked as he pulled the trigger again, and pushed him all the way

through until he lost his balance. I got my knee up onto his back and drove him into the ladder, twisting the gun out of his hand. It fell away from both of us, clattering across the deck.

He swung around and elbowed me in the gut, knocking the wind out of me. Then he tried to drive the crown of his head into my nose. I turned away just in time, but everything went white when I caught most of the blow right in the cheekbone.

I tried to hold on to him, but I could feel him slipping away from me. I tackled him from behind as he went for the gun. He kicked at me, caught me a few times in the stomach, in the hip. I dug my fingers into his sides, grabbed onto his belt, and pulled him back as hard as I could. He had the gun in his hand. He tried to turn over to shoot me. I grabbed his wrist, tried to bend it back. I needed to get up on my knees, get some leverage on him, but he was beating me to it. He was pulling himself up off the deck.

I got up on one knee. Then the other. I got one foot under me and put my shoulder into him. I felt all the air go out of him as I drove him hard into the gunwale, right next to Rhapsody's body.

Whatever leverage I had now, I lost when I stepped in the blood. There was just enough of it on the wooden deck to make us both start sliding around like we were on ice, until I finally got both hands around his right wrist. I pounded his arm against the edge of the gunwale. Again. Then again. I could see the gun slipping from his hand. One more time and it was free.

It fell into the water and sank. It disappeared forever, just like Rhapsody's gun, like all the other guns that were down there, every gun in the world on the bottom of the lake.

Every gun except the small pistol still strapped to my ankle.

Cap swung at me a few times without connecting. I hit him in the gut. Then I hit him in the face. He went down on the deck and rolled over. When he came back up, he had Rhapsody's black bag. Before I could get to him, he reached inside and pulled out a switchblade. He hit the button and I saw the long gleam of metal.

'I'm going to carve you up like a turkey, McKnight.'

I bent down for the ankle holster. He came at me, faster than I would have thought possible. I dived backward, reaching out one leg to trip him as he made his rush. I felt the lick of the blade against my forehead.

When I turned around, he was getting back to his feet. Blood trickled into my left eye.

He stood there for a moment, breathing hard. He spat blood as he wiped the blade clean against his coat.

'Everything was just great,' he said. 'Until you came along.'

'I feel the same way,' I said. I pulled up my pant leg and drew the pistol. I pointed it right at his face.

'Oh, fuck me.'

'Drop the knife.'

'I don't believe this. What next?'

'Drop it,' I said. 'Throw it overboard.'

He tossed the knife in the water. He stood there with his arms hanging at his sides.

The blood was really flowing into my eye now. I picked up Rhapsody's bag and turned it over. Her wallet fell out. Her cell phone. A makeup bag. A little dispenser of tissues. I pulled out all the tissues and held them to the cut on my forehead. There was blood all over my face, all over my hands. My clothes. Rhapsody's blood mixed with Cap's mixed with mine.

'So what are you going to do now?' he said. He wiped more blood from his mouth.

It was getting dark now. There was no fog tonight. The stars were starting to appear high above us. The only sound now was our breathing and the boat creaking gently as it drifted in the water.

'I'm not moving,' Cap finally said. 'I'm going to stand right here.'

'Good. You'll make an easier target.'

'You can't shoot me.'

'Why not?'

'You can't do it. You know that.'

I kept the gun pointed at him. I didn't say anything.

'You don't have it in you, McKnight. Neither did Brucie, remember? Hell, neither did Rhapsody, it turns out. There aren't many people in this world who can kill a man in cold blood.'

'Brucie didn't have a good enough reason,' I said. 'Neither did Rhapsody.'

'It doesn't matter. Either you can or you can't.'

I stood there. I held the gun.

'You're not a killer,' he said in a low voice. It was almost a whisper. 'You can't do it.'

He stared into my eyes. He didn't blink.

'You can't do it.'

I picked up Rhapsody's cell phone off the deck and turned it on. After it played a few notes of music, I could see in the faint glow that it was getting a weak signal. She obviously had a much better phone than I did.

I fumbled with the buttons, looking up at him every couple of seconds, finally found the menu, then the call history. I went through the numbers, saw my own number in the outgoing calls, the three times she had called me, kept going, saw another number appear several times. I recognized the 416 area code. I knew it well from every time I had called Natalie in Toronto.

'What are you doing?' Cap said.

'Just a little trick I learned from you guys.'

I hit the talk button.

'McKnight,' he said. He couldn't keep the panic out of his voice. 'Who are you calling?'

'You're right,' I said. 'I'm not a killer. I can't shoot you in cold blood.'

The signal was weak, but the call was going through. It was ringing.

'But I know someone who'd be happy to.'

He grabbed one of the plastic deck chairs. He threw it at my head and made a diving lunge for the gun.

I ducked the chair and shot him dead.

23

The warm weather finally arrived in September. It stayed for ten and a half days. The sun was bright and in the evenings it shone against the trees and made everything look like a postcard. The sunsets were the very definition of breathtaking. You would literally stop breathing when you stepped outside to see them.

Far from being lost on me, I think I felt those days more deeply than anyone. They were so beautiful, but the beauty was tinged with a great sadness because you knew there would be so few of them. Each perfect day making you wonder if it would be the last.

A white man would have called these ten and a half days an Indian summer. I asked Vinnie what the Ojibwa called it. He said it was *dagwaging*.

I had apologies to make, to Vinnie more than anyone. I had shut him out, had treated him like no brother should ever treat another, even before I shot him with a fifty-thousand-volt stun gun. Someday maybe we'd be able to joke about that one. But not yet.

Vinnie finally asked me what had happened that day, after I left him. I figured I owed him the full story. We sat outside and watched the sunset while I told him. When I got toward the end, the moment of truth, I wasn't sure quite what to say.

'He told me I couldn't kill him in cold blood,' I said. 'I wanted to. I really did. But I couldn't do it.'

'You had the only gun at that point,' Vinnie said. 'He was defenseless.'

'After what he had done, that shouldn't have mattered.'

'No . . . but it still came down to shooting an unarmed man.'

'That's why I called Laraque. I knew he'd have no problem with it.'

'So when he figured who you were calling . . .'

'He came right at me. He probably thought it was his last chance.'

'You had to shoot him then.'

'Yes. I did.'

'So what's the problem?'

'I couldn't do it straight up,' I said. 'So I had to force his hand. I think I *knew* he'd try something.'

'But it wasn't a bluff. You really did have Laraque on the line.'

'If the situation was reversed, Cap would have shot me right away. No hesitation. So does this make me a better man, Vinnie? A weaker man? What?'

He looked at the sky while he thought about it. It was painted with every shade of red, orange, yellow. Some blue, some purple. Even some green. A painter would have lost his sanity trying to capture it all.

'You did what you had to do,' he said. 'You found the one way to get it done. I think you can let it go now.'

I didn't say anything to that. We both sat there for a while.

'So what happened with Laraque?' he said. 'What did he say when you called him?'

'I didn't really get to talk to him until after I shot Cap. Then I tried to explain everything. He told me to give him my GPS so he could send somebody out to meet me. He had those men with a boat on St. Joseph Island.'

'They wouldn't have let you live. I mean, talk about loose ends.'

'Yeah, I know.'

'So what did you say?'

This was the only part I didn't tell Vinnie — the part about me sitting there in the boat, asking Natalie what I should do. Wait for the men, let them find me so I could join her, wherever she was? Or find a reason to keep on living in this world for a little bit longer.

'I came up with some coordinates, miles away from where I was. I gave those to him and told him I'd wait. I figured those guys would be going out no matter what, might as well send them in the wrong direction. Then I called the Coast Guard.'

'That must have been some scene . . . '

'Two dead bodies. Me standing there covered with blood. Yeah, that got their attention.'

'Sounds like you still have their attention.'

He knew I'd already been interviewed by the ATF and the Mounties. The ATF agent in particular wanted to hold an obstruction of justice charge over my head, but Sergeant Moreland called me himself to tell me the guy was just blowing steam. Laraque was still out of reach, he told me. The guns at the bottom of the lake could be tied back to Gray, but Gray was already dead. Moreland told me they might want me to testify against Laraque someday, if it ever came to it. I thanked him for all the times he had been watching out for Natalie. He thanked me, totally off the record, for killing the man who had killed her.

'It's ironic,' Vinnie said. 'You wanted to go after Laraque so bad, and it turned out he had nothing to do with it. Now he might have reason to go after you.'

'He wouldn't dare right now. Things are still a little too hot for him.'

'Yeah, but someday . . . '

'We'll see about that.'

'You'd better sleep with a gun, Alex.'

'I can't. They're all on the bottom of the lake, remember?'

The sun disappeared. The colors stayed in the sky, darkening one degree at a time.

'I miss her, Vinnie. I really do. It's not getting any better.'

'You're done running around for a while. It's time to grieve now.'

He was right, of course. It was time.

★ ★ ★

Vinnie helped me move all my stuff to the second cabin. We left the first cabin empty for now. I'd figure out what to do with it later.

We worked on the new cabin at the end of the

road. We built the interior stairs. Then we started in on the kitchen.

I spent my evenings at the Glasgow Inn. I sat by the fire and remembered the one night Natalie was there.

Ten and a half days. On the eleventh day, it was gone within an hour. You knew it wouldn't be back for a long time. The leaves all seemed to turn at once and you could feel the cold wind coming. You could practically smell the snow in the air.

I asked Vinnie what the Ojibwa word was for fall.

'It's *dagwaging*.'

'Wait a minute, that's the same word you gave me for Indian summer.'

'There's no difference,' he said. 'The sun may be shining. Or it may be cold and gray. It is what it is. It's still *dagwaging*. You accept it and you go on living your life.'

★   ★   ★

That night, Vinnie came to me and told me that Caroline was having some real trouble again. Things were getting bad with Eddie, now that she wasn't making those few bucks on the side selling her prescription painkillers. He asked me to drive over to the Soo with him, so we could both have a little talk with Eddie, maybe suggest to him that beating up his wife wouldn't solve any of his problems.

He drove. I sat in the passenger's seat of his truck, watching the leaves blow around in the cold wind. He could have done this himself, I thought. He's taking me with him for a reason, maybe to show me that I still have some fight left in me.

I looked over at him, at his stone-calm face. 'You won't give up,' I said, 'will you.'

He kept his eyes on the road. 'Never.'

Caroline was at work that night. Eddie was at home, sitting at his kitchen table with his beer and cigarettes, just like the first time I had met him. Here was a man lucky enough to have a woman who loved him, lucky enough to spend every day of his life with her. I could barely stand to look at him.

I'd run into my share of domestic violence before, back in Detroit. A beat cop sees it all the time. There's only so much you can do about it. You can arrest the man, talk to the woman, help her with her options. You may feel like bouncing the man off the walls a few times, but you can't.

I wasn't a cop anymore.

By the time we left him, I think he was thoroughly convinced that Vinnie would be watching over her every day in the casino. Looking for a bruise. The slightest mark on her. Red eyes, maybe from crying. A bad hair day. That's all it would take for us to pay him another visit.

It was one thing I could do. One good thing for one person who needed help. Maybe another thing the next day, for someone else. Maybe getting one step closer to being the kind of man who'd deserve having someone like Natalie

Reynaud in his life, if only for a short time.

Yes, being that man, living with the *dagwaging* I'd been dealt. Then getting through another long winter so I can see how the world looks when springtime comes again.

Other titles published by
The House of Ulverscroft:

ICE RUN

Steve Hamilton

Winter has come late — and all the more brutal — to Paradise, Michigan. For the first time since moving there, Alex is taking a hard look at his life. This is what happens when a man long used to solitude falls in love. The woman is Natalie Reynaud, an officer from the Ontario Provincial Police whose cop partner has recently been killed. As far as the OPP are concerned, Natalie is responsible for his death. She needs a break — from the past as well as the present. Alex and Natalie brave a violent storm to spend a romantic weekend together in Soo, Michigan, but they are disturbed by someone who knows all about Natalie. An old blood feud is reignited; one that goes back to a dark episode buried in her family's past . . .

A COLD DAY IN PARADISE

Steve Hamilton

Apart from the bullet lodged close to his heart, former Detroit police officer Alex McKnight thought he had put the nightmare of his partner's death and his own near-fatal injury behind him. After all, Maximilian Rose, the killer they convicted in their last case together, has been in the state penitentiary for years. But in the small town of Paradise, Michigan, where McKnight has traded his badge for a cosy cabin in the woods, a murderer with Rose's unmistakable trademarks suddenly emerges. With Rose locked away, who else would know the intimate details of the old murders — not to mention the signature blood-red rose left on his doorstep?

THE WATER'S LOVELY

Ruth Rendell

One summer's day, Ismay's stepfather, Guy, was found dead in the bath. Now, nine years on, she and her sister Heather still live in the same house in Clapham. But it has been divided into two self-contained flats. Their mother lives upstairs with her sister, Pamela. And the bathroom, where Guy had drowned, has disappeared . . . Ismay works in public relations, and Heather in catering. They get on well. They always have. They never discuss the changes to the house, still less what had happened that day in August . . . But even lives as private as these, where secrets hang in the air like dust, intertwine with other worlds and other individuals. And, with painful inevitability, the truth will emerge.

THE SECOND HORSEMAN

Kyle Mills

Brandon Vale is a career thief, the best there is. He's never been caught — until he is arrested for a crime he didn't commit. Then, one night, he is broken out of prison by Richard Scanlon, the former FBI agent who framed him in the first place. Scanlon has discovered that a Ukrainian crime organization is auctioning twelve nuclear warheads to the highest bidder, but he can't convince the government that the sale isn't a hoax. His solution: arrange for Brandon to steal the $200 million necessary and buy the warheads himself. As the day of the warhead sale approaches, though, their plan begins to break down, and Brandon starts to suspect that the deal has higher stakes than he could ever have imagined . . .